EARTH UNKNOWN

Forgotten Earth, Book One

M.R. FORBES

Published by Quirky Algorithms
Seattle, Washington

This novel is a work of fiction and a product of the author's imagination.
Any resemblance to actual persons or events is purely coincidental.

Copyright © 2018 by M.R. Forbes
All rights reserved.

Cover illustration by Geronimo Ribaya

Acknowledgments

THANK YOU for picking up this book. I truly hope you enjoy reading it as much as I enjoyed writing it.

THANK YOU to my editor and beta readers for making the copy sparkle.

THANK YOU to my wife, for your feedback and input, on both the plot and life in general.

Chapter 1

"Mr. Yamaguchi isn't taking visitors."

Nathan Stacker shifted his gaze to the well-dressed man standing on his left. The one who had spoken. He regarded the thug for a moment in silence. He hadn't come all the way to Dome One to leave without completing the job. This guy had to know that.

"You know who I work for, right?" Nathan said. "Mr. Yamaguchi is late with his payment."

"Tell them it's coming," the guard replied. He started reaching for something behind his back, under his perfectly tailored black jacket.

The movement caused Nathan to start shifting his hand too, deeper into the pocket of his overcoat where his plasma pistol was waiting.

"Careful," he said.

The guard locked eyes with Nathan. "Relax." He

took hold of something and lifted it slowly into Nathan's view. A small, thin rod of metal. Platinum. A fortune's worth. "Mr. Yamaguchi authorized me to offer this as a partial payment for debts owed."

He held it out.

Nathan eyed the platinum. The metal was rare on Proxima, available only in small quantities from the mining expeditions in the nearby asteroid belts. He knew exactly how Yamaguchi had gotten it. Asteroid mining was dangerous work. Way too dangerous for civilians. Criminals, on the other hand? There was no question some of Yamaguchi's lackeys had wound up in front of the Proxima High Court, convicted and sent to the rigs as punishment for their offenses.

Hell, he had only escaped life as a miner because of a technicality.

The bit of platinum was a treasure to a former Centurion Space Force pilot like him.

It was worthless to his employers.

"I need to speak directly to your boss," Nathan said, not giving any ground. "Don't make this hard. I'm not getting paid that well."

The guard on the right smiled at the comment. The other one wasn't amused. He pushed the platinum forward again.

"Take this now. Your employer will have the rest in a week."

"That's a week late."

"Plus interest. Mr. Yamaguchi gives his word."

"Mr. Yamaguchi gave his word that he would pay in full today. Therefore, unless Mr. Yamaguchi pays in full today, Mr. Yamaguchi's word is as fucking worthless as that platinum."

The two guards didn't like that response. Nathan hadn't expected they would. The one on the left returned the platinum to his back pocket. Of course, when the hand reappeared it wasn't empty. It was holding a small laser pistol, military grade, silent and deadly. Nobody outside of Centurion Space Force should have had access to that kind of weapon, but then again, the plasma pistol he was carrying was military issue too.

The crooked smile the thug responded with was anything but friendly. "Mr. Yamaguchi will be sure to apologize to the Trust for his late payment. He was expecting a courier to come and pick it up, but unfortunately, the courier never arrived."

Nathan didn't wait for the man to finish talking. He took two quick steps forward and lunged at the thug, throwing his overcoat out like a cape to distract the man's attention. He brought a hard chop down across the guard's wrist, forceful enough to knock the pistol out of it, getting behind him and locking ankles, driving him back with a hard shove that twisted him over and onto the ground.

Nathan kept moving with the man, preserving the momentum, dropping low while the guard's head slammed into the floor with enough force to put him out. His other hand had been busy the entire time, getting a grip on the handle of his pistol and aiming through his coat. The other guard had drawn his sidearm, but he wheezed and collapsed as a red bolt burned through Nathan's coat and caught him in the chest.

Nathan stood up, exhaling his pent-up breath and trying to calm the sudden and rapid rise in his heart rate. Why couldn't they have just made it easy? The eight hundred he was getting for this would barely be enough to cover his share of the rent.

He considered grabbing the platinum from the unconscious guard. It was easily worth a million or more. He didn't dare. If word got from Yamaguchi to the Trust that he had stolen anything, they wouldn't hesitate to make him their next problem.

He glanced at the door. A small red light blinked beside it. He grabbed the unconscious guard under the arms, lifting him and dragging him to the light. He positioned the man's wrist in front of it, and a moment later the door slid open.

Nathan dropped the guard, stepping over him and past the threshold. He was half-expecting ninjas to come bounding out of the shadows to confront him. He smiled at the thought. This was reality, not a stupid entertainment stream.

Instead, he stood facing the middle of a factory floor. A replicator factory. An older model scheduled for reconditioning. It had produced a lot of the original equipment that had helped build the other equipment that had allowed humankind to settle and survive on Proxima B. After two hundred years, it was about time for the newer replicators it had printed to return the favor.

Even though everything on Proxima was technically owned by everyone, the factory had been operated by the Yamaguchi family for nearly all of those two hundred years. It was essentially theirs, and they didn't only use it as a standard profit center. The illegal operations were much more lucrative than the government contracts, but scaling meant retrofitting, and retrofitting had a certain cost attached. That was where the Trust came in.

Right now, the factory floor was empty. The workers had all gone home for the night. Large metal boxes rose on either side of Nathan, some up to thirty meters tall. Robotic arms of various sizes rested near them, and thick conduits dove in and out of them, providing power for the sculpting lasers and shapers inside. There were smelters behind the replicators that were kept heated full-time, and he could feel the warmth and smell the molten alloy.

In the corner to his left, finished product waited to be packed and shipped. Parts, mostly. Newer replicators did most of the final work nowadays. A cursory glance revealed pallets of water filtration drive units and other bland crap. A deeper dive would have uncovered other materials like firing pins, bullet casings, and who knew what else.

Nathan didn't care about any of that. He kept his eyes forward and slightly raised. He could see Yamaguchi's office on the second floor, a massive wall of glass allowing the owner to look down on his workers and monitor the flow of the goods he was producing.

He could see Yamaguchi inside, looking back.

He kept walking, maintaining a steady pace across the factory floor. There weren't any ninjas to jump out at him. There weren't any other guards. Maybe Yamaguchi had thought the Trust would send some other courier to deal with this payment. The two he had dropped weren't rookies.

They also weren't like him.

He watched Yamaguchi open the door to his office and begin descending the winding stairs to the floor. The businessman wasn't rushing. It would look bad for him to appear hurried or afraid.

Nathan noticed someone else appear in the glass of the office. A woman, petite, dark hair and narrow lips. She had predator eyes that landed on him and glared like she wanted to cut his throat. Yamaguchi's bodyguard. He scanned her for a firearm but didn't see one. That didn't mean it wasn't sitting on a couch or a desk — just out of reach.

He stopped walking when Yamaguchi reached the floor. The man's shoes clapped on the tiled surface, a smooth cadence that brought him within a few meters. He paused, making eye contact and holding it.

Nathan bowed first. It was proper etiquette. "Mr. Yamaguchi," he said.

The other man returned the bow. "Mr. Stacker."

Nathan was surprised the man knew him by name. He opened his mouth to repeat the words the Trust had imparted to him to deliver. "The terms of our—"

"Enough," Yamaguchi said, putting up his hand to cut Nathan off. "I don't need to hear it. I know what I agreed to."

"Then why didn't you meet with me instead of making me drop your goons?"

"I was otherwise occupied." His eyes shifted back toward his office. Insinuating what, exactly? "It's no business of yours, courier."

He reached into a back pocket, repeating the motion his guard had made a few minutes earlier. He retrieved a second stick of platinum.

"You can get the first from Iko," he said, holding it out.

"The Trust doesn't accept payment in—"

"The Trust didn't specify how they would accept payment in the contract. You can read it yourself if you need proof. This is how I choose to pay."

Nathan smiled and held out his hand, palm up. Yamaguchi dropped the platinum into it.

"Thank you," Nathan said, bowing again.

Yamaguchi bowed in return.

"That wasn't so hard, was it?" Nathan asked. "You could have left both sticks with your man if you didn't want to be disturbed."

"I could have," Yamaguchi replied. "But I had other business with the Trust. They asked me to delay you."

He looked back at the woman in his office. Nathan looked too, in time to see her short nod.

"It seems both our tasks are completed for the evening, Mr. Stacker," Yamaguchi said. "Sayonara."

He turned around and started walking. Nathan stared at his back for a moment, confused.

"Why did they ask you to delay me?" he said.

Yamaguchi didn't turn around. "Why don't you ask your wife?"

Chapter 2

Nathan hurried away from the replicator factory, barely noticing the historic sights of Old Praeton. Dome One was the first of the now twenty-three domes that composed the largest city on Proxima B. It was the place where the original settler's new lives had started after arriving from Earth.

Why don't you ask your wife?

Yamaguchi's words echoed in Nathan's mind as he descended into the loop station. He reached the entry gate and swiped his wrist over the red beam of light spitting out from it, letting it hit the small patch expertly glued over his real identification. The entrance kiosk flashed an image of someone who wasn't him, told him his credit balance, and opened the gate for him to reach the platform.

Why don't you ask your wife?

He stood at the edge of the platform, waiting for the vehicle to arrive. He was tense. Nervous. His heart was pounding. He wanted more than anything to stop at a comms terminal and ping Niobe, but if he made contact with anyone before he reported his job as complete, he would be in deep shit.

Why don't you ask your wife?

The statement made him feel like he was in deep shit already. The Trust didn't do anything for no reason. Were they angry with him? Had he fucked something up? He didn't think so. He couldn't think of anything he might have done wrong.

He heard the soft whooshing of air that signaled the pod's approach. He turned to look into the tunnel to his left, at the headlight that appeared there.

The pod was long and cylindrical, able to carry two hundred riders at a time. It was shaped like a bullet, its outer shell treated to make it as frictionless as possible, its interior appointed with simple, common synthetics. It glided to an easy stop at the edge of the platform, doors opening at either end to allow embarking passengers to swap places with departing passengers.

Nathan joined the group of people boarding the pod, staying near the doors so he could get off quickly.

Why don't you ask your wife?

What could Niobe have done to draw the attention of the Trust? She was a scientist and a professor of mathematics. She had been stupid enough to marry him, but otherwise she was a smart woman. Smart enough not to get involved with anything the Trust was involved with. While the syndicate was a myth to most people and claimed as non-existent by anyone working for them, he had passed enough hints in quiet moments she knew what he really did for a living. She didn't agree with it, but she also knew why he had to do it.

He had been a Centurion Space Force pilot. An officer. A Captain. He was a Stacker, which meant he was top-of-the-line and destined to rise through the ranks of the CSF as he gained experience. During his five years in the military, he'd become a top-scorer in the simulators completed nearly a dozen exploration missions.

Then one day, he and his squadmates were granted some leave. They had gone out for a drink. One of them had too much and started getting rowdy with one of the female patrons, making advances she clearly didn't want. All he had intended to do was break them up, to get his man to calm the fuck down and chill the hell out. They exchanged words, and then they exchanged fists.

It was only one punch. He had underestimated his strength. He hit his brother-in-arms just right and killed him on the spot. A freak accident. A stupid mistake. There were a number of labels, but the most important one was *murder*.

He had spent fifty years on the mining rigs, court-martialed and disgraced. They would have never let him go, except he was a Stacker. A first-generation Stacker at that. The decorated veteran from whose DNA he had been designed had a flaw, and that flaw had led all of the first-gen Stackers to develop problems with their mental stability.

They said they couldn't blame him for that.

He wasn't so sure.

Even so, the Space Force had released him, though they had no intention of helping him restart his life. The social climate for replicas was bad enough, and he had still killed a man.

It had never gotten easier to live with.

Ex-cons on Proxima had two options: Live in a containment center and take whatever few shit jobs you could find, or work for the Trust.

He had gone with the second option. Containment centers were prisons with unlocked doors and no guards. Dangerous, violent, filled with the worst kinds of society. The Proxima Civilian Council claimed they reduced recidivism by eighty percent. The truth was the cons were too busy fucking one another over to mess with the general population.

Why don't you ask your wife?

The pod took eight minutes to reach Dome Six, where he and Niobe lived. As soon as the doors slid open, he shoved past the other riders and ran to the exit, excusing himself past another group of people to get to the top faster. He ran across the street, barely avoiding the traffic, cutting through an alley, crossing another street and through a second alley, and then running to their apartment building.

He had to slow to wait for the entry doors to slide open. He had to wait again for the lift to carry him to their eighth-floor cube. He reached their door, cursing as he fumbled at the patch over his real identification chip, finally getting it off and swiping his wrist over the all-seeing eye.

The door slid open.

Why don't you ask your wife?

"Niobe?" he shouted her name, though he didn't need to.

The cube wasn't large. A small living area, a bedroom in the back on the right, a smaller bedroom ahead of it. A kitchen and bathroom on the left.

The doors to the rooms were all closed. Was she even here? It was late enough. He could have checked the rooms first, but he didn't. He had to call the job in. That was how it worked.

He went to the comms terminal on a table in the corner. He tapped on the single button there. "Oleksy Dostoyev," he said.

He waited a few seconds for the system to do the lookup, and then for the man to answer. Oleksy was middle-aged and balding, thin and ugly.

"Stacker," he said. "Is it done?"

Nathan retrieved the two sticks of platinum and held them up to the screen.

"Leave them on the table. We'll have someone pick them up in the morning."

Nathan nodded. He put the platinum on the table in front of the terminal. Then he reached for the button to disconnect the link. He didn't need to say anything.

"Tell your wife I said hello," Oleksy said with a smile, just before Nathan tapped it.

The terminal went dark. Nathan's heart rate leveled up.

"Niobe?" he shouted again. Was she here? She should have heard him the first time.

He went right to the bedroom, reaching for the door. If she wasn't here, did that mean the Trust had taken her? If she wasn't here, where would she be? Why?

Why don't you ask your wife? Tell your wife I said hello.

He pushed the door open.

Chapter 3

The first thing Nathan noticed was that the window's transparency was set to one hundred percent, offering a view into the alley below and the next apartment a few meters away. He could see across to the cube to his neighbor's living space.

She was standing there, looking back at him, her face pale.

What was her problem?

He shifted his attention from her to the bed. When his eyes landed there, they didn't move. His body froze in place. His heart felt like it stopped beating. A dull roar sounded in his ears, and he could hear the real pace of his pulse within it, thumping so hard he could barely believe he was still upright.

His entire world collapsed.

The strength fell away from his body. He tumbled forward onto his knees, the move putting him at the edge of the gel mattress.

He kept looking at his wife, trying to disbelieve the truth.

She was on the bed. She was wearing the same suit he had seen her in when she had left for work. It was a gray suit, but now it looked nearly black. It was soaked with blood. Stained and wet. There were marks all over her chest and stomach and arms. Her face was intact. Her eyes open. Peaceful.

"Niobe?" he said as if calling out to her would bring her back to life. "Nye?"

He reached out, putting his hand on her ankle and squeezing. She didn't respond. Her flesh was still warm. She couldn't have been gone more than a few minutes.

They had killed her. The Trust had fucking killed her! Why would they do something like that? It didn't make sense.

His anguish to boil away with the sudden rage that consumed him. He had done everything they asked. Delivered every message. Picked up every payment. He was a good and loyal soldier.

They had done this. There was no question. Worse, they had hurt her to hurt him.

And he had no fucking clue why.

His jaw clenched. He pulled his hand away from Niobe's ankle, balling it into a fist. He tried to catch his breath, his chest heaving as he stood up. He was a soldier. He had seen death before. This? This was too much.

His eyes returned to the window. The neighbor was there, but she had moved to her terminal. He glanced from her to Niobe and back. Privacy was secondary to efficiency on Proxima. She had a good enough angle to see the body.

Nathan looked away. His eyes landed on the floor beside the bed.

On the knife.

It was twenty centimeters long, with a thick, wide blade. He had seen knives like it before. Yamaguchi made them in his factory.

Son of a bitch.

He left the room, hurrying back to the terminal. He tapped a few of the controls. He had installed a hallway camera above the entrance to his cube, just in case. It recorded whenever there was movement in front of the door. He needed to know who had done this.

Whoever it was, he was going to find them, and he was going to kill them.

He had a clip of himself entering the apartment. He went to the one before that and froze again.

What the fuck?

It was another clip of him entering the apartment. Same clothes, different timestamp. Thirty minutes earlier. He swiped his wrist across the scanner, and the door opened. He walked right in.

Except it wasn't him. It couldn't be.

It had to be another Stacker. Another of his kind. As first-gens, limited numbers of Stackers were made to be identical before Proxima Command decided it might not be a benefit to their interpersonal development to feel as if they had come off an assembly line. Nathan just happened to be one of the lucky ones.

He double-checked the terminal. There was no record of the man leaving. Was he still here?

He spun around, looking at the two closed doors. There was nowhere to hide in a cube. It was too small. He clenched his fists and walked toward the second bedroom. If his life were perfect, there would have been a nursery inside. His life was far from perfect. Replicas were sterile, and Niobe had chosen him over motherhood.

She had chosen him, and now she was dead because of it.

He kicked the door open. It cracked on its hinges. They used the room for storage. Personal effects. Keepsakes. That was all he found inside.

He turned back to the bathroom. He pulled his pistol from his pocket and walked over to it. He kicked that door open too, aiming the gun into the room.

Empty. It was empty. What the hell?

He heard a buzzing noise outside the window,

growing in pitch. He looked out in time to see a small drone rising from the street toward him, a small red and blue light flashing on top of it.

He hit the controls for the transparency, making his window opaque. He could hear the drone move closer, and then a green beam split through the glass and the tint was overridden. He found himself staring directly into the front of the drone, a red light beaming out toward him.

The peace officers already knew?

He remembered his neighbor.

She must have called them. Had she seen his twin murder his wife?

"Nathan Stacker." The drone blared through the wall in a tinny mechanical voice. "You are under arrest for the murder of Niobe Rivera Stacker. Put your hands above your head and remain in position until the peace officers arrive."

Nathan had no intention of waiting for the peace officers to arrive. He turned away from the drone, moving back to the terminal. It shifted its position to stay behind him and keep him in its sights.

"Nathan Stacker." It's order was louder this time, as if that would make him more likely to follow it. "Do not move."

"Oleksy Dostoyev," he said, ignoring the drone. He knew the man knew what had happened here. Would he tell him why they had done it?

The terminal remained dark. A moment later, the screen turned red.

Account locked.

They were closing in on him. Damn it.

He hurried back to the bedroom, leaning over Niobe. Tears ran from his eyes, down his cheeks and off onto her lifeless body. He kissed her on the cheek.

"I'll find whoever did this. I'll fucking kill them. I promise."

He looked down to her hand. It had a large gash in the palm, as though she had tried to catch the knife as it stabbed her. His stomach churned at the sight of the wound, but he forced himself to take the hand. He picked it up, holding it gently while he slid her wedding band from her finger.

"I love you, Nye. Real love."

He kissed her forehead, barely able to contain himself. He had to force himself to pull away. To leave her behind. He couldn't do anything for her by staying here.

He ran out of the cube and out into the hallway. He turned his head toward the lifts at the end of the corridor. He could see the counter on the wall, showing one of the lifts was rising, another descending. Both were going to cross his floor.

He made a run for it, charging toward the lift banks and the stairs beside them. He had to get down before they could stop his escape.

By the time he reached the end of the hallway,

one of the lifts had arrived, the doors beginning to swing open. He saw three peace officers inside, dressed in dark blue uniforms and linked tactical helmets.

He didn't slow, hitting the wall to slow his momentum and turn to his left. Three long strides carried him to the stairs, and he shoved his way through the door, nearly crushing one of his neighbors in the process.

"Nate?" the man said, pressing against the wall to get out of the way.

Nathan took the steps three at a time, hopping down, turning, going down, turning. He had dropped three floors when the door on the eighth floor opened, the peace officers catching up. They didn't shoot at him, retreating instead, hoping to cut him off at ground level.

He didn't slow. He was committed to running, and he was committed to making it to the bottom of the stairwell.

He was on the second floor when the door beneath him opened, a pair of officers moving in. They saw him coming, turning to aim their rifles at him. He knew the guns would be loaded with stunners, not lethal ammunition. He reached the last platform and jumped, throwing his large, muscled body at the law men.

They both fired. One of the stunners got caught in Nathan's overcoat. The other hit him in the shoulder. He felt the high-voltage shock, and he grunted lightly at the pain it caused, at the same time his arm went numb. He still couldn't change gravity. He hit the two officers like a wrecking ball, using his shoulder to slam into one and his working arm to gather the other and push them both over. They hit the wall, the air knocked out of them. Nathan grabbed the door and pulled it open, yanking himself through.

Another peace officer waited outside the door. She tried to get her rifle trained on Nathan, but he grabbed the end of it and turned it aside, maintaining his forward momentum and putting his good arm across her chest, using his strength to drive her back off her feet and onto the ground.

She grunted as she hit the floor. He didn't slow, exiting into the lobby. He could see a pair of marked cars coming to a stop outside the building, and he turned and headed for the 'employees only' door that led into the loading dock.

Fortunately, it was a regular locked door, meant to keep people from accidentally wandering back there instead of trying to prevent entry. A powerful kick convinced it to move aside, and Nathan burst into a service hallway, shoving past a technician and heading straight for the back of the apartment building.

He didn't have much time before the place would be surrounded.

He passed the restrooms and a break room, reaching the door to the loading dock. He shoved through it, nearly falling off the edge of the bay, catching himself and jumping instead. A transport was reversing into it, and he rolled beneath it, the pressure of the pusher-coils shoving roughly into his body as he did. He got back to his feet, breaking out through the open bay door and into the wider back alley.

He came to a stop, looking in both directions and up. He could hear the drones nearby. He could see flashing lights around the corner.

He sprinted to the closest cross-alley, squeezing past garbage collection units. When he reached the corner, he leaned out to look around.

He knew where he wanted to go; he just had to get there. He wasn't going back to the asteroid mines without doing something about this. At the very least, he was going to find out why they had burned him, and why Niobe had been used to do it.

He walked quickly across the street, pausing when he noticed the clothing exchange. The small store had a few of its wares on display on the sidewalk, beside the open door. He waited a few heartbeats for the other pedestrians to clear the front of the store. Then he walked over, reaching out and snatching a broad-brimmed hat without slowing.

He pulled it low over his head and flipped up the collar of the overcoat. He diverted at the next alley as the peace officers reached the street. He took it another block over and then began to make his way back.

He had to get to the loop station.

His wife was dead, and someone was going to pay.

Chapter 4

Nathan lowered his head as a large Peacekeeper drone whined down the street, a red laser scanner pouring out from its belly like it was pissing on the populace. The identification chips implanted in every resident responded to the laser, feeding it back information and giving it a detailed map of who, what, when, and where.

The Peace Office claimed the drones helped reduce crime across the Domes by up to fifty percent. It was all bullshit. A lie, like the facts about the containment centers. Like so much of the tech they had come to rely on, it was easily manipulated. It didn't stop the real criminals from doing whatever the hell they pleased.

It only made it easier for them to get away with it.

The drone passed him by, its laser sweeping over

his tag without registering his identity. Of course, he knew how to avoid the drones. He knew how to do a lot of things the normal population didn't.

He scanned the street ahead of him for peace officers. He was clear for now, though he could still hear the commotion nearby.

He started walking, crossing the street by navigating between the scooters that raced back and forth along it; the small transports the only personal vehicles permitted in the domes. He made it to the other side, turning left and going one block over to the loop station there. He would need to take it from Dome Six to Dome Nine.

He thought about Niobe. He couldn't stop himself. Nausea crept up from his gut, heading for his throat. He coughed to keep himself from groaning or crying. He needed to soldier the fuck up. He was a Spacer, damn it. At least, he had been.

He remembered back to when he had gotten out of prison and swore to himself he would stay out of trouble. Get a job. Find a wife. Live the normal, peaceful life. He used to repeat the mantra in his head like a song.

In the beginning, he had wondered if he could do it. Life was hard for replicas in general, harder for replicas who weren't soldiers, and hardest for replicas who had been to prison. The Trust had changed that by giving him a job. Niobe had changed that more by giving him someone to love.

You can't trust the Trust. That's what all the replicas at the center had told him. Sooner or later, you're going to get yours. He had always thought if he stayed loyal to them, they would stay loyal to him. After all this time, he had even started to believe it was true.

They had screwed him over in the worst way possible. It seemed his time had come. He still couldn't believe it.

Nathan descended into the loop station. The walls on the way down were alive with color and light and text, marketing all kinds of pop culture garbage he had always struggled to find interesting. A woman with a small face and huge eyes spun around in a long sparkling dress, belting out the same two lines to the same awful song. A happy couple perched on their sofa cradling a brand new baby, the latest in replica technology with up to eighty-percent parental DNA. A Centurion in full armor held a plasma rifle to his chest and saluted the viewer.

Wouldn't you be proud to join the Space Force?

He reached the platform, approaching the automated kiosk against the wall of the station. He would have to scan his chip to pay for the ride, and the gate wasn't going to open for him unless he did. He was hesitant to do it. Once he scanned it, they would trace him here in no time.

Would he be on his way to Dome Nine by then?

He paused at the kiosk. When he was running a job for the Trust, he would stick a throwaway they provided him with on his arm over his real chip. It was usually a stolen dupe of some poor, innocent soul's biometrics. He would do his business and then go home as if nothing had ever happened.

To a PO trace, it would seem as though he was hanging out in a bar or watching a stream or was at a ballgame the whole time, instead of transporting illicit goods or shaking down someone like Mr. Yamaguchi. If the Peace Office was curious enough to follow up, they might question the civilian who had their bio lifted, at which point they would discover the duplicate entries and the whole thing would be forgotten.

Assuming of course, that the Trust hadn't already paid them to look the other way.

Nathan had already removed his stolen identification. He hadn't been prepared to come home to find his wife slaughtered. How the hell could anyone prepare for that?

"You gonna go through?"

Nathan glanced back at the man who had gotten into line behind him. The man flinched slightly, recognizing Nathan as a Centurion Space Force replica before finding his courage and standing his ground. Nathan considered commenting, but he didn't need to draw more attention to himself.

He made his decision, taking the last step to the

kiosk and raising his wrist to the scanner. It beeped as the gate swung open, allowing him through.

He walked out onto the platform, eyes passing over the people already waiting there. It should be less than a minute before a pod arrived that would carry him to Dome Nine, a trip that only took a few minutes more. Five minutes from the station to his destination, and then he would find out what all this was about.

He leaned against one of the columns that lined the platform, keeping his hand up to wipe the tears from his eyes. He had gone soft over the years. When he had been in the brig, the other inmates had been scared shitless of him. And why not? He was bigger and stronger than most of them. And he was a Stacker.

He kept his head moving, sweeping the platform left and right. The crowd was getting thick with men and women in fancy suits, a lot of them with Oracles over their left eyes, giving them a modularized connection to the rest of their lives. Work, kids, wife, hobbies. Take your pick. You could do it all with an Oracle. At least, that's what the billboards said.

He froze when he spotted a peace officer at the gate, dressed in a dark blue uniform, a stun baton on his hip. The man swiped his wrist to open the barrier, stepping onto the platform. His body language told Nathan the PO wasn't doing a general patrol.

He was looking for Nathan.

Nathan cursed under his breath, shifting to the other side of the column and out of sight of the officer. He reached up and lowered the brim of his hat, trying to put his face in shadow. The pod would arrive any second. All he had to do was stay in one place and wait.

He closed his eyes, gripping the handle of the pistol in his pocket. He didn't want to shoot a peace officer. The guy was doing his job. But he couldn't let himself get caught, either. He had questions. He needed answers. If it hadn't been Niobe, maybe he would have let it go.

But it was, so he couldn't. No matter who he had to hurt.

He opened his eyes again, leaning out slightly to see past the column. He could hear the hiss and whine of the pod now, approaching the station and slowing. He eyed the crowd, searching for the peace officer. He found the man moving away, walking along the north end of the platform. He breathed a sigh of relief, turning his head the other way as the pod's forward lights lit up the darkness of the tunnel.

Thirty seconds and he would be on his way. Once he was in the pod, he was assured to make it to Dome Nine. They couldn't shut everything down that fast.

The pod came to a stop, the doors opening. Nathan walked briskly from his spot near the column to the closest door at the ass end of the pod. He stepped over the threshold, even more relieved now that he would definitely make it to his destination. Passengers piled in after him, slipping past and taking the seats on either side of a narrow aisle, filling them before he had a chance to claim one of his own. They didn't look at him, but he was used to that. Replicas existed to protect the Proxima Republic, not to take up seats on the loop.

He pulled his hat off so it wouldn't knock into the other passengers, crumpling it in his free hand and shoving it into his other pocket. He turned to look out the window, back to the platform. His heart skipped when he saw four more peace officers at the gate, rifles in hand.

They were here for him, and the doors to the pod were still open.

Chapter 5

"Come on, close," Nathan whispered, as if that would convince the doors to close. He watched the peace officers open the gate. They would be in the pod in seconds, and they had the power to stop it from going anywhere if they chose.

He took a step deeper into the vehicle, pushing past a woman to do it.

"Excuse me," he said softly.

"Watch yourself, clone," the woman replied.

He clenched his teeth, bristling at the term. Clone suggested he was a copy, which wasn't accurate. At all. Replicas were derivations of the original, using the best parts of the root DNA and blending it with a lab-modified genome. He was stronger, faster, and more resilient than any real human. Newer replicas were often smarter, too, though the powers that be made sure not to let them get too smart.

He didn't react outwardly. To make a scene would give the PO a reason to hold up the pod. He took the insult in stride, continuing to look back at the platform. The officers had entered, but they didn't move straight to where he was. They were heading north, in the direction of another guy with a similar build. Another Stacker? Maybe his luck wasn't all bad.

The doors to the pod slid closed on a hiss of air. A tone sounded to alert the riders they were about to accelerate. Nathan grabbed a handle on top of the pod, using it to keep his balance as they got underway. He bent over slightly to see through the windows as the pod raced along the north side of the platform. He saw the Officers had surrounded a replica like him. He was right; it was another Stacker. They could have passed for brothers, and technically they were.

Was he the one who had killed Niobe?

He stared at the Stacker, eyes burning with anger while the pod cleared the station, gaining speed when it entered the tunnel. There was nothing to see through the windows now. No light. No scenery. They were fifty meters underground, traveling through the rock that composed most of Proxima.

Nathan stayed on alert as the pod made its stops in Dome Seven and Dome Eight, the passengers around him coming and going, a sea of normalcy that he wished he was still sailing in. There were no Officers on the platforms. Not yet. The loop was quick enough to make a fast reaction challenging.

The pod pulled out of Dome Eight Station, gaining speed. Nathan could feel his anxiety growing with his anger. Once he caught up with his contact, there was going to be some sort of hell to pay. It didn't matter if it brought the weight of the Trust pressing down even harder. They had killed his wife. What else could they do to him?

He was busy with his thoughts. Busy enough that he didn't notice the first peace officer from Dome Six was in the pod with him. He didn't notice the officer coming toward him either, making his way through the passengers to get a closer look and a positive ID. Not until the PO was right on top of him, stunner in hand and making a hard face like he wanted Nathan to challenge him.

"Nathan Stacker," the officer said. "You're under arrest for the homicide of Niobe Rivera Stacker."

Nathan didn't react. He stared at the PO, holding his gaze long enough the other man started to get intimidated. Most peace officers were replicas. Like him, but not like him. Stackers had a reputation, and sometimes silence was the best weapon.

"Don't move," the PO said.

"I haven't moved since I got on this thing," Nathan replied softly. He had one hand on the support, the other in his pocket, still on his pistol.

The officer reached to his hip, retrieving a restraining device.

"I didn't kill Niobe," Nathan said. "The Trust—"

"Is a myth," the PO replied, cutting him off. "A story made up by second-rate assholes and replicas to use as an excuse for becoming criminals. I've heard this story a hundred times before."

He reached out and up for Nathan's neck. His hand was shaking while he did.

Nathan knew from the officer's answer he was either an idiot or on the take. In this case, probably both. He eyed the puck coming for his neck. Then he eyed the officer's Oracle. The time was visible on it, backward from Nathan's perspective.

"The Trust owes me answers, officer," Nathan said, at the same time his free hand dropped from the handle and wrapped around the PO's wrist. He held it easily, despite the man's effort to pull it away. "If you talk to them, tell them they fucked with the wrong replica. One way or another, I'll make them pay for what they did."

The officer stabbed the stunner into Nathan's stomach, activating the shock. Nathan felt it like a tickle along his flesh. He had been designed to stand up to much worse threats than this. He released the plasma pistol and took his other hand from his coat, using it to grab the officer's other wrist and pull the stunner away.

The pod started to decelerate, having nearly reached Dome Nine Station.

The officer looked up at him, white with fear. "You're a murderer."

"Not this time," Nathan said. "But I'm getting closer to doing it again."

He held the man's wrists, leaning back and kicking him in the chest, letting go as he did. The peace officer stumbled backward, crashing into a few of the passengers before falling to the floor.

The pod came to a stop, the doors sliding open. Nathan hesitated for a second while the officer reached for his sidearm. Then he shoved two passengers out of the way and moved out onto the station's platform. A quick glance to the gate showed him a squad of soldiers coming toward it. Not peacekeepers. Fucking military police.

Fortunately, the entrance and the exit were separated by a tall, unbreakable glass barrier, intended to keep people from trying to sneak in through the out without being scanned. Nathan walked briskly toward the gate, meeting eyes with the MPs as he drew near.

"Stacker," one of them said, raising his rifle toward the gate. It was a stunner, more powerful than the officer's version but just as nonlethal.

That didn't mean Nathan wanted to get hit with it.

He burst forward, ducking slightly as he charged

into a passenger in front of him, grabbing the woman by the waist and holding her in front of him. She screamed and tried to pull away, but she couldn't fight his strength. The MPs held their fire, afraid to hit her as Nathan brought her to the exit gate.

"Sorry," he said, letting her go to pass through the gate.

"Asshole," she said in reply.

He cleared the gate. The MPs were already on the move, headed back up toward the surface, intending to grab him there.

The race was on.

Chapter 6

It was easier for Nathan to ascend on the proper side of the mover than it was for the MPs to go up the wrong way. He was rising with the flow of traffic, while they had to turn and push against the incoming civilians, yelling for them to move aside and let them through while trying to get a shot off on him.

Nathan shoved the people ahead of him aside, always to the right to block the MP's fire, ducking behind them and staying in motion. One moron tried to be a hero and stop him, sticking out his foot as Nathan passed him. He was rewarded with a sharp kick on the ankle, hard enough to break the bone and leave him howling in pain.

Nathan didn't care. Not now. The peace officers had moved faster than he expected. The MPs? He hadn't been expecting them to send MPs. But they knew what they were dealing with, and who they were dealing with. They weren't taking any chances.

The soldiers on the descending mover started shooting, getting more desperate as he put distance between them. He was rising fast enough to clear the station before they reached the surface. The rounds were high-powered stunners, and they flashed when they ricocheted off the railing beside him or hit the civilians around him by mistake. Non-lethal meant they could knock a few people down without too much repercussion.

Drones were swooping in toward the station as Nathan crested the top. He used his shoulder to shove another man aside, grabbing his plasma pistol from his pocket and taking quick aim. Three bolts sizzled through the air, slamming into the first drone and sending it hurtling to the ground.

He could hear sirens approaching, the echoing wip-wop gaining in volume as he raced across the street, sparing only a moment to look up at the semi-transparent dome keeping the breathable atmosphere contained. A fake sunset was projected across it, and he could see the Dove through the orange and pink hues. Today it served as the seat of the Government, as well as a sports stadium and barracks. Two hundred years ago, it was one of the seventeen colony ships that carried the settlers from Earth to Proxima.

The massive starship rose high above the Dome,

a sentinel against the backdrop of space and the unknown threat that was out there.

Somewhere.

They didn't tell the Centurion Spacers all that much about who or what it was they were being trained to fight. The government kept a lot of things need-to-know, and that was one of them.

He sprinted toward an alley, the clapping of gunfire loud at his back. The MPs were shooting in desperation, their rounds skipping off the ground or whipping past him. One of them hit him in the shoulder, and he fell to the ground as the stun charge went off, blasting him with close to one hundred thousand volts.

He groaned in pain, spending a few seconds on the ground before rolling back to his feet. He turned, aiming back at the soldiers and squeezing off a few bolts from his pistol. He wasn't trying to hit them, only slow them, and he succeeded in that.

He made it into the alley, between two of the common ten-story apartments. The space between was too narrow for something as large as a Peacekeeper to follow, but it didn't keep smaller tracker drones from buzzing overhead.

He spun and fired, three more bolts pouring from his pistol and hitting a tracker. Smoke poured from it as it sank and crashed into the wall of the cube before falling to the ground. The commotion brought the residents of the cube to their windows, looking down into the alley at him. He ignored them, emerging from the alley and into the next street, immediately looking to his right.

The capital city of Praeton was contained within twenty-four separate domes, and was home to nearly ten-million of the one-hundred million people living on the planet. Each dome was very much a self-sufficient unit, containing everything from farms and apartments to factories and recycling. The zoning of the domes moved from the outside in, starting with A-District. Those were the apartments and shops of the wealthy and had the best views of the landscape beyond the city. That fed into B-District, which was the business center of each dome, as well as a neutral gathering place for people from all walks of life.

The poorest residents were on the inner side in C-District. Their views were of the Centurion Space Force complex and shipyard, and the edges of the other domes that surrounded it.

Oleksy was a low-class merchant with a storefront in C-District. When he wasn't middle-managing jobs for the Trust, he was a med-peddling asshole who only sold the lowest quality garbage. He was Nathan's only real connection to the Trust, which meant he was the only option Nathan had for getting any answers.

Nathan passed through the next alley before making another turn and running along a more lightly populated street. He sprinted along the sidewalk, maneuvering around the few civilians in his path. The sirens were closing in again, having changed direction to give chase, and he could see a Peacekeeper drone approaching on his left.

He pulled to a stop when a pair of MPs cleared the alley in front of him, turning his direction and bringing up their rifles. A civilian on a scooter was about to zip past, and Nathan didn't hesitate to leap out into the street, wrapping his hand around the man's arm and holding him tight. Momentum pulled the scooter out from under the man, yanking him back and off the vehicle. Nathan strained against the force, planting his feet to stay upright and dropping the rider to the ground before heading for the scooter.

"Stop!" one of the MPs said, getting to the machine first, his rifle pointed at Nathan.

Nathan faked to the left before dancing to the right. The MP's shot missed him by a hair. The soldier only had time to squeeze the trigger once before Nathan was on him, grabbing the weapon with a strong hand and hitting the soldier in the head with his plasma pistol. The MP tumbled to the ground, and Nathan pocketed the pistol and slung the rifle, grabbing the scooter and lifting it upright. Another stunner round hit him in the leg at the same time he mounted the vehicle, causing the whole thing to go numb.

Nathan didn't slow as he mounted the scooter. He

let his right foot drag while he accelerated away, just barely getting ahead of the Peacekeeper drone when it passed overhead and turned, fans whining to change its direction and put it back on Nathan's course. He leaned over the controls, gaining speed.

Peace officers came screaming around the corner to his right, their cars making a thrumming noise as they slipped sideways to make the turn, three of the vehicles giving chase in a tight line. Nathan could hear more of them up ahead, getting in position to set up a roadblock and shut him down.

He pushed the throttle to the max, lowering his head to become more aerodynamic. As if that would make a difference. He wasn't a small man.

He whipped through the intersection, turning his head to glance back as the peace officer vehicles came to a quick stop, their intended roadblock already slipped. He was nearing C-District, the buildings ahead losing more of their luster the closer he got. He would have been living in a C-District for the last ten years if not for Niobe, in a containment center with the other unemployable ex-cons and losers the Trust didn't want.

Her love had saved his life.

His love had taken hers.

He clenched his teeth, fresh anger renewing his motivation.

The MPs were slow to catch up to him. So were the peace officers. They would get him sooner or later, he knew they would, but not before he got to Oleksy. Not before either the man talked or the man died. Taking out one member of the Trust was better than going down quietly, and letting Niobe die with zero consequences to her killers.

He skipped the scooter over a low curb and onto the sidewalk, cutting around the other personal transports that had yet to peel off the road in response to the chase. He was nearing another intersection where the traffic was flowing perpendicular to him. Pedestrians and scooters were in his path, but he didn't dare slow down.

"Move!" he shouted at the top of his lungs, his voice deep and loud and getting the attention of the civilians ahead. "Get out of the damned way!"

He angled the scooter and jumped the sidewalk, coming close enough to a woman's back that her long hair whipped him in the face on the way past. He kept shouting, trying to get the people to evacuate. He didn't want to hurt them, only Oleksy.

He reached the intersection, guiding the scooter through an opening in the pedestrians and into the street. A PO car had settled ahead of him, the passenger side door open and an officer leaning against the hood, rifle aimed in his direction.

Nathan didn't hesitate. He squeezed the scooter tightly between his legs and lifted, the vehicle going airborne, the front end just barely clearing the hood of the car. The pusher coils that let it float a few millimeters off the ground slammed into the metal and dented it before lifting him up again. The peace officer took the shot, the stun round hitting the frame of the scooter. Nathan lashed out with his good leg, hitting the side of the officer's helmet and sending him tumbling away.

The scooter crashed down on the other side, the coils planting into the street and bouncing hard. He almost wrecked, the scooter wobbling beneath him, but somehow he managed to keep it going without crashing into anyone on the other side.

He continued along the street, risking a glance behind him. The other cars giving chase had been forced to slow while they cleared traffic, letting him open up some distance between them and giving him a clean break to one of the bridges that connected B-District to C-District.

The Centauri river was the lifeblood of Praeton, and the reason the generation ships had landed here in the first place. While the atmosphere outside the domes was incredibly unfriendly to the needs of humankind, Proxima had an abundance of surface water in the form of long, deep rivers and pools. Not quite oceans, but more than suitable for civilization.

The domes for all twenty of the planet's cities had been organized based on the flow of the rivers, and in Praeton's Dome Nine, the Centauri had been contained to a dozen meters across and a dozen meters depth. Its reduced flow was used for hydroelectric power, among other things. It had greenery and parkland on either side, including trees and other vegetation that had been brought all the way from Earth.

Nathan looked to his left as he started up the bridge's incline. There were always people walking along the banks on both sides, though there was a stark contrast between the upper and middle-class on the B-District bank and the lower-class opposite them. Not that Nathan cared that much about either one at the moment. He was looking for Oleksy's storefront on the other side, in the first row of buildings close to the river.

He found it as he reached the top of the bridge, noting that the front door was open, meaning Oleksy was inside. He looked back at the road, cursing under his breath when he saw a pair of Centurion Defenders blocking his path.

He slammed on the brakes, letting the scooter drop and holding it close to his body. The Defenders were robots, machines designed to protect the Centurion Space Force base from any potential threats, whatever those might be. They were human-sized, though bulkier and blockier than humans, with thick arms and squat legs. He had heard them called gorillas before, but he didn't know what a gorilla was. He couldn't believe they had been requisitioned from the base to deal with him.

Stun rounds burst from the turrets mounted on

their shoulders, flashing off the scooter right in front of him. He closed his eyes to keep the light from blinding him, staying down in the face of the assault. Dozens of rounds detonated all around him, and when they stopped he could immediately hear the two Defenders stomping his way.

He let go of the scooter and stood, opening his eyes. He didn't hesitate, turning to his left and charging toward the lip of the bridge. The Defenders tried to rotate to follow the motion, but he managed to stay a step ahead, leaping up and over the railing.

He straightened out, or at least tried to, his stunned leg not responding as well as he would have liked as he dove toward the river. It was illegal to swim in the Centauri, not to mention cold as fuck, but what else did he have to lose?

He hit the water, plunging underneath, squirming his body to get out of his coat to keep it from slowing him down. He kicked his feet and moved his arms, taking long, powerful strokes beneath the water, fortunate to be moving with the current.

He went deep, swimming underwater for nearly three hundred meters. His lungs were on fire by the time he came up.

A Peacekeeper was already hovering over his head, its red scanning laser pissing down on him. He could hear the peace officer sirens getting closer. The MPs wouldn't be far behind.

He made it to the bank, pulling himself onto the grass. The people around him stared. A few of them cursed at him for being another dirty criminal clone. He ignored them, sprinting across the greenway to the street. Oleksy's shop was right on the other side.

He looked to his right. An army of peace officer cars were closing, along with the MPs and the Defenders. He had given them a good chase, but it was about to end.

He pushed harder, gaining an extra burst of speed and using it to make it to Oleksy's storefront ahead of his pursuers. The asshole was sitting behind the counter, and he stood, bringing a shotgun with him. He managed to fire it before Nathan got to him, the buckshot spreading across Nathan's stomach and digging in deep. Nathan ignored it, grabbing the muzzle of the shotgun and ripping it from Oleksy's hand at the same time he jumped the counter and slammed into the man, pushing him back against the wall.

He threw the shotgun aside, shoving his forearm against Oleksy's neck. The man looked back at him with too little fear in his eyes.

"Why?" Nathan asked, barely containing his fury. "Just tell me why."

"She had too many questions," Oleksy replied. "And she found too many answers."

"What? What does that mean? You didn't kill her to punish me?"

Nathan heard the peace officers move into the store behind him.

"Let him go," one of them said. "Turn around with your hands up. It's over, Stacker."

Oleksy started laughing. "You have a perfect record, Nathan. Why would we want to punish you? No. Your wife was curious. Too curious. Tell me, what do you know about Earth?"

Nathan pressed his forearm harder into Oleksy's throat. Niobe had never said anything to him about asking questions or finding answers. And she had damn well never brought up Earth.

Nathan was sure he didn't know any more about Earth than anyone else. The generation ships had left it behind because there was some kind of political trouble or some other bullshit, and they had decided to settle here. Earth cut off relations, and that was that, at least until recently. He had heard Command was re-establishing communication with their homeworld, and they had brought in the first new settlers in nearly two hundred years, though they were being kept segregated from the rest of the population while they acclimated to their new homes.

What had Niobe done behind his back? What had she learned that had gotten her killed?

"What about Earth?" he hissed, sticking his face close to the other man's.

Oleksy only laughed harder, refusing to offer any

new clues.

"I said, turn around," the peace officer repeated.

Nathan held Oleksy under his forearm. The man's face was beginning to turn red; his breath choked off. His laughter faded to a choking whine, but the smile didn't vanish with it.

The officers didn't warn him again. They opened fire, half a dozen stunners hitting him in the back. Nathan winced against the pain, the strength draining from his body. He brought his other hand up, trying to get more leverage against Oleksy's neck.

Three more stunners hit him in the back. It was too much for him to take. He fell to his knees, losing his grip on Oleksy, leaving the man to stumble away, clutching at his neck and coughing.

"How is he still alive?" Nathan heard one of the officers behind him say. "Never mind still upright."

Four more stunners hit him in the back.

Finally, he toppled forward, landing on his face.

"We're sorry it had to be this way," he heard Oleksy say, the man's voice raspy from being choked. "It isn't personal."

The world started fading away. An image of Niobe crawled into his mind. She had been perfect. Everything he had ever wanted or needed, and they had taken her away from him.

Not personal?

Fuck that.

It was now.

Chapter 7

Nathan woke up in the hospital.

A robot was at his side, four wiry, mechanical arms reaching in and downward toward his gut, doing something with it he couldn't see. It hurt like hell. It probably hurt more than hell would have. He could feel every movement the machine was making as it reached into his flesh to remove the shrapnel from the shotgun.

Hadn't the nurses bothered to give him anything? Had they stuck him on the table and left him to wake up?

"Nurse!" he shouted, trying to get someone's attention.

He shifted his head slightly to see off the side. Medical robots weren't supposed to operate unsupervised, and there was no reason why an anesthesiologist wouldn't be in the room to monitor him.

What the hell was going on?

He clenched his teeth against the pain, the robot's arms twitching slightly in an unnatural movement. He realized he knew exactly what was going on. Fucking Oleksy and the fucking Trust. Was this their kind of twisted justice? What had happened to it not being personal?

He balled his hands into fists, trying to raise them from the table. He wasn't surprised to find them restrained, shackled to the gurney and keeping him down. His feet were the same, his whole body held against the table and unable to move.

The robot raised a shard of buckshot between a pair of narrow fingers, turning the hand and opening the fingers to drop it in a clear bag. Nathan eyed the bag, noticing the blood and the number of fragments there already. At least the robot had to be almost done.

"Nurse!" he shouted again. He didn't expect anyone to come to help him, but there was no harm in trying.

He heard a nearby door open. He had to flip his head the other way to see who had entered. He groaned at the sight of a woman in a too-stylish business suit, with a fitted skirt tight near her calves and a long, fancy jacket going nearly as far, hanging open to reveal a white blouse with a round collar beneath. She had a full Oracle over her eyes, a pair of the screens sitting just in front of her and feeding her data. Two narrow black bangs hung over them, partially obscuring dark eyes.

"You aren't a nurse," he said, grunting slightly at a fresh wave of pain. Any born human would have been unconscious by now, unable to handle the intensity of the metal fingers digging around in the buckshot wounds.

"No," she replied, glancing down at his chest and making a face. "That has to hurt."

There was no compassion in the statement. Curiosity. Amusement. Those four words told him everything he needed to know.

"You're my attorney, right?" he said. "The one the Trust sent to make sure there's no way in hell I manage to get out of this?"

"You're a parolee of a Centurion Space Force maximum security prison," she said flatly. "You murdered a fellow officer. There was already no way in hell you were getting out of this no matter what. You're also technically still property of the system, which means you don't get an attorney. I'm just the unlucky bitch who has to deal with you for the next three days."

"Three days?" Nathan said. "Don't civilian cases normally take up to six months to process?"

"Wake up, Stacker. There is no case. No judge. No jury. Didn't you hear me? Once a Centurion, always a Centurion. That's how the system works."

"That's how the system works because the Trust wants it that way, you mean."

"I'm a judicus. I work for Proxima Command, not some mythical crime syndicate."

"Then why are you letting a medical robot operate on me while I'm still awake?" he hissed, trying to dislodge his binds. He wanted nothing more than to break free of the shackles and use them to wring her neck.

At least the anger was distracting him from the pain in his abdomen.

And from the pain of losing Niobe.

"Everything appears in order to me, Mister Stacker," she said. She moved closer to him, leaning over his face. "You should have handled things gracefully. You might have wound up on one of the labor rigs working the asteroid belt. Not a great life, but you probably could have carved out a niche for yourself, made some friends, adjusted and survived.

"But you decided you were going to, what? Take on the entire planet on your own? The population, they barely tolerate replicas, and only because Command tells them to or because their sister or neighbor just picked up one of those new infant models they've been hawking all over the loop. You decided you were going to go on a rampage across Dome Nine, all to reach some lowlife med dealer in C-District and choke him out. Do you know what that looks like for Command? For the Civilian Council? They spend half their time trying to get you accepted, and all it takes is one wayward asshole like you to make everybody tense again."

"Your boss should have thought about that before they had my wife killed," Nathan said.

"Really, Stacker? Is that really the story you're sticking with? We have surveillance video of you entering your apartment. Thirty-seven minutes later, the same you in the same exact clothes goes running out. Meanwhile, the coroner has already nailed the time of death. I bet you can guess when it was?"

Nathan stared at her. He couldn't decide if she was working for the Trust or not. The way they were treating him suggested she was. Then again, Command had a reputation of its own. Law demanded that his wounds get attention. It likely didn't specify that anesthetic or pain meds accompany it.

"Another Stacker and a data wipe could falsify that evidence in less than a minute," he said. "Even a homicidal asshole like me can figure that out."

"If that evidence were presented tabula rasa, maybe it would be worth digging into, but probably not. Combined with your record? Not a chance in hell. Out of control replicas will not be tolerated. Today or any day in the future."

"We don't have capital punishment here."

"Why would we kill you, Stacker? If that were

enough, we didn't need to bring you here and patch you up."

"You're doing such a great job of that."

"You think you understand how things work here. You think you know all the machinations that help define the daily lives of you and everyone around you. For all of that, you didn't even stop for half a millisecond to consider the reasons or the consequences of your actions. You murdered your wife, and then you went after some lowlife in Dome Nine. Did he sell you bad pills? Do you blame him for the rage that made you stab your wife twenty-eight times?"

"I didn't kill my wife!" he shouted, as loudly as he could. For some reason, knowing the number of wounds made it that much worse.

She smirked, lifting her left wrist and using her right hand to tap on the small computer there.

"It doesn't matter that much if you did or didn't," she said. Nathan could see the data streaming across her Oracle. He couldn't make out what it was. She was probably submitting his statement of innocence for the record. "The Justice Department has already reviewed the evidence. We can't afford to let you integrate back into society. You're not only a risk to commit further violence, but you're a public relations disaster. Do you understand?"

He winced as the medical robot hit a particularly

sensitive area. "So that's it? I get what? Locked up again?"

"Not exactly," the judicus replied. "Command has other plans for you."

Nathan hated the tone of her voice when she said it. He hated the idea of Command making specific plans for a specific soldier, especially when that soldier was him. "What kind of plans?"

"I'm not authorized to say. I've recorded our conversation and passed it to the Department. Your surgery should be completed shortly. You'll have a brief recovery period, after which we'll transfer you to a Centurion Spacer facility on the dark side of the planet. Unfortunately, I'm required to stay with you until you're delivered, so get well soon, Nathan."

She stood up straight and turned to leave.

"Judicus, wait," Nathan said.

"What is it?"

"The ring. My wife's wedding band. Can I have it back?"

"If it was on you when you were brought in, it'll be impounded as evidence."

"Judicus, please. It's all I have left of her."

"Maybe you should have considered that before you killed her."

Nathan clenched his jaw to keep himself from shouting again. It wasn't going to help. New tears formed in his eyes. "Do you really think I'm a monster?"

"I've seen your file," she replied. "Yes, I think you're a monster. I also think if Command had been smarter, they wouldn't have overlooked the loophole that let you walk free. Does it make you feel better to hear me say that?"

Nathan grunted at another sharp pain in his gut. He wasn't sure why he had asked the question, or what he had expected her to say. It had been a long time since he had committed that crime. A long time during which he hadn't harmed another soul. His squadmate would have been eighty years old, wrinkled and retired, while he still didn't look a day over forty. It didn't matter. Nobody had ever forgiven him for that mistake, including himself.

Nobody, except Niobe.

"She believed in me when no one else did," he said. "Do you think I would ever hurt her?"

She stared at him for a long moment. Then she shrugged. "I told you. It doesn't matter. Even if I tell you I believe you, it doesn't change a thing."

He smiled through the pain. "Maybe not for you. It does for me."

The judicus turned around again, leaving the room without another word.

Chapter 8

Three days. To Nathan, they felt like three years. The medical robot had done a decent job of patching him up, but the recovery hurt almost as much as the surgery, and as before the Spacer infirmary refused to waste any of its precious chemicals on a murderous replica. He was forced to get better without medication, to bear the pain like a good little soldier, to lie there in agony while his body knitted back together.

In that sense, he was fortunate to be a Stacker. His enhanced DNA gave him a strong healing factor, and by the third day he was well on his way to recovery. The wounds still hurt a bit, and they would leave a nice bit of scarring, but he would live.

He hadn't seen the judicus after her first visit. He had hardly seen anyone. After the medical robot finished, the gurney had been remotely controlled, guided from the operating room to a cell, the heavy steel doors clanging closed behind him. Only then had his restraints unlocked. Only then did he even have the option to sit up.

He had spent the time doing his best to think. The pain was a distraction, a constant reminder of the reality of his situation. He barely thought about that, though. He barely considered what the judicus had told him about being shipped to the dark side, despite the fact that he knew what was on the dark side. The Centurion Spacer base there was R&D, a research station segregated from the rest of the populace, just in case anything went wrong. The work being done there was hush-hush, highly classified and only truly known to two or three of the most powerful people in Proxima Command.

Instead, he thought first about Niobe. About the day they had met. She had smiled at him from across a row of network access terminals in the Dome Nine Central Datastore. He had been off the mining rigs for almost a year, and she was the first person who had made direct eye contact with him. He had gone over to talk to her, and they had hit it off. When he told her who he was and what he had done? She empathized with his guilt and pain, and he wound up in her arms, bawling like a baby. So what if he was a replica? So what if he had killed someone? He was sorry, and he had changed.

She had allowed him to change when nobody else did.

When he couldn't handle those thoughts anymore, he moved on to what Olesky had said about questions, answers, and Earth. He still couldn't remember Niobe ever mentioning Earth. He didn't recall her speaking of being curious or concerned, or looking up anything about humankind's homeworld. What could she have discovered? Why didn't she say anything to him? Did she know she was going to attract the wrong kind of attention? Was she trying to protect him? Or had her overall kindness and compassion helped support her naivete?

The questions swirled in his head, repeating themselves over and over. He could never get answers directly from her. He would never get answers at all. Whatever happened to him, he was going to do it knowing there would be no resolution to her murder. No closure.

The idea of that nearly drove him mad.

Three days.

The judicus finally showed at the tail end of the third. She was wearing the identical suit from her first visit, a standard uniform for her department. She was carrying a Spacer pack.

"I took the liberty of grabbing some of your things from your apartment," she said as she reached his cell. He was already standing by then, looking out at her through the bars.

"You went into the apartment?" he asked.

"This morning. It'll be cleaned out and sealed for the next three months as per procedure, and then it'll be put up for occupancy. Your wife did well for herself. Her place is in high demand."

"She was a scientist," Nathan said, angry that she had invaded their home and gone through their things. "She was working on extending the relative strength of our space-fold drives." He didn't know what that meant, but it was what she had told him she was doing. The goal was to allow their exploration ships to travel further from Proxima and still make it home.

"I read her file," the judicus said as if that meant she knew Niobe. She shook the Spacer pack in her hand. "You'll find a few changes of clothes and a couple of keepsakes. Your wedding ring, for one. You didn't have much."

"I didn't need much."

"You'll need even less soon enough."

"Still not going to tell me what's going to happen to me?"

"It's not part of my job description." She dropped his bag, reached around her back and producing a pair of restraints. "Give me your wrists."

He held them out. She slapped one of the metal rings on to each. Immediately, powerful magnets activated and pulled his hands together. He tested the strength of the restraints, unable to move them at all.

"I know you're strong," she said. "You aren't that strong."

She took a step back as the cell unlocked and the door slid open. He moved out in front of her, towering over her now that he was upright.

"She would have figured it out," he said.

"What?"

"Niobe. She would have figured out the algorithm. She was making good progress. Or so she said."

The memory hurt more than the shotgun blast had. Sitting on the couch, her head in his lap, looking up at him while she described her work. She had jumped up excitedly, grabbing the blanket off the bed and spreading it out on the floor. She went into a lot of detail he didn't understand about how spacetime was ordinarily flat, but with enough energy and the right math, it could be bent, and the distance between two points could be dramatically shortened.

"The technology isn't new," she had said. "Albert Prackoff invented the first space-fold drive around the time you were made." She always said 'made' without hesitation and without judgment. "But right now, it works kind of like this." She folded the blanket in a certain way. "I have a theory that if we can change the generation fields, we can make it bend like this." She changed the wrinkles, tightening the gaps. "Which will extend our range by two, maybe three-fold." She paused at the pun, smiling in that way she had, sheepish and smart and cute.

"Okay, but extend our range why?" he had asked. "I've had the same question for sixty years. If we aren't looking for a planet with a more Earth-like atmosphere, then what are we looking for?"

"I've never heard anyone say we aren't. But who knows what else is out there, either? The Spacers lead the way. They make sure it's safe before the colony ships leave Proxima again."

"Stacker."

The judicus' voice pulled Nathan back out of his head. He locked eyes with her.

"Let's go," she said.

"Are you sure this is enough?" he asked, shifting his bound hands. "I'm a Stacker. And a monster."

He expected her to respond to the comment, but she held his Spacer pack out to him instead. "If you want this, take it."

He did.

Chapter 9

The judicus brought him out of his cell and into the corridor. He should have guessed earlier he was in a military hospital inside Praeton's Space Force complex. A pair of guards filed in behind them as they entered the hallway, their expressions flat. They were wearing dark navy uniforms, carrying rifles no doubt loaded with stunners.

The nurses eyed him cautiously as he followed his handler from his cell through the building. So did the doctors, orderlies, and other guards they passed. They had heard about him. The Stacker that murdered his friend, and later killed his wife. Their looks were accusing, sometimes fearful. Nathan kept his eyes on the floor, but he could see them in his peripheral vision. It was almost enough to make him feel guilty.

They reached one of the outer doors of the building. It slid open ahead of them, revealing a transport already waiting. A pair of guards stood on either side of a rear hatch, and Nathan could see the pilot sitting in the cockpit behind a wedge of glass. Short wings helped give the craft stability in both the inner atmosphere of the Domes and the outer atmosphere of the planet, while powerful thrusters provided the lift and control.

The judicus climbed in first, settling into a jumpseat on the stern side of the transport. The interior was sparse and functional, metal-framing with just enough cushioning, security belts and little else. Resources on Proxima weren't that tight, not with the numerous mining efforts both on the surface of the planet and in the nearby asteroid belt, but there was no point wasting anything on grunt movers.

She strapped herself in, watching Nathan as he dropped back into his seat opposite her. He was tall enough his legs nearly met hers in the middle. One of the guards climbed in beside him, helping secure him since he didn't have a full range of motion with his hands.

When the guard finished, he dropped into the seat beside Nathan and buckled up. The second guard took the remaining seat beside the judicus. Then the hatch slid closed.

"Let's go," the judicus said.

She could probably see the pilot's back from her

seat, through a small gap between the cockpit and the rear. The transport began to whine slightly as power transferred from the battery to the thrusters.

Nathan couldn't see outside, but he had taken enough rides to know what happened next. The transport would skim the surface, angling to the large airlock that kept them insulated from the planet's true nature. They would wait there while the mechanisms adjusted the atmosphere from inside to out, and then they would climb away, up and over the domes and the ships before accelerating and heading for the dark side of the planet.

It wouldn't be a long trip. A couple of hours at most.

And then?

He had no clue.

He looked across the small aisle at the judicus. He hadn't really noticed her before. He had been in too much pain the first time they met.

It was hard to identify the origins of most of the residents of Praeton. The generation ships had come from all over Earth; delivering pilgrims from the United States, Russia, India, China, Japan and plenty of other locales. The need to settle and survive had stripped away bias and racism, at least until the first replicas were successfully produced. Intermarriage meant hardly anyone was one hundred percent of any single race or nationality.

She looked like a blend of Chinese and African,

maybe with a little bit of Indian tossed in. Darker skin, a small nose, round eyes. High cheekbones, a small frame. He liked the shape of her lips and their natural fullness. They reminded him of Niobe. She had been a real melting pot too, able to trace her family history through six different parts of Earth.

She had been beautiful.

He looked away, glancing at the soldier opposite him. There was no doubt he was a replica, but he was smaller and more compact, his skin pale and his face square and hard. He was staring back at Nathan, and they locked eyes for a few seconds before Nathan turned his head enough to get a look at the other Spacer. That one was more his size, though not quite as tall or muscled.

He put his eyes back on the judicus, noticing her lips first, now that he had associated them with Niobe. He had loved the feel of them on his. He had loved kissing her. He had loved making love.

He felt the tears forming in his eyes, and he blinked to try to stop them. He was going to embarrass himself in front of the soldiers. He was a Spacer, too. He needed to stop getting so damn emotional.

"Stacker," the judicus said, drawing his attention from her lips to her face. "Is there a problem?"

"Just thinking about Niobe," he said. "Your lips remind me of hers."

"You want to cut her throat, too?" the guard beside him asked.

Nathan shifted his head to look at the Spacer. "Go fuck yourself, asshole."

The guard punched him, his hand a rocket into the side of Nathan's face. "Watch your mouth, Stacker."

"Stand down, soldier!" the judicus barked, glaring at the man.

Nathan felt a trickle of blood on his face. He turned his head back to glare at the soldier, anger pressing into his chest.

"Captain, stand down," the judicus said.

The transport shifted, coming to rest in the airlock. The whine of the thrusters vanished, leaving the four of them sitting in silence.

"We have a hard enough time dealing with the birthers," the guard sitting next to the judicus said. "Your bullshit has put us back twenty years."

"They should have never let you out of the brig in the first place," the other one said. "Stackers have always been the worst mistake the program ever made."

"I didn't kill my wife," Nathan said.

"All of you, shut the fuck up," the judicus snapped. She turned to the guards. "Another word from you two, and I'll be filing an insubordination report with your XO."

The guards shifted their eyes downward, remaining silent.

The judicus leaned over to Nathan's bag, unzipping it and pulling out one of his shirts. She unbuckled herself and leaned forward to wipe the blood from his face.

"Ma'am, please sit back," the guard said.

"I can't bring him in bleeding," she said.

She touched the shirt to his temple, dabbing at the cut. Their eyes met. He was surprised to see compassion in them. A touch of kindness, despite her job. Maybe she was starting to believe him?

It was almost enough to stop him from doing what he did next.

Almost. But not quite.

Chapter 10

She had gotten too close. She should have listened to the guards.

He moved fast. Too fast for the Spacers to stop him. He brought his hands up and over her head, using the magnetic attachment of the bands to hold his arms locked around her as he squeezed back, dragging her toward him and down, and crushing her face against his chest, her neck choked by his arms.

In the same movement, he kicked out with his right foot, the length of his reach more than enough to catch the Spacer across from him in the throat, the force of his blow crushing the guard's larynx and leaving him choking for air.

The guard next to him reacted, grabbing his sidearm at the same time he started unbuckling himself, turning to put it against Nathan's head.

Nathan threw his elbow up, hitting the weapon and knocking it away.

"Unbuckle me, or I'll kill you," he said to the judicus.

She responded by reaching for the belt's release, struggling to find it since he had buried her face in his chest.

The guard next to him recovered, unstrapping himself and shifting his weight, throwing another hard punch into Nathan's head. Nathan absorbed it, clenching his teeth and grunting against the blow. He took a second before the judicus managed to hit the release for his security straps, and then he threw himself into the guard, still holding her tight against him. All three of them were shoved into the corner; the guard pressed tight between Nathan and the wall.

The pilot had noticed the chaos and was climbing out of his seat and moving through the opening into the rear. Nathan kicked out, catching him in the side and pushing him into the wall. He kicked again, getting the pilot in the head and knocking him down.

The guard struggled to get Nathan's weight off him, throwing badly leveraged punches into Nathan's side. The other guard was still gurgling and choking, clutching at his neck.

Nathan let go of the judicus, bringing his hands back up and over and using them to shove her back across the aisle. She hit her original seat, coughing and trying to catch her breath. Nathan backed off the guard he had trapped, shifting his weight and then swinging his hands like a sledgehammer, hitting the soldier in the face with the restraints. The metal shattered the Spacer's jaw and knocked him out, too.

The judicus was reaching for the other guard's sidearm when Nathan grabbed her again, getting his two large hands back around her throat from the front.

"Open the restraints," he growled.

She looked at him, terrified. He felt a wave of guilt for hurting her. He didn't want to hurt anyone, but they weren't giving him a choice. He wasn't going to become a part of some fucking experiment. He wasn't going to let the Trust kill Niobe and blame it on him.

The judicus had the guard's stunner in her hand. She fired it into his side, the round punching hard into his already tender stomach at close range.

He hissed at the pain of the shot and the charge coursing through his body, but he didn't let go. Her eyes met his, wide with surprise. She shot him three more times, but he still didn't release her.

She dropped the weapon, reaching up to the bands and tapping on the releases. He let go of her neck as they powered down, unclasped, and dropped free.

He scrambled to his feet, grabbing his Spacer pack and one of the stunner rifles.

"What are you going to do?" the judicus asked, her voice soft and husky. "You can't get out of here alive. You just made everything so much worse for yourself."

"How can it get any worse?" he asked. "You take away everything a man has, what the fuck do you expect him to do?" He aimed the rifle at her. "How much are you worth to them?"

She shook her head. "Not enough," she replied. "Not to keep them from doing whatever it takes to contain you."

Nathan slapped the control to open the hatch. He looked through it. The transport was in the airlock between the dome and the outside, the planet's natural atmosphere filtering in. The air was thin, too thin to keep him alive for long.

"You're killing both of us, Nathan," the judicus said. "He's going to die too."

Nathan looked at the Spacer with the crushed larynx. "Trach him," Nathan said. "If you went through basic, I'm sure you know how." He shifted to the hatch, pausing at the edge. "For whatever it's worth, whatever happens, I'm sorry for choking you."

He jumped out, hitting the outer control to close the hatch again and keep the atmosphere out. He held his breath, scanning the airlock. It was a massive space, big enough to allow some of the larger ships to come and go.

He froze, logic catching up to his emotion. What the hell was he doing? He had gotten out of the transport, but so what? The judicus was right. There was nowhere to go, especially here. He couldn't get back inside the Dome; there would be an entire base of Centurion Spacers waiting for him. He couldn't go outside. There wasn't enough air.

He had one choice, and that was to go back in the transport. And then?

And then nothing.

They would be waiting for him wherever he went. They would catch him again, and deliver him to the R&D facility. Or he could stand here and suffocate. That was better than the other option, but it wouldn't change anything.

Nothing he did would change anything.

Niobe would still be dead, and the Trust would have gotten away with it. He was sure she wasn't their first victim. He was sure she wouldn't be their last.

He was a dead man walking, no matter what he did. He released his breath, trying to draw a fresh one in. It was a strain to get enough oxygen like someone had their hands around his neck again.

It was better to go this way. At least it was his choice. At least he was free. He raised his head, turning to look out at the inner side of Dome Twenty. There was a restaurant in that dome with an amazing view of the mountains that rose in the distance, and if you were there at the right time, you could watch the red dwarf sun sink behind them, casting them in mesmerizing hue of reds and blues. He had been there with Niobe a few times, her treat. He could never afford anything like that. Except for that one time, when he had asked her to marry him. And she had said yes.

The worst mistake of her too-short life.

He was surprised to find his view blocked. A small ship sat between him and the other side of the airlock, and the edge of Dome Twenty beyond. It was an Explorer, twenty meters long, six meters tall, with longer wings than the transport, swept back and joined to a rounded fuselage.

More importantly, it had a space fold drive.

He had been in the ships plenty of times before, though they had evolved in the years since his first mission. The fold drives had gotten smaller and smaller, the fabrication more precise. Blocky shapes had turned into smooth lines, become sleeker and more refined.

If he could get onto that ship, he could...

He stopped himself. He could what? Jump to some random place in the universe? Strand himself in the middle of nowhere? How would that help?

He turned his head, looking back to the other side of the airlock. The dome was separated by a pair of large, transparent doors, sealed closed. He could see the Centurion Spacers racing toward it, prepared to intercept him as soon as they reversed the atmospheric interchange.

And they were reversing it. He could feel the air changing, his breathing becoming easier. He had two minutes to do something, and then he was going to be caught again.

He looked back at the Explorer. There was one place he could go. He had no idea what the consequences would be, but it was something.

He started running toward the ship, at the same time the bottom of its hull began to separate and lower on a pair of hydraulic arms. He glanced up at the cockpit. The pilot was looking at him, lips moving as he reported back to whoever was in charge of capturing him again.

A squad of Spacers were coming down the ramp. The guns they carried wouldn't be loaded with stunners.

He brought his stolen rifle up and started shooting. He hit two of the soldiers in the legs, the stunner rounds instantly causing the appendages to go numb and knocking the Spacers down. The other three cleared the ramp, taking up a defensive position behind the hydraulic arm, two high and one low.

Nathan dove to the ground, lowering his profile and rolling to the side as plasma bolts started hissing off the floor of the airlock where he had just been. He sighted down the rifle's barrel and fired, his first burst clipping the Spacer standing on the right, a perfect shot few Centurions could make or match.

Then he pushed himself back to his feet, charging forward again. Bolts whipped past him, and he dropped to the ground a second time, one of the shots catching the edge of his shoulder. He grunted in response to the burning pain, returning a stream of fire that forced the spacers behind the arm.

He jumped up and charged forward, still shooting. He was only a few meters away from the ship when the rifle ran out of ammunition. When the two soldiers emerged from behind the arm, he lunged at one of them, batting his rifle aside and throwing a heavy punch into his head. The Spacer crumpled and didn't get back up.

Nathan threw himself behind the hydraulic arm, barely avoiding a bolt that hissed past his gut. He spun around it, catching the Spacer trying to turn to meet him. He grabbed the side of her weapon, tugging at it. If she had let go, she might have had a chance. She didn't, and he pulled her into him, tucking his shoulder and throwing her up and over to the ground.

The two soldiers whose legs he had stunned were trying to sit up and aim their weapons. He hurried to them, pulling the weapons away and throwing them down the ramp and off the ship. He ran up into the lower cargo hold, smacking the controls to close the ramp before turning back to a metal staircase leading to the cockpit. The pilot was coming out to meet him, sidearm in hand. He fired smaller plasma bolts at Nathan, who found cover behind a metal crate containing some of the exploration team's supplies.

"Get the fuck off my ship!" the pilot shouted.

Nathan peered around the corner of the crate at the pilot. The Spacer was returning to the cockpit, probably to lower the ramp again.

He couldn't let that happen.

Nathan came out of hiding, charging toward the metal staircase. The pilot heard him, spinning and firing in one smooth motion. The bolts weren't aimed, and they went wide, hissing past Nathan and striking the containers behind him. He took the steps three at a time, catching up the pilot in three quick hops. He grabbed the pilot's gun hand, pushing it aside and throwing the soldier back into the wall.

"You're an idiot," the pilot said. "There's nowhere for you to go."

"There's one place for me to go," Nathan replied. "Earth."

The pilot started laughing. It was cut off when Nathan hit him with the handle of the gun, knocking him out.

It took time, but Nathan didn't want complications. He carried the pilot back to the hold, opening the smaller personnel hatch at the side and lowering him out to the ground. He looked back at the inner airlock as he did. The atmosphere had nearly been equalized, and once it was the doors would open and he would be in real trouble.

He hurried back to the Explorer's cockpit and dropped into the pilot's seat, hoping they hadn't changed the ship's controls too much since the last time he had flown one nearly seventy years ago.

He started tapping on the control surface, powering up the thrusters, and then took the stick. So far so good. As he started to bring the vessel off the ground, and the inner airlock began to slide apart to allow the Centurion Spacers in, he couldn't help but wonder...

What the fuck was so funny about going to Earth?

Chapter 11

Nathan guided the Explorer off the surface of the airlock, rotating the vessel away from the incoming Centurion Spacers as he did. A light was already blinking on the control surface ahead of him, signaling an incoming communication from Flight Control.

He ignored it, keeping the ship on a vertical ascent, the thrusters whining at the strain. There was a matching set of doors on this side of the airlock as well, sealed and locked to keep Proxima's atmosphere out where it belonged.

He tapped a button on the control surface, and a display illuminated up and to his right, giving him a view out of the ship's rear end. He could see flashes behind him, the Centurion soldiers firing plasma into the back of the starship. If they damaged the main thrusters, he wouldn't have enough power to break free of the planet's gravity.

He pulled on the stick, spinning the craft back around in a one-eighty that left him facing the approaching soldiers. Plasma bolts zipped past the cockpit, a few of them striking the metal skin around it. He put his finger over the stick's main trigger, making the quick decision to use it.

A round of heavy bolts fired from twin turrets on either side of the Explorer's cockpit, heavy balls of superheated gas hitting the ground a few meters ahead of the lead Spacers. The front line dove to the ground, while the rest of them came to a stop, hesitating before backing away.

Nathan guided the Explorer forward before turning it around again, the momentum pulling him sideways in the seat. He flipped up the safety on the stick's top trigger at the same time the craft's comms system was overridden.

"Captain Stacker," a deep male voice said calmly. "This is Colonel Jonathan Bard. Set the ship back on the tarmac and power down, or you will be destroyed. Do you copy, Captain? Power down or be destroyed."

Nathan wondered if the Colonel thought that kind of threat would work? If he gave up now, he was beyond screwed.

He pressed down on the thumb-trigger. A pair of rockets launched from tubes near the Explorer's wings, streaking toward the airlock in a sidewinding motion. He hit it twice more for good measure, following the first pair up with two more.

The rockets hit the heavy iron-glass, detonating against them and sending shards of material spreading back and into the airlock. By the time the last one hit and exploded, the outer airlock doors were cracked and nearly pierced. He fired four more rockets at it, causing the control surface to complain that he had used all of that particular ammunition.

Nathan checked behind him at the same time the last missiles finally broke through the airlock, leaving a gap plenty large enough for the Explorer to pass through. The soldiers were scrambling now, running back toward the inner airlock, which was already starting to close. He noticed the transport was with them, retreating away from the scene.

He used the control surface to adjust the throttle, accelerating toward the damage, main thrusters bright in the rear camera view. He nudged the stick, adjusting his flight path, angling toward the broken part of the airlock. The hole wasn't as big as it had originally looked.

He winced as the Explorer passed through it, half-expecting a jagged shard of the blasted doors to hit the craft and knock it violently to the ground or into Dome Twenty in front of him.

He was grateful when that didn't happen. He grinned tensely as the Explorer cleared the airlock and broke into the open atmosphere, raising the pitch. The ship ascended quickly, rising over the closest dome and giving him a quickly fading view of Praeton and the Dove while he continued to climb.

The control surface started blinking again, a shrill tone accompanying the flashing lights, indicating a potential collision. Nathan checked the sensor grid, finding what the Explorer called friendlies coming at him from his left. Five of them in a tight wedge pattern.

Damn, that was fast.

He rolled the starship to the right, angling away from them with the hopes of outrunning them into space. The Explorer was armed like all of the smaller Centurion spacecraft, but that didn't mean he could take on an entire squadron of starfighters.

He checked his six as he pushed the main thrusters to their maximum, then returned his attention to the sensor grid. The fighters were still approaching, and while the collision alerts had stopped, they were also still gaining, green triangles drawing ever nearer to him in the center of the screen.

If that wasn't bad enough, a new set of triangles appeared, again on his left, coming up from one of the other Centurion bases. The pilot might have thought Earth was a funny destination, but it was obvious Command didn't intend for him to reach it.

He was already maxed out on the throttle, so

there was nothing he could do but watch the sensor grid and wait. He didn't realize he was holding his breath until the sensors picked up smaller objects released from the starfighters and the warning system went crazy.

Missiles.

One from each of the fighters trailing him. The smaller dots were gaining fast, on a direct course to plant themselves right up the ass end of the Explorer.

Nathan cursed, watching the grid, keeping an eye on the second squadron cutting in from the left. Command was probably loving the chance to give the pilots a real combat scenario, instead of having to rely on the simulators.

He didn't love it at all.

He kept watching the grid until the missiles were nearly on top of him. He glanced up into the camera view, barely able to make them out as black specks on the screen. He clenched his jaw and cut the throttle all the way to zero, pitching the Explorer almost straight down.

His body was pressed back into the seat as the craft started its descent, dropping so rapidly he felt like his head was going to be crushed under the force. The missiles flashed past, going over the ship, their targeting computers adjusting and trying to get them turned around. The trajectory had burned a lot of fuel, and as they started to descend they ran out, rocket thrusters shutting down and leaving the warheads to crash back to the planet's surface, well away from any of the domes.

Nathan reached to the control panel on his left side, sliding the throttle back up. The thrusters fired, at first driving him downward at an increased rate, until he pulled back on the stick and began to level off.

One squadron of fighters had followed him. The other had slowed, waiting to see what he was going to do. What was he going to do? If he didn't make it to space on the next climb, he was never going to make it to space.

He brought the Explorer back into a positive pitch, trying the climb again. He rolled the ship to the port side, cutting it at a sharp angle that carried it toward the second group of starfighters. He didn't even try to aim as he began firing the plasma cannons, sending balls of gas launching out at the nimble craft.

It forced them to react, to accelerate or decelerate. It distracted the pilots and gave him a little more space. He checked his grid. The first squadron was behind him again, climbing with him. He had nearly doubled the distance. It would be too hard for them to catch up, and too far for their missiles to close the gap.

He rolled the Explorer back to starboard, keeping

the cannons firing. The spray of plasma cleared a path ahead, all he had to do was keep from being hit.

The warning systems blared again, and a quick glance showed a projectile coming his way, fired so close he had seconds to react. He rolled hard to port, leveling his pitch and screaming out loud when he saw the missile headed directly for the cockpit.

"Come on!" he said, firing the plasma cannons at the weapon. It was a one in a million chance to make a lucky shot and save his ass.

The shots missed. All of them.

But Nathan hadn't left his fate up to luck. He gripped the stick, manipulating it expertly, all of his muscle memory coming back. At the last second, he dipped the craft, the projectile scraping past.

Then he was through the gauntlet, the Explorer continuing its ascent. He reached for the control surface, navigating to the space-fold drive menu. Was Earth already programmed?

He found it was. He selected it as his destination before sitting back and guiding the Explorer out of the planet's gravity well and into space. Once he was there, he leaned forward again, tapping the button that cut the main thrusters and left him drifting. A moment later, the universe began to wobble in front of him, the fold-projectors casting massive amounts of energy ahead of him. As Niobe described the process, it was like manually grabbing the spacetime of the universe and doing a controlled crumple in your hand.

The space around the Explorer became both elongated and compressed, the light bending, the stars all shifting their positions. It stayed that way for a few seconds. Then the fold-projector shut down, putting the universe back into its proper place.

In less than a dozen seconds, the ship had crossed the four light-years from Proxima Centauri to the Sol System. The imperfectness of the fold had left him a fair distance away from Earth itself, but at least he had made it this far.

He heaved a sigh of relief, using the controls to put himself on a direct path to humankind's home world. He had no idea what kind of greeting he would receive when he got there. He had no idea what would be waiting.

Whatever it was, it had to be better than what they had planned to do to him on Proxima.

Chapter 12

Nathan leaned back in the pilot's seat, closing his eyes. His side was throbbing, the wounds from Oleksy's shotgun not completely healed. His head was throbbing too.

He still couldn't believe he had gotten away. He couldn't believe he had survived.

He climbed out of the seat, dropping to his knees and then falling onto the floor. The adrenaline poured out of him, and the reality of the situation slammed him like an asteroid.

He curled into a fetal position, a big, strong soldier sobbing like a baby, the tears running freely from his eyes. There was no-one around to see him like this.

He stayed that way for thirty minutes, crying while the powerful waves of sadness and loss flowed through him. Once the tears had slowed to a stop, he sat up, wiped them off, and got to his feet.

He glanced out the viewport at the stars around him. The universe was beautiful. It had always been beautiful. Light pollution made it hard to see everything from inside the domes. He had promised Niobe he would take her on a cruise beyond the planet's surface to see everything in all its glory.

It was another promise he would never get to keep.

He climbed from the cockpit to the cargo hold. He had dropped the Spacer pack the judicus gave him on the floor when he boarded. He approached it and picked it up, carrying it back through the ship, to the racks near the stern. He sat down on one of them and opened the pack.

He picked the clothes out first. He didn't know what he would have done with them in the Centurion R&D facility, and he didn't know what he would do with them here. A t-shirt and a pair of soft lounge pants. A few pairs of underwear. He looked down at himself. He was sweaty and slightly bloody. He smelled awful. He put the pack off to the side and stood, peeling off his utilities. The ship wouldn't have any means to clean them except in the shower. It probably had water stores for six, not one, so he could afford to waste it.

He would clean himself off, but not yet. He sat back down, looking into the pack.

Judging by the collection of items, the judicus had grabbed all of the smallest keepsakes he and Niobe kept in their spare room and tossed them in. He picked out his wedding ring first, surprised to find it inside. It was a simple black carbon band with a satin finish. Nothing special, just like him. He slid it on his finger, having to push a little harder to get it over some swelling. He stared at it.

They had only been dating for eighteen weeks when they decided to get married. Nathan had wondered at the time if he was doing the right thing. Not because he didn't love her, but what if his love was because he was too desperate to not be alone and to feel accepted? If his love was for the wrong reasons, it was no love at all.

He had gone through with it anyway, and it had all worked out. At least, until today.

He felt the tears threatening to spill again. He looked away from the ring. Why hadn't she told him what she was researching? Why hadn't she come to him if she had found something connected to the Trust?

He reached for the pack, digging through it until he found her wedding band at the bottom. He picked it up, holding it in his palm, feeling the weight of it. It was carbon, too. A little fancier than his with a half carat diamond embedded in the top. He had paid for the ring himself, with credits he had earned from his first few courier jobs. He had felt guilty buying it for her with dirty money, but that was the only money he could earn. Like most things, she didn't care. She wanted his love. That was it.

He closed his hand around it, squeezing it tight, a surrogate for being able to hold her in his arms. He closed his eyes, gripping it as hard as he could, wishing he could change the past or rewrite the future or do something that would put her here on this ship with him.

He would never have noticed the way the center stone was pressing into his hand if he hadn't been holding it so tightly. After gripping it for a few minutes, he started to get a tingling sensation in the middle of his hand. He would never have thought anything of it, except Niobe had demanded a completely inset stone with no extended surface to scratch anything or get caught on anything.

He opened his palm and picked up the ring, looking at the small indent it had left in his skin. It was definitely not flat.

He brought it up to his face, giving it a closer inspection. He ran his fingertip across the stone. He could feel the small bump in it. He turned the ring over and over, examining it from every angle. Was this even Niobe's ring? Had the judicus tried to make him feel better by giving him a cheap fake?

He had gotten a laser-etched inscription burned into the inside of the band the night before their wedding. He found it there, right where he expected it:

Real Love.

It was a simple statement, both the answer to his doubts and his status as a replica.

What he wasn't expecting were the two words that had been added to it. Instead of reading *Real Love*, the inscription now read *Real Love Never Dies*.

He stared at the ring. When had Niobe added the extra words? Did she put them there because she suspected what was going to happen to her? Was it intended to be a message that only he would understand?

He ran his finger along it. Then he turned the ring back over and looked at the stone. He left the racks still carrying it, making his way to the rear of the ship and the reactor compartment. He opened a small service panel beside the compartment entry, revealing a toolkit. He pulled it out and opened it, looking through it until he found a small screwdriver. Then he carefully pressed it against the edge of the stone until it sank in, allowing him to pop the diamond out.

There, resting beneath it, was a data chip.

He leaned against the wall, staring at the small green and gold and silver bundle of circuits. She had left this for him to find. He was sure of it. Maybe she had guessed the Trust would come for her. She hadn't guessed they would bring him down too.

He knew from experience there was nothing on the Explorer that could read from a chip like this. What she had given him was specialized tech, a massively dense storage medium for crazy space-fold algorithms. As far as he knew, there was only one place he would be able to access the data on the chip.

In her lab.

On Proxima.

He punched the bulkhead. "Fuck!"

He could only hope Earth had kept up a similar pace of technological advancement. He could only hope they would have something that could read it.

"I won't let your death be for nothing, Nye," he said, snapping the diamond back into the setting and back over the chip.

He would figure something out. He had to.

Chapter 13

Special Officer Austin Bennett looked out the window. The hustle and bustle of the night time traffic inside Dome Three left a field of color and light across the city below. He watched it for a few minutes, unmoving in his spot at the corner of his office and taking it all in.

Every few seconds, he would shift his gaze from the city below to the dome above. The projectors were shut down at night, allowing all of the residents to get a look at the billions of stars that spread above the planet. So many of the people had no idea how many of those stars never became visible through the light pollution of their civilization. They thought the night sky was beautiful the way it was.

They had no idea.

He caught his reflection in the glass as he turned his head, looking for the river that split B-District and C-Districts. His new job was making him age so much faster than the old one, surprising since he was a hell of a lot less active now. He hadn't lost any of the muscle or put on any weight, but that was typical for his kind. He had always planned on a career as a Spacer, and the turn of fortune that had caused him to switch roles couldn't take away the discipline. Still, he had noticed the budding gray hairs, the wrinkles on his face, the crow's feet around his eyes. He would take a battlefield over his new responsibilities any day.

He spun around when he heard the door to his apartment swish open. His office door was also open, and he waited near the window for his visitor to find him there.

She entered a few seconds later, a big smile growing on her face to find him there.

"You're back," she said, walking over to him. He started moving, going to meet her halfway.

They embraced. Then they kissed. He held her for a minute before she backed away. He stared at her.

"I wasn't expecting you home so early, Rico," he said.

Evelyn Rodriguez. She had been out of the Centurion Space Force for months, but he still found himself referring to her the way he had always known her best — by her call sign.

"You know, the private sector is a bit more unpredictable than government life. I finished up for the evening, and now I'm here. And now you're here." She smiled. "Staring out the window. You haven't been back for long."

"It's hard to readjust sometimes, but you know that. Things are so different here than they are on Earth." He looked out at the city again. "I always feel like we should be doing more."

"We have been doing more, thanks to you."

"It isn't enough."

"It takes time. You know that."

He nodded, looking back at her again. "There's one thing that always makes it easy to come home." He reached out and took her hand. "I've missed you."

"I've missed you too, Sarge," she said, squeezing his hand.

"Have you eaten?"

"Not yet. I was going to make something."

"Fuck that," Austin said, pausing. "Forget that," he corrected. Sometimes it was hard to take the soldier out of the man, but he needed to practice. He was a special officer now. His words had become his weapon, and they needed to sound good for the politicians. "Let's go out. The farms in Dome Six have a fresh crop, and I've heard Riccardo's already got some of the eggplants."

Rico laughed. "How did you hear that?"

"Lucie told me. She's dating Riccardo's brother."

"And your secretary is giving you culinary advice?"

"I've got the inside track."

They shared another laugh.

"I'm game, Sergeant," Rico said. "I could use a nice, romantic dinner with my husband."

"Then let's hit the shower and suit up, soldier," Austin said.

They started toward the door to his office. A soft tone sounded from the communicator pin on his collar, and then a voice came out of it.

"Special Officer Bennett, this is Colonel Bard, sir," the man said. "We have a situation. Can you meet me at the barracks right away?"

Austin glanced at Rico. There went their dinner. She returned a knowing look and a slight nod.

"Affirmative, Colonel," he replied. "I'll be there."

He tapped the communicator to shut it off. He knew better than to ask what the situation was before he got there. Since the Colonel had used the comm pin's emergency override to contact him, he knew it had to be important.

"Don't wait for me," he said. "I don't know how long this is going to take."

"Roger that," Rico replied. "I know how it is." She leaned in and kissed him again. "If you get out early, I'll be at Riccardo's. If you don't, I'll bring some eggplant back for you."

"That's why I love you," he said.

"Eggplant?" she replied, laughing.

"Because the whole of Proxima could be under attack, and you wouldn't change at all."

"Let's hope I never have to prove that."

They moved out into the living area. Austin grabbed his navy dress coat and slid it on, making himself more presentable. He headed to the door, looking back at her as it slid open.

"I'll see you later tonight."

"Yes, sir," she said.

He went from the door to the lift and down the forty floors of his building in A-District. The building liaison had already been alerted he was on the way by scanners in the lift. He was there to meet Austin when he stepped out on the ground floor.

"Sir, a transport will be outside in three minutes," the man said.

"Thank you," Austin replied.

The liaison walked with him in silence as they crossed the lobby. There were a few other residents scattered around the space, which was well-appointed with plush sofas and fancy rugs, a few of which had actually come from Earth. They passed sidelong glances at Austin, trying to look at him without looking at him. He could almost feel the thickness of their disdain, not that he gave two shits about what they thought. He kind of enjoyed being the fly in their snobby soup. The crap on the bottom of their shoes.

Being promoted to special officer had meant special privileges, including new digs in the fancy-ass section of Dome Three, living the high-life as one of the elite, at least when he was back home. He knew the others hated him for it. He and Rico both. A pair of replicas invading their fortress against change and progress?

It was fucking heresy.

He smirked, making eye contact with one of the residents, an older man in an expensive suit. Probably a banker, or maybe one of those same council members he hated dealing with. They all looked the same to him. The man shifted his head, returning the focus of his attention to his Oracle.

The liaison went outside with him, standing at attention beside him while he waited for the transport. He checked the man out of the corner of his eye. The stance wasn't as good as Spacer attention, but it wasn't bad for a civilian. He wondered what the liaison would think if he told him he had just gotten back from Earth?

Lies. So many damn lies. The people on Earth? They didn't know about Proxima. Well, most of them didn't. The people on Proxima? They didn't know the truth about Earth. It had been buried on both sides a long time ago. Almost two hundred years, supposedly for their protection. It was the kind of intel that was kept need-to-know, and the Spacers who found themselves on humankind's first planet were held to the strictest measure of secrecy at home, and a no contact protocol abroad.

Those walls were starting to show cracks, though. The no contact protocol had become a minimum contact protocol, in part thanks to him and his contact a few light years away. He was doing his damndest to take a nuke to the old ways of handling the past and blowing them into rubble. His promotion was only the start of a long process, but at least it was a start.

He was worried about whatever Bard had to say. If the Colonel was desperate to talk to him, that could only mean one thing:

It had to do with Earth.

Chapter 14

Austin arrived at the Centurion Space Force complex in the center of Praeton within ten minutes of receiving the message from Colonel Bard. He had been picked up in a car, carried through the interconnected tunnels reserved for official business and deposited directly in front of the complex's administration building.

It was impossible to miss the state of the place as he stepped out of the vehicle. To his left, a planetary transport was resting on solid ground, its hatch sitting open and a team of investigators milling around it, talking to one another and taking notes. The complex's outer airlock system sat behind the craft, and looking through the steel-glass of the inner doors allowed him to see the disastrous state of the outer doors.

He was no genius, but it didn't take one to put

two and two together and make a quick conclusion about why he had been called in.

Then again, the devil was in the details.

"Special Officer Bennett, sir."

The man who emerged from the building was tall and lean, sharp in his full Spacer blues, heavy rows of hardware lining the outer chest of his jacket. His insignia gave his identity away immediately, though Austin already knew him well. The soldier stopped and saluted, standing at attention.

"Colonel Bard," Austin replied, returning the gesture. It still felt strange to be ahead of the colonel in rank when he had spent all but the last six months saluting Bard and calling him sir. Such was the way of things on Proxima these days. "At ease. Let's keep this informal."

"Yes, sir," Bard said, relaxing his posture. "I'm sorry to have to drag you here. Especially when I know you just got back." He pointed toward the damaged airlock. "You can see we had some trouble."

"What kind of trouble?"

"Did you have time to catch up on current events?"

"Not yet. It usually takes a day for me to get re-acclimated."

"I can only imagine. Does the name Nathan Stacker mean anything to you?"

Austin thought about it for a few seconds. "It sounds familiar, but there are other Stackers running around Space Force. And probably more than one Nathan."

"This is a specific Stacker," Bard said. "Come on inside, and I'll give you the full debriefing."

Austin followed the colonel into the admin building, letting the man lead him to a nearby conference room. Three other soldiers were already there, and they rose to attention as he entered.

"Special Officer Bennett," Bard said. "This is Judicus Imani Shia, Captain Everett Lane, and my assistant, Private Xi."

He returned their salutes. "At ease, all of you. Please, sit."

They sat down again. Austin grabbed the chair next to Colonel Bard.

"Private Xi, if you will?" Bard said.

"Of course, sir," he replied.

The private tapped a control surface on the conference table, and the wall immediately displayed a high-resolution photograph of a tall, muscular man in a Spacer uniform.

"Nathan Stacker?" Austin said.

"Yes, sir," Bard replied.

"I can tell he's an original. Am I right to assume they made him before they implemented the replica aging protocols?"

"Correct, sir," the judicus said. "He's a little before all our times."

"Am I also correct to assume he punched that hole in the airlock out there?"

"Yes, sir."

"And he's headed for Earth?"

"Yes, sir."

Austin nodded. "And the million dollar question?"

"Why," Bard said. "Judicus Shia?"

"I'm transferring Captain Stacker's complete record to you now," the judicus said.

"Can you give me the short version?"

"Of course, sir. Sixty years ago, the Captain was involved in an incident with one Lieutenant Clive Davis. They got into an argument, and Stacker lost his temper and punched him. Unfortunately, Lieutenant Davis didn't survive the hit. He had massive hemorrhaging on his brain and died on his way to the hospital."

"The original Stackers were known to be a little unstable," Austin said.

"The real Stacker was a little unstable," Bard said. "It was coded out by third-gen."

"But Nathan here is first-gen. How long was he in the brig?"

"Fifty years," the judicus said. "His crime was reevaluated after the ruling that first generation Stackers couldn't be held fully responsible for their actions. He was provided with mental health treatment and released into the population with a dishonorable discharge."

"Even though the court said it wasn't his fault."

"They didn't specify how the Space Force should resolve the status of the Stackers who wound up incarcerated. Our courts handled it on a case-by-case basis."

"How long ago was he let out?"

"Ten years."

"And he's stayed out of trouble?"

"Until a few days ago."

"It was all over the news," Colonel Bard said. "But you've been gone."

"What happened?"

"He murdered his wife," the judicus said. "Peace officers were called to her cube when she didn't show for a tutoring lesson. They found her with her throat sliced. We put out a bulletin for Stacker, and when the Officers caught up to him, he ran."

"He made it to the complex to steal a starship?" Austin asked.

"Of course not," the judicus said. "He headed to Dome Nine, C-District. He managed to evade both peace officers and Centurion Military Police and get to a medicinal supply shop there, owned by a man named Oleksy Dostoyev."

"Why did he run to a low-quality herbal shop?"

"We aren't sure. We questioned Mr. Dostoyev. He claimed Captain Stacker was pissed about an erectile dysfunction treatment that supposedly didn't work."

Austin shook his head. "And you say claim because you aren't buying that bullshit, right?"

"Not at all, but that doesn't change the fact that Stacker killed his wife."

"You're sure?"

"We have correlating stream data, a past conviction, and he ran. What do you think?"

"I think the council likes to jump to conclusions, but I know that's not why I'm here. You were handling the case. You caught him, and you were planning to bring him somewhere."

"The research facility on the dark side of Proxima," the judicus said. "Yes, sir."

"What were you going to do with him there?"

"That's classified, sir, above my clearance."

"And probably mine," Austin said. "So how did he escape?"

"We had him secured in the transport. One of the MPs made a comment about his wife, and Stacker got pissed. The MP decided the solution was to punch Stacker in the face."

"We already reprimanded him for his actions," Colonel Bard said.

"The punch left a cut on Captain Stacker's head, and he started to bleed. I leaned over to wipe it off, and he grabbed me and started choking me." She shifted her head to show him her bruised neck. "He made me unbuckle him, and then he disabled the guards."

"One man disabled two MPs?" Austin said. He knew Stackers were tough. He didn't know they were that tough.

"And the pilot," Bard said.

"But you were on a planetary transport, not a starship."

"Correct, sir," the judicus said. "He escaped from the transport. There was an Explorer nearby, also waiting for the airlock to open."

"My Explorer," Captain Lane said, speaking up for the first time. "I saw the whole thing from the cockpit. That cloney stunned out my entire squad in fifteen seconds."

"Cloney?" Austin said, eyeing the pilot.

"Sorry, sir," Captain Lane said. "No disrespect to you intended. Just a little sore over what he did to me and my squad."

"He took out five Spacers on his own?"

"Six, counting me."

"Eight if you include the MPs," Austin said. "This guy is dangerous."

"He knocked me out and dropped me out of the Explorer," Captain Lane said. "Then he made a run for it."

"You sent starfighters after him?" Austin asked.

"Of course," Colonel Bard replied. "Two squadrons."

Austin could feel his mouth dropping open. "And he still got away?"

"You know how things are, Austin," Bard said. "Our Spacers are prepared for an encounter we all hope we'll never have with an enemy we all hope we'll never meet. It's simulator training or bust. When they started facing live fire, they panicked."

Austin nodded. He couldn't exactly relate to their situation, but he understood it. He had seen plenty of lollies on Earth. "How do you know his destination was Earth? He could be going for one of the mining rigs. It wouldn't be the first time someone disappeared there."

"He told me," Captain Lane said. "I probably shouldn't have laughed at him when he said it, but I couldn't believe he thought he would be better off there."

"What does that mean?" Judicus Shia asked. "What's so bad about Earth? I know we left a long time ago and we aren't on speaking terms, but are they openly hostile to Centurions?"

"It's complicated," Austin said. "And classified."

"This whole conversation is classified," Colonel Bard said. "If any of you utters a word of this to anyone outside this room, you'll be court-martialed and sent to the asteroid mining rigs. Do you understand?"

"Yes, sir," the Spacers said.

"So, this replica is on his way to Earth," Austin

said. "I get why you're out of sorts about it considering the damage he did. But why were you so eager to call me here? What do you want me to do about this?"

"No contact protocol," Bard said. "There's a good chance he's going to break it. That might become a big problem for us."

"It would probably be the best thing that could happen for Proxima, and for Earth."

"That isn't your call to make, Austin," Bard said. "Word from Command is they want him found, and they want him dealt with before he can fuck things up too badly."

"And since I'm the bridge between here and there, that makes it my problem?"

"Affirmative."

Austin glanced at the image of Nathan Stacker, still displayed on the wall. This wasn't the kind of dealing with Earth he wanted.

"We've already got a ship prepping for departure," Colonel Bard said. "And a platoon of our best Spacers to accompany you."

Austin continued staring at the image. His strategic mind was going, considering the options.

"Special Officer Bennett?" Bard said. "Did you hear me?"

Austin glanced at Bard, and then looked at the judicus. "Did Stacker say anything to you? Anything that seemed strange?"

She hesitated a moment before nodding. "Nathan was insistent that he didn't kill his wife. That he was framed by the Trust."

Austin's heart began to pulse. In an instant, everything had gone from bad to worse. Everyone said the Trust didn't exist. That they were an excuse for criminals to do criminal things and have some bogeyman to blame them on. He knew better than that. Still, if Stacker was involved with the Trust, if he had gotten on their bad side, it complicated things a whole lot more.

"The Trust doesn't exist," he said, keeping his outward appearance the same. It was the rote answer. Another lie to stack on top of the rest.

"Of course not, sir."

Austin turned back to Colonel Bard. "I don't want an entire platoon. I'll take the five best, most trusted Spacers in the group."

"Are you sure?" Bard asked. "I've heard—"

"If we're going to catch up to Stacker, we need to get close. We can't do that if there are thirty of us chasing him."

"Command doesn't want him caught," Bard said. "Command wants him dead."

Austin figured as much. He would see about that. "We still need to get close to kill him. Anyway, this is my problem, right? Then we go with my solution."

"Of course, sir," Bard said.

"Special Officer Bennett," Judicus Shia said. "I'd like to come with you."

"That would be incredibly unorthodox," Austin said. "Not that I have a problem with unorthodox. Why?"

"I'm the judicus assigned to the case. It's my job to ensure justice is meted out as documented by the Justice Department. Losing Stacker is a personal and professional affront."

"That may be, but you have no idea what you're getting yourself into."

"I understand that Stacker is dangerous. I'm a trained Spacer, just like you."

"You aren't just like me."

"Okay, I'm not a replica, and I don't have first-hand experience." She paused. Austin could tell she was trying to decide if she should say what she wanted to say. She did. "I think Captain Stacker and I have a rapport. I think I can help you get close to him."

"I think if he spots you, he'll run."

"Only if he knows it's me. I can cut and dye my hair, and put in colored lenses. There's something about my face that he seems to find comforting."

"I can imagine a lot of men would find your face comforting," Austin said. He couldn't argue she had a look to her. He paused to consider the request. "Maybe you're right. Worst case, you get yourself killed. That's the job. I can live with it if you can."

Her face flushed slightly, but she nodded. "Yes, sir."

"Fine, you're in." Austin stood up. "We leave in sixty minutes. If you'll all excuse me, I have to go let my wife know I'm not going to be around to eat Riccardo's eggplant, which I'm certain would have been a hell of a lot more enjoyable than any of this."

Chapter 15

Austin exited the Space Force barracks exactly sixty minutes later. He had contacted Rico to tell her he had to make an emergency trip back to Earth. She was completely understanding. She knew how things were. She wished him good hunting and promised him something special when he got back.

He could guess what that something special would be.

He was carrying a Spacer pack he had requisitioned, containing a few pairs of basic utilities and some underwear — clothing for the weeklong trip aboard the Kiev. Armor and weapons would be provided on board, along with other equipment they might need for the mission. Since Command was concerned about the NCP, it was more likely they would be getting most of what they needed once they arrived.

The damage to the Praeton CSF Complex's airlock meant there wouldn't be any ships going in or out that way until the repairs were completed, a process that would take at least a week according to Colonel Bard. It was the only reason they would be taking the Kiev in the first place.

The dropship was an older model — larger, heavier, and more importantly louder than any of the newer droppers in the fleet. It was kept in the Dove's hangar, used more as a training vessel nowadays than a mission-capable craft. Bard had needed to call in an emergency provisioning for the ship, scrambling to get it stocked and loaded in the timeframe Austin had declared. He hated to make the soldiers rush on his account, but the longer Stacker had on Earth, the more trouble he might get himself into, and that was bad for everybody.

He crossed the tarmac to where his new team had assembled, dressed in utilities and standing at attention from the moment he appeared in the barracks' doorway. They were positioned in front of a truck that would take them from the base to the Dove.

He had thrown the pad containing the soldiers' records in his pack, and he made a point of identifying each soldier's face and matching it to their image and name as he neared them.

He came to a stop a meter ahead of them. They didn't shift a muscle, waiting for his commands. Even the judicus, Shia, managed to stay stiff and still at attention. He was impressed.

"Spacers," he said, his voice shifting to a deeper, rougher tone. "I'm Special Officer Bennett, but from this point onward, you'll be calling me Sarge. Do you copy?"

"Yes, sir," they all barked in unison.

"Good. I'll be making less formal introductions with each of you once we're underway. In the meantime, I want you to know that you were selected by Colonel Bard as the best of what Praeton CFS has to offer. You should be proud of yourselves for your accomplishments."

"Yes, sir!"

"I also want you to know that this mission is highly classified. Whatever you see, do, or experience during your time with me, you relay to no one without my express consent or the consent of a sitting member of Space Force Command. Do you understand?"

"Yes, sir!"

"Good. Then mount up, soldiers, and let's get this show on the road."

The squad turned as one, Shia slightly behind, and then filed into the truck, gaining their seats. They remained silent, ready for any instructions he offered.

He looked at them. It felt good to be in charge of a team again, even if he wasn't thrilled with the mission parameters. He had never intended to become a so-called diplomat. Fate had a good sense of humor.

"At ease, Spacers," he said. "Relax and enjoy the ride."

The soldiers relaxed visibly, their posture shifting before they started talking to one another in quiet tones. Bennett grabbed a seat next to Judicus Shia, and the truck got underway.

"How are you feeling?" he asked her.

"Fine, sir," she replied. "A little nervous. A little excited. I always imagined going to Earth."

"You did? Why?"

"Curiosity, I guess, sir. Though I am a little fuzzy on the exact nature of our mission. Don't we need to get clearance from Earth's government before we go hunting a fugitive there?"

Bennett smiled. "Of course. And we will."

"How are the people there, if you don't mind me asking, sir? The Earthers? Is it a lot like Proxima?"

Bennett didn't answer right away. He stared straight ahead, responding with a question.

"Do you have a lot of family here, Judicus?"

"Some, sir. My parents. A sister. She's in the judicus program too. Some aunts and uncles."

"Husband? Wife? Boyfriend? Girlfriend?"

"Not currently, sir."

"Good."

"Permission to speak freely, sir?"

"Sure, go ahead."

"Are you trying to unnerve me? You keep making these veiled hints that Earth is not a safe place for Centurions to go."

"No, I'm not trying to unnerve you. I'm trying to prepare you. The truth is, Earth isn't a safe place for anyone to go."

Bennett almost laughed at the way she looked at him after that statement. It was sad because of the way Command had decided to cover-up the reality of the situation. So sad it was funny.

"I don't understand, sir," Shia said.

"You will." He glanced at the other soldiers behind them. "You all will."

"Should I be afraid?"

"Hell yes. If you aren't afraid, you're going to wind up dead for sure. Follow my lead, and hopefully we'll ace the mission, and all seven of us will make it back alive."

Shia looked away, remaining silent.

"You can still change your mind," Bennett said a minute later.

"No, sir," she replied. "I'm in."

"Suit yourself."

He stopped talking, making the rest of the ride to the Dove in silence.

Chapter 16

None of the Centurion Spacers Bard had selected had ever been in one of the generation ships before. Bennett found that surprising. Praeton schools took field trips to the seat of the planetary government all the time. There were no kids there now, of course. It was night time, and unless they had bad parents, they should be asleep.

He found he appreciated walking through the starship more now than ever. The last one he had entered hadn't been this quiet or in such good condition. He liked the big, open, clean spaces of the corridors and the soft hum of the reactors that kept the ship's power on.

A team of techs were waiting for them when they reached the hangar. Bennett heard Shia gasp beside him, seeing the massive space for the first time in her life, amazed by what humankind had been able to build over two hundred years earlier. He barely noticed it himself; his attention fixed on the Kiev. The bulky, boxy craft was resting in the center of the hangar, a team of techs hastily clearing the space between it and the closed hangar blast doors.

The starship was nearly forty meters long and twenty meters high, with four decks, a central bridge, a large bottom cargo hold, and its own hangar capable of holding a pair of starfighters and a few atmospheric drones. He doubted the prep team would provide any of those, but that was okay. Drones weren't a common sight in Earth's skies.

The outer hull was ragged and bumpy. Four rotating plasma cannon turrets lined the top of the vessel heading bow to stern, while a pair of projectile launchers sat exposed on the sides. The rear of the craft was all thrusters, with four large, round nozzles sticking out from the armored ass, and smaller vectoring nozzles poking out from points surrounding the ship. The cargo hold ramp was extended to the floor of the hangar, a pair of techs rolling a weapons module into the craft.

"Special Officer Bennett, sir." A young woman approached him. She was wearing a pair of navy overalls stained with different types of fluids. A pair of goggles rested on her short red hair, and a pair of gloves stuck out of her pocket.

"Is she ready to fly?" Bennett asked, pointing to the Kiev.

"Yes, sir. It took some amazing work by my team, but she's ready to go. Your pilot, Captain Danethi, is running the preliminary checks now."

Danethi. His file was in Bennett's pack. A replica with over a dozen years of flight experience, though all of his combat was simulated, of course.

"Thank you for taking care of this on short notice," Bennett said. "You and your team have done a great job, and I'll be sure to commend you to Colonel Bard when we get back."

"Yes, sir. Thank you, sir."

Bennett guided his squad across the hangar, to the ramp into the Kiev's hold and up into the ship. The troops had gone silent and attentive again the moment they stepped off the truck.

"At ease, Spacers," he said for the second time. "Bunks are on the second deck. Pick your racks, drop your packs, and assemble for launch."

"Yes, sir!" they said as one, heading to the stairs in the stern of the ship.

He went the opposite direction, taking an alternate stairwell in the bow to the third deck and moving back to the bridge, located in the center of the craft. The door slid open as he approached, revealing a pilot's seat surrounded by a control surface and displays that offered a full view of the outside of the Kiev. A raised command chair was positioned behind it, flanked by two other seats.

A short, dark-skinned man sat in the pilot's seat, running through the pre-launch checklist, tapping on controls and checking different status screens. He didn't realize Bennett was there until he received a tap on the shoulder.

"Captain Danethi," Bennett said.

The pilot shifted his head, not as startled as Bennett had expected. "Can I help you?" he asked.

"Special Officer Bennett."

"Oh." The Captain turned the chair, saluting. "I'm sorry, sir. I didn't know you were you. I mean, I didn't know the special officer was you. I mean, I didn't know you were the special officer."

"Don't worry about it, Captain," Bennett said. "At ease. Feel free to go back to what you were doing. I just wanted to stop in and introduce myself."

"Yes, sir. Thank you, sir."

"Give me a holler when we're ready to lift off. I'll have my pin synced by then."

"Yes, sir."

Danethi faced forward again, continuing through the checklist. Bennett left the bridge, heading to the officer's quarters behind it. He was due the biggest of the four staterooms, though it wasn't really that big. A twin bed, a desk with a networked terminal and ship's log, a full-length closet and a private head. Big deal. He dropped his pack on the bed, used the terminal to sync his communicator with the ship's network, and then headed back out, returning to the bow of the craft, ahead of the bridge. There were a dozen seats there, six rows of two for use by the crew during takeoff and sometimes landing. Half of them were already filled, the Spacers getting settled as quickly as he had.

"Nice work, Spacers," he said, moving to the front of the line. "As soon as Danethi gives the word, we'll be on our way. Once we've passed through the fold, I'll give you a rundown on what to expect when we arrive. It won't prepare you for the real thing, but at least it'll keep you from pissing your armor." He glanced at Shia, to see her expression. She was keeping her face level, her emotions flat. Good. "And remember, whatever happens, whatever you see, it stays with you until you're dead or you will be charged with treason, and you will have a very painful existence after that. Understood?"

"Yes, sir!" they replied.

"Special Officer Bennett," Danethi said, his voice coming out through Bennett's pin.

Bennett tapped it. "Captain Danethi. Please, call me Sergeant or Sarge. It's less of a mouthful."

"Yes, sir. We're ready to go, sir. Preliminary checks are completed. All systems are go."

"Roger that," Bennett said. "Patch us in to Control."

"Roger."

"Kiev, this is Control," a woman's voice said a moment later, coming out through loudspeakers hidden in the Kiev's walls.

"Control, this is Special Officer Bennett. Captain Danethi has completed his checks, and we are go for launch."

"Roger. You are cleared for launch from the Dove's main hangar bay. Activating atmospheric shielding and opening blast doors. Please stand by."

Bennett didn't need to look at the displays on the bridge to know what was happening. The two massive doors that protected the hangar from Proxima's environment would be sliding open, an energy field replacing it to keep the atmosphere at bay. Once the doors were open, the energy field would stay lit except for the few seconds the Kiev was pushing through it. Once they were out, the blast doors would close, and the field would shut down again. It was all standard operating procedure.

He felt the ship begin to vibrate as the main thrusters fired. They rattled slightly, the Kiev lifting off her skids and into the thin air. He grabbed his seat and buckled in, leaning his head back and relaxing while Danethi got them underway.

The old dropship wasn't as smooth as he was accustomed to, but it didn't bother him. He had dealt with hard maneuvers before, and this was hardly that. He felt the pressure change as the Kiev cleared the Dove and started to ascend.

"Reaching orbit in t-minus four minutes, eighteen seconds," Danethi said.

Bennett closed his eyes. This was the quickest turnaround he'd ever had from Proxima to Earth.

He wished it was under better circumstances.

Chapter 17

Nathan was woken up by the beeping of the ship's computer, alerting him that he was finally nearing his destination.

It had been a long, lonely week aboard the Explorer, drifting through the Sol System on his way to Earth. It reminded him of his days in the Space Force when he had participated in over a dozen of similar sorties. Command would send the ships out to different spots in the universe; they would spend a week to a month traveling around on sublight engines, mapping the area and searching for anything of interest. After that, they would fold back to Proxima Centauri, spend another week or so on the return to the planet, rinse, and repeat.

There was a difference between then and now. A major difference. Being in solitude had given him too much time to think. Too much time to reminisce about Niobe. His heart ached every hour of every wake cycle, and his dreams were a fucking mess. They didn't all feature his wife, but they were dark and violent, and he usually wound up killing or being killed.

The time to think wasn't all bad. He had come to realize that if the Trust had killed Niobe because of something having to do with Earth, then maybe he would be able to find some answers there, with or without the data chip she had left him. Maybe he could solve the mystery of why she had been murdered regardless. And maybe, just maybe, he could find some way to see justice done.

It was a long shot, but escaping from Proxima had been a long shot too. He would never have believed it possible if he hadn't done it. So maybe anything was possible.

He had claimed the bottom left rack in the small sleeping area intended to be shared by the Spacers. He stood up, his body cracking as he stretched. The head was right next to him, and he squeezed himself through the small hatch, relieved himself, and then ran the shower, washing himself off. The one thing the Centurions had in abundance was water, both because of the capabilities of their recycling systems and because of the rivers that flowed around Proxima. It was the cheapest, easiest, most compact way to get clean on a ship like the Explorer.

He went back out to the racks, grabbing his

clothes from the opposite rack. None of the Spacers he had removed from the ship were close to his size, so he had been forced to wear the same dark blue utilities they had put him in for transport. He would have been okay with that, but even after spending most of the week naked to preserve them, even after scrubbing them in the shower, they had retained a sickly smell of sweat and blood and body odor.

He could only imagine what the people of Earth were going to think of him.

That was the other thing he had spent a lot of time considering. In order to do anything on Earth, the first thing he had to accomplish was being granted safe haven there. He had to convince Earth's government that he was being unfairly persecuted, and hope they would let him land and remain, and refuse any efforts by Proxima to have him extradited.

Maybe the condition of his clothes would help convince them of his need to escape?

He headed through the small kitchen, grabbing a bottle of water and an MRE. He tore the instant meal open on his way to the cockpit, revealing a dark brown bar of nutrients. He scarfed it down, barely noticing the bland taste, and then swigged the water, finishing both by the time he settled in the pilot's seat and finally turned the proximity alert off.

"Let's see what we've got," he said, looking over at the ship's sensor grid. There was nothing on it, so he extended the view, gaining a bigger picture of the space around him.

The computer marked the moon and the Earth near the far end of his grid, at the top of his central triangle, still a few hours distant if he maintained course and velocity.

Other than that, there was nothing.

He wrinkled his face, confused. How could that be? The colony ships had left over two hundred years ago, but Earth didn't have any spacecraft?

He wondered if maybe some of the fire he had taken escaping Proxima had damaged the sensors, preventing him from seeing anything smaller than a moon or a planet. There was nothing he could do about what the computer was reporting, except let the Explorer get closer and judge it with his own eyes.

Two hours passed. Nathan leaned back in the pilot's seat, glancing at the sensor grid every few seconds, and then back out through the viewport. The sensors still hadn't picked up any ships or any activity from beyond the planet's atmosphere. He didn't know what he had been expecting, but considering that every ship the Centurions produced was armed and armored, he had thought Earth would at least have some smaller patrol ships or something. Maybe a satellite or two? He was still too far out to see any potential objects smaller than a starfighter.

Another hour and the Earth was growing large in

front of him, its moon off to his right. He should have been able to make visual contact with anything the size of a dropship, and soon enough he would be close enough to see a ship the size of the Explorer. There was still nothing. No sign of orbital technology of any kind. He tapped the control pad, opening a comms channel on a wide band of radio frequencies.

"This is Captain Nathan Stacker of the Proxima Centauri Space Force, requesting permission and coordinates to enter planetary orbit. Over." He waited a few seconds for a reply, repeating the message when none came. He tried those bands a few times, then switched to another set of frequencies, duplicating the effort.

He followed the procedure for the next thirty minutes, while also beginning to fire retro-thrusters and slow the craft's velocity. He was almost as close to the Earth's atmosphere as the moon, and while his sensors had finally registered a few objects the size of satellites, they weren't picking up any electrical current, heat, or radio emissions from them.

They were all dead.

"I did fold to Earth, didn't I?" Nathan said, going into the ship's computer and double-checking the flight log.

It confirmed he was in the right place.

He rubbed his chin, his heart starting to pulse. How could this be Earth? Where was everybody?

He switched the comms unit to last potential band of transmission frequencies.

"This is Captain Nathan Stacker of the Proxima Centauri Space Force, requesting permission and coordinates to enter planetary orbit. Over."

Nothing.

He sighed. Whatever was going on, he couldn't exactly go back to Proxima. He would enter the atmosphere and descend toward the surface, to see if there was anything to see.

He had a sinking feeling there wasn't.

Chapter 18

The front of the Explorer glowed orange and red as it passed down through Earth's thermosphere, the field of heat blocking Nathan's view of the landscape below.

He had approached cautiously, cycling through the radio frequencies a second time and repeating his message, adding a suffix to the end requesting a response from anyone who could hear him. Again, no reply.

The lack of activity was unnerving. Frightening. Nobody on Proxima had ever said anything to him about Earth being deserted. It couldn't be, could it? He had heard the rumor that they had brought a bunch of Earthers back to their planet. Had that been a lie?

Why would anyone lie about something like that?

He was worried they were maintaining radio silence and watching him. Did they know the Centurions were building ships that carried weapons? Did they know about the Space Force? Were they trying to appear defenseless, to lure him in and take him out?

It seemed ridiculous, but the other option seemed impossible.

The Explorer settled down as it broke through the thermosphere, its thrust and short wings keeping it aloft against Earth's gravity. Nathan looked down at a thick layer of cloud cover, obscuring his view of the surface below. He had wanted to descend somewhere clear, but he would have had to sync his orbit and wait for hours to make his entry, and he was eager to figure out what the hell was going on.

He continued his descent, watching his sensor grid and the view out of the cockpit. His mind wasn't quite ready to register the existence of a livable atmosphere, or the blue ocean and green and brown landscape he had seen during his approach. He knew a little bit about Earth from Proxima's internet. He knew about some of the vegetation and the animals, and a portion of the planet's history. He had always been intrigued by the American Civil War and the concepts of slavery and emancipation.

He entered the clouds, guiding the Explorer ever downward. Rough air started bouncing the craft, but it didn't concern him. Proxima had rain and rainstorms, with lightning and thunder and high winds. He had been to other worlds that featured the same. None with a human-appropriate atmosphere, though. None that were already home to intelligent life.

He didn't pay much mind to the rain or wind, or the flashes of light around him. The cloud cover was thick, continuing for a few kilometers toward the surface. When he emerged, he would only be ten kilometers or so from the surface, plenty close enough to see if there was anything interesting on the ground below. He was both scared and excited, more excited now that he was committed to the course.

He was so fixated on the viewport that he didn't notice the small dot that appeared on his sensor grid. He didn't see it tracing up from the left side of the starship and angling toward him on an intercept course.

Not until the ship's computer started beeping, sending out the shrill tone of a collision alert.

"What the?" Nathan managed to say, whipping his head around to view the grid. He saw the dot and he grabbed the stick, yanking it hard as he tried to throw the Explorer into a sudden, violent evasive maneuver.

Too late.

The dot, whatever it was, hit the side of the craft and exploded.

Nathan cursed as the Explorer was pushed violently sideways, the hull in the cargo hold suddenly ripped open and allowing the outside air to pour in. He gripped the stick with both hands, holding it tight in an effort to say under control as the ship suddenly wanted to do nothing more than plummet out of the sky.

The craft spun wildly, pinning Nathan to his seat. He growled, reaching over to adjust the thrusters, fingers working quickly along the control surface. Warning tones sounded in the cockpit, a secondary display switching to show the known damage to the craft. The entire starboard side lit up in red, multiple control systems reported destroyed.

He started to shake as cold air moved through the hold and up into the cockpit, threatening to distract him from saving his life. What had hit the ship? Where had it come from? There had been no sign of anything, and then he had been attacked?

The Explorer continued to fall, all of Nathan's effort serving only to stop the uncontrolled spinning. He couldn't stop the crash, not with so many systems down. He knew the old saying as well as anyone. As long as he could walk away.

He forced himself to stay focused, gripping the stick tightly and keeping his eyes ahead. He was losing altitude fast, but not as fast as before. As long as he didn't emerge from the clouds right up against a mountain range, he had a chance.

Six thousand meters. Five thousand. Four thousand.

The Explorer continued to drop.

The ship's computer began beeping again, suddenly signaling another collision alert. Nathan's heart felt like it stopped from the sudden shock. He looked at the sensor grid. Another projectile was incoming and would strike the craft in less than ten seconds.

Damn it; he hadn't come all this way to die before he made it to the ground.

He quickly set the computer to maintain the Explorer's settings, rising from the seat and abandoning the cockpit. He jumped down the ladder to the hold below. Freezing air pummeled him as he rushed to the Spacer deployment station, opening one of the lockers and grabbing an emergency jump pack while ticking off the seconds in his head.

He didn't have time to open the cargo ramp or make it to the standard exit hatch. He had a few seconds at best.

He ran toward the gaping wound in the Explorer. The metal around it was slagged and sharp, and one wrong move would leave him sliced open and tumbling to his death. It didn't matter. It was his only way out, and he was out of time.

He reached out, grabbing the edge of the impacted metal. It sliced into his hand, but he ignored it. He pulled himself up and over, holding onto the ship with both hands and leaving himself to dangle outside, the EJP over his shoulder.

He turned his head at the sound of the sharp whine, his eyes landing on the missile an instant before it hit the ship.

Then he let go.

He had only dropped a few meters when the projectile smashed into the starship and exploded, the fury of the warhead tearing through the already damaged vessel and making it to the fuel stores at its rear. They detonated under the impact, creating a fireball and a wash of heat that shoved into Nathan as he fell, pushing him through the sky. He tumbled end over end, fighting to stay calm and under control, to right himself the way he had been taught in training. Proxima's gravity was ninety-five percent of Earth's, comparable enough that the EJP could save his life as long as he didn't panic.

He came clear of the clouds and into rain as he started to straighten out. Grabbing the other strap of the EJP in his bloody hand, he painfully pulled it over his shoulders and onto his back. He could see the ground below, his experience judging the distance at three thousand meters. He didn't see any mountains, but he did see buildings.

Broken, battered, dirty and destroyed buildings. Crumbling and decayed and falling apart. An entire city of them was approaching beneath his feet, threatening to leave him with no place to land. There was no green to be found. Only brown and gray, dull and drab and lifeless.

What the hell happened here?

He didn't have time to think about it. He reached back to the side of the EJP, pulling the control sticks out from the hard shell and bringing them around to the front. He pressed down on the triggers, the bottom of the pack breaking away and revealing a pair of small, powerful thrusters underneath. They started firing, giving him lift and slowing his fall.

He kept the triggers depressed, watching the fuel gauge on the left stick as his descent began to slow. He looked back up, just in time to see the remains of the Explorer break out of the clouds, trailing smoke and mist as the main fuselage fell.

He followed it, from the clouds to the ground, watching as it struck the top edge of a partially collapsed building, pulling stone and dirt with it as it cut through the structure, tumbling more wildly before hitting another, tearing through it and slamming into a third, right near the base of it. The impact was enough to bring the building down on top of it in a growing cloud of dirt and debris.

Nathan used the controls of the EJP to guide himself as far away from the crash site as he could, his drop under control, the pack allowing him to drift downward and angle toward a gap between two buildings. He scanned the landscape on his way down, noting that the city occupied almost all of a small island, connected to a large land mass by multiple bridges, though they all looked to have collapsed to some extent. There were a few smaller islands nearby, and he noticed one that looked to be man-made, in the shape of a star, with a statue rising from it.

The Statue of Liberty.

He had seen it during his study of Earth's history.

He had come to Earth looking for liberty. For freedom from the Trust and the Centurions who wanted to blame him for something he didn't do.

Now that he was here, looking at the condition the planet appeared to be in, he didn't feel liberated or free.

He felt like he had completely fucked up.

Chapter 19

Nathan touched down between two dilapidated buildings just as the EJP's fuel indicator reached the red zone. His hand was killing him, his body sore from tension and effort. His feet hit the ground, and he dropped to his knees, lowering his head in thanks that he had at least survived this long.

He shrugged the EJP off his back, bringing it around in front of him and pushing on the top. It flipped open, revealing a small compartment beneath.

He took the plasma pistol from it with his good hand, checking its condition. It had a one hundred cell magazine, and it was loaded and ready to go. He slipped it into the pocket of his fatigues before picking the other contents out of the pack. It included a multitool with a ten-centimeter knife, a weeks supply of MREs, a flat waterskin, and a med-kit. He tucked those into his pockets too.

The last thing in the pack was an emergency transponder. It was supposed to go on his wrist, and once activated would help the Space Force locate him from as far away as the planet's orbit. He left it in the compartment and closed the top.

Then he stood up, looking around. There was no sign of anything living nearby. The buildings on either side of him were in terrible shape. There were abandoned and rusted vehicles all over the street. Moss and other plant life grew everywhere they could break through the cracked, faded stone.

He had come down in a ghost town. Or rather, a ghost city. He could guess from the Statue where he was. He knew this place used to be one of the most populated places on the planet.

Where had everyone gone?

Hoping to find out, he picked up the EJP, carrying it with him as he sought cover in a hole in the building on his left, getting himself out of the rain. The temperature was comfortable enough. He guessed the time to be early morning. He used the spent pack as a bench, sitting on it facing out toward the street. Reaching into his pocket, he retrieved the med-kit. He opened it up, pushing aside the patches and sterilization ointments until he found the stitches. The kit didn't contain fancy med-tech like a starship might. It was simple and functional. He just wished he had thought to use his off-hand to grab the jagged metal of the Explorer's damaged fuselage. He was going to have to stitch the right hand with the left, and it was going to come out messy.

There was nothing he could do about it now. He opened one of the tubes of ointment and spread it over the wound, gritting his teeth against the sting. Then he started stitching.

His hands were shaking while he did it, the adrenaline jolt starting to subside. It took him too long to start closing the wound, his stitches big and uneven and sure to leave a scar. Not that he cared about a scar. He was lucky the metal hadn't sliced through the nerves and muscles.

He tried not to think about his situation while he did it. One thing at a time. One stitch at a time. He couldn't wrap his head around all of this at once. If he did, he would be overwhelmed, and from overwhelmed he might fall into the panic trap. Remember the training, keep calm and carry on.

He was halfway through the job when he thought he heard something, a soft scrape like the sound of rubble shifting nearby. He looked up and out into the dim morning. The small cave the building collapse had created was just that. A cave. Broken stone and bent metal were all around him. If there was anything moving, it could only be outside.

He was silent and still for a few heartbeats. When he didn't hear anything else, he lowered his head and resumed the stitch job. He pulled the needle through his flesh, watching the two sides of it pinch together. He let go of the needle and grabbed a bit of gauze, clearing the blood from the wound so he could see what he was doing. He ran the needle through again.

He heard another sound, similar to the first. It came from the opposite direction, registering in his right ear. He turned his head again, double-checking his hiding spot. He knew Earth had an abundance of animal life, and some of it was pretty small. Maybe there was a crack large enough to let something in? If there was, he wasn't afraid of it, but he did want to see it.

He looked out into the rain again, still listening. He didn't hear any other noises, so he returned to what he was doing.

The moment he lowered his head, he heard a louder clang, like something big had smacked into a piece of metal. It echoed in his small chamber, and he jumped to his feet, leaving the needle hanging from the thread in his hand and reaching for his plasma pistol. He stared out into the street, slowly approaching the edge of his cover.

Another sound echoed from his right, and he ducked low, leading with the pistol as he pivoted and leaned out over the threshold. He thought he saw a black shape vanish behind one of the rusted vehicles, but it was so quick he wasn't sure.

He stared at the car in question for a moment

and then slowly pivoted back the other way, keeping his pistol out ahead of him.

He scanned the street but didn't see anything. The black shape had probably been his imagination, an after-effect of his near-death drop to the surface.

He returned to cover, sitting back down on the EJP. He put the pistol down and picked up the needle again, finishing the stitches and tying it off.

With that done, he picked up his head to look outside again. He needed to figure out what to do next, and he had no clue where to start.

He froze, finding himself face to face with a monster.

Chapter 20

A week traveling through the Sol System at sublight speed gave Bennett plenty of time to get to know his new team. Beyond Judicus Shia, who he had given the call sign "Judge," there was Private Hafiz "Happy" Johnson, Private Harold "Frank" Furter, Private First Class Carlos "Animal" Suarez, Corporal Lin "Neko" Smith, and Sergeant Nancy "Seventy" Illario.

They were an interesting bunch of career Spacers, each pulled from their units and shoved into what needed to become a cohesive group of Earthbound grunts if they were going to survive long enough to locate Stacker.

When the soldiers had first boarded, they had been too busy showing off to bond, spending the time making jokes at one another's expense, or telling exaggerated stories about their days in boot camp or their time exploring the outer reaches of space. While the Kiev was larger than a more modern dropship, it still wasn't large. A week crammed together in her confined spaces had settled the machismo and bravado into something Bennett began to recognize as a solid unit.

He was pleased with the outcome, though he was also a little jealous of their situation compared to his own. He was the outsider, the commanding officer, and as such not part of the group. He felt it every time he walked into the mess and the squad was playing cards, or when he entered the gym to exercise. He got along with all of them fine, and he knew they respected the hell out of him for his extended deployment on Earth. Still, there was an undercurrent of separation he wasn't accustomed to and didn't like.

Not that he could do anything about it. He had been like them not that long ago, but he wasn't like them now. He had accepted the assignment as liaison to Earth because somebody had to do it, and after what he had witnessed he didn't trust anyone else not to use the situation to take advantage. The people of Earth had gotten screwed over by their own enough already, left behind when things got rough and forced to fend for themselves.

He had witnessed it firsthand. Hell, he had participated in it. He had been a good soldier. He followed orders. He didn't ask questions.

Then, one thing had changed, and everything else had started to change with it.

Wasn't that the way it always seemed to go?

The No Contact Protocol was still in place, but he had gotten it relaxed just a tiny bit. There was one place on Earth where they could touch down and interact with the locals, and that's exactly where they were going.

"Sergeant, we're nearing Earth's orbit," Captain Danethi said, his voice coming out from Bennett's pin. It was resting on a counter a few feet away from him, a few centimeters away from a plasma rifle.

Bennett reached over and picked it up, tapping it to open the channel. "How long to ingress?" he asked.

"Twelve minutes, sir," Danethi replied.

"Roger."

He put the pin back down, turning to look at his squad. They were all in a state of half-dress, each of them in their underwear while they ran routine inspection on their body armor.

"Twelve minutes, Spacers," he announced, drawing grunts of affirmation from the soldiers.

Judicus Shia was the furthest along in the preparations, her hands grabbing at the clasps that would pull the two sides of the armor together.

Space Force armor was composed of a high-tensile, synthetic spider-silk woven cloth that sat fitted against the wearer, and a series of hardened, high-strength ceramic plates that ran along the length of the material, providing a primary layer of protection above the secondary, highly-energy absorbent defense.

Once it was fully realized and clasped, it gave the wearer the appearance of a futuristic medieval knight, the dark blue material of the cloth only visible in the joints and bends of the even darker ceramic. It had enough toughness to stop almost any small caliber projectile without concern and was also capable of taking damage from higher-caliber, hollow-point or depleted uranium rounds without allowing the round to pierce the cloth and enter the flesh. The ceramics were also uniquely suited for both laser and plasma defense, owing to their incredible heat resistance and dispersive molecular chemistry.

The armor was the culmination of hundreds of years of iteration, beginning before the Centurions had ever dreamed of leaving Earth to head for the stars. The outward appearance hadn't changed much over the years, but the protective factor had improved dozens of times.

Judicus Shia picked up her plasma rifle and swung it to her back. It clicked as it locked into place against the large plate protecting her there. Then she turned back to her locker, grabbing the helmet resting inside.

It matched the body armor in color and overall

look, the smoothly molded helmet made of the same material as the ceramics and painted just as dark. The Space Force logo, an eagle with a star on its chest, had been printed on the forehead, black to match the tint on the helmet's visor.

Of course, the visor wasn't a simple bit of protective transparency. It was similar to an Oracle, only much more advanced in function and processing power. Networked to the other helmets, it would provide real-time battlefield updates and reporting. Everything from the health of each of the soldiers to the precise positioning of both the squad and any marked targets would be automatically transferred to each of their visors, giving them valuable zero-second intel.

Used in conjunction with compatible firearms, it would also provide a targeting reticle for the weapon, which would adjust automatically based on the weapon's current position. It meant the Spacers could literally shoot from the hip and still have a high probability of hitting their target.

She pulled the helmet over her head, connecting it to the body armor with a small plug. She turned left and then right, surveying the input the helmet was providing her.

"First time in a shoot suit?" Happy asked, pausing in his preparations to watch her. He was the largest man in the group, two meters plus and nearly one hundred thirty kilograms of muscle, with a peach fuzz haircut and a massive grin. He was the only soldier in the group who could challenge Stacker in terms of size.

"Second," Judge replied. "First was in training. But that was twelve years ago. The optics have improved since then."

"What was the estimate? An effective doubling of effectiveness every eighteen months?"

"Sixteen months," Neko said. She had gotten to the armory late and was only now stepping into the body armor, which was held slightly above the floor by a hook that extended out from her locker.

She was the complete opposite of Private Johnson, her body petite and pale, her face soft and thoughtful. She had a blend of features from a dozen origins, but her straight black hair was undoubtedly Asian.

"I stand corrected," Happy said. "Anyway, it's about eight times better than when you wore it last time."

"I can tell," Judge said.

"Judge, if you're prepped and ready, head on up to the jump seats and wait for ingress," Bennett said.

"Yes, sir," she replied, pulling off the helmet and tucking it under her arm. She turned back to an array of firearms magnetically locked to the wall, picking out a standard issue plasma pistol and snapping it to her hip. "That should do it."

She saluted him before leaving the room.

"That should do it," Animal said, mimicking her. He was the smallest male soldier in the group, stocky and powerful. His call sign was Animal, but if there were an Earth animal he most resembled, Bennett would have said a badger or wolverine. "What the hell does she know about off-world missions?"

"Am I sensing a little animosity, Animal?" the squad leader, Seventy, a tall and lean blonde with a stoic, handsome face, asked. "Or did you wake up on the wrong side of the rack again?"

"Please, Sergeant, the way he sleeps?" Frank said. "He should be the happiest fucking grunt on this boat." The Private was finishing the clasps on his armor, forcing it to stretch almost uncomfortably around his barrel chest. Once he'd managed to get it closed, he snapped his rifle to his back and selected a laser pistol from the wall as a sidearm. He tucked his helmet under his arm and ran his hand over his bald head as if he had hair to straighten. "Looks like I'm all set too. See you Spacers topside."

"I think Judge thinks she's tough shit because she's a Judicus," Animal said, replying to Seventy's comment. "She could put any of us away without much effort, and she knows it."

"Except she's on our side," Happy said.

"Nothing against Imani," Frank said, reaching the doorway out of the room. "But I don't get how a Judy managed to get the call for this mission?"

"She volunteered," Bennett said, speaking up.

"She was assigned to Stacker's case. As far as I'm concerned, she's going above and beyond the requirements of her duty and taking responsibility for the prisoner's escape, and I respect her for that."

"I don't mean any disrespect, sir," Animal said in response. "She just doesn't seem... I don't know... Tough enough for this kind of work."

"And you don't say that about me?" Neko asked, clasping her body armor. She had dressed faster than any of the others, smoothly adjusting the fit and grabbing her rifle.

"I don't know you well enough to make that determination," Animal said. "It's not because she's a woman. She's got no combat experience and no drop experience. But she's so eager to get to Earth. Maybe too eager."

"None of us have real combat experience," Seventy said. "Simulations and war-games only. And if you were in charge of a dangerous criminal and you let them get away, you would be pretty eager to catch up to them, too."

"I can't argue that."

"Then cut her some slack and shut up," Neko said.

"What are you, her girlfriend?" Animal asked.

"Not yet," Neko replied, winking. "We'll see how it goes."

"All right, all right," Bennett said. "Happy, you good?"

"Yes, sir," Happy replied.

"Then get your ass to the jump seats." Bennett finished clasping his armor, grabbing the pin and sticking it to the collar. He wouldn't need it once he put the helmet on, but he wasn't ready to wear it just yet. "Let's go, Spacers. Five minutes."

Happy headed out of the room, with Seventy right behind him. That left him alone with Neko and Animal.

"Sir, the things you told us about Earth," Animal said. "You weren't exaggerating?"

"There's a reason this stuff is all need-to-know and hush-hush."

"I get that sir, I do. But." Animal paused. "I don't know. It doesn't seem right."

"It isn't right, but it is what it is. I've got a plan to keep relations moving in the right direction."

"What are you thinking, sir?" Neko asked.

"A joint operation," Bennett replied. "If the Earthers help us grab Stacker before he can make too much noise, it might give me a little more leverage at the next policy meeting."

He shuddered slightly at the idea of the next policy meeting. Playing politics was by far the worst part of his new career, so much so he was almost looking forward to getting out into the field despite knowing what was waiting.

Almost.

Chapter 21

"Captain Danethi," Bennett said, walking onto the bridge.

"Sir," Danethi replied, shifting slightly to acknowledge him before pointing at the forward display. "Earth, dead ahead."

"Interesting choice of words, Captain. Did you put in the coordinates I gave you?"

"Yes, sir. Though I don't understand why we're setting down there? Based on Stacker's time of departure from Proxima, approach vector, and the planet's rotation, we're going to be thousands of kilometers off his estimated trajectory."

"The short answer is because I'm in charge, and I said so," Bennett said. "The longer answer will come soon enough."

"Of course, sir. I can't believe we're here." The captain stared at the display and the big blue and green and brown ball floating in it, so close it was consuming the entire spread of the camera's lens. "I never thought I would see it in person."

"It's pretty incredible, isn't it?" Bennett said. "I can still remember my first time." He stopped himself before he said more. His original mission on Earth was highly classified, and there was nobody on the ship with him who had clearance to hear about it. "Of course, it's a hell of a lot nicer from up here than it is on the ground."

"Sir," Danethi said, his voice confused and concerned. "I'm picking up a directed transmission from the planet."

"Open the channel," Bennett said. He expected the call.

"Dropship Kiev," the voice said. "This is Lieutenant Graham at CSF-LM. Do you copy?"

"We hear you, Graham," Bennett said, responding to the lieutenant.

"Bennett, is that you?" the man said. "I thought you just went home?"

"I did," Bennett replied. "I made it about six hours before Command turned me around and sent me back."

"In the Kiev, for that matter. This doesn't have anything to do with the Explorer that showed up on sensors twelve hours ago, does it?"

"It does. What can you tell me about it?"

"Not much. It appeared on sensors once it hit

orbit. Since it was unauthorized, we maintained comms silence and started tracking the ship. Standard operating procedure." Graham paused. There was something about the way he had ended the sentence that made the hair on Bennett's arms stand up.

"And then what happened?" Bennett asked. "You've got something."

Graham was hesitant. Why?

"We picked up something else on our sensors. Well, two something elses. Ground-to-air missiles. They both hit the Explorer."

"And destroyed it?" Bennett asked.

"It seems that way," Graham said. "The signature flared and vanished after the second strike. I assume it was vaporized. Whatever was on that ship, whatever you came back for, I'd say you wasted your time."

Bennett stood in silence, staring out at Earth through the forward display. The news was shocking, and it made it so tempting to order the Kiev to a stop, turn it around, and head home. He had missed his dinner date with his wife, and he wouldn't mind getting back to Proxima early. If the Explorer was destroyed, there was no Stacker to worry about. Lieutenant Graham's report would reinforce the decision.

Except it wasn't that simple, as much as Bennett wanted it to be. It made the whole scenario worse. Much worse.

Someone had fired on the starship. More than that, the missiles had hit it twice. It wasn't like the Explorer was a massive target floating lazily through the sky. It was a twenty meter long spacecraft traveling at nearly a thousand kilometers per hour. To accomplish that kind of feat, either the launch operator had gotten extremely lucky, or the missiles in question were more advanced than anything that should have originated from Earth.

If they hadn't come from here, then they had come from Proxima. And if they came from Proxima, somebody had brought them to Earth's surface and had likely broken the No Contact Protocol to fire them.

He could only think of two groups who might be able to pull something like that off. One was Centurion Space Force Command.

The other was the Trust.

He swallowed hard. There was the safe thing to do, and then there was the right thing to do. Fuck Nathan Stacker for making him make the decision.

"Bennett, you still there?" Graham asked.

"I'm here," Bennett replied.

"I'm assuming by your silence you want to check things out?"

"Want? No. Going to anyway? Yes. If you have a location, send it over. Have you tried to contact Sheriff Duke?"

"I passed a message down to the link in Sanisco,

but according to the governor he's out at the Eastern Expansion Zone."

"Roger that. Did you say anything to the governor?"

"The Explorer didn't pass over the west coast. It didn't seem necessary to mention it."

"Good man. Let's keep it that way. I'll plan to meet the Sheriff out at the EEZ."

"You're the boss," Graham said. "Good hunting, Austin."

"Thank you. Kiev out."

The comm channel closed. Danethi looked back at him.

"I didn't understand most of that conversation, sir," the pilot said.

"It seems someone may have already done our job for us," Bennett said. "Which wouldn't be too much of a problem, except as far as I know CSF doesn't have a presence in what used to be the eastern United States."

"You're saying someone on Earth somehow got their hands on Space Force ordnance?" Danethi asked.

"Or someone from Proxima brought the ordnance to Earth to use. This whole thing is a growing fucking mystery to me right now, one that I don't like or trust."

"Roger that, Sarge," Danethi said, pausing to look back at him. "What's the Eastern Expansion Zone?"

Chapter 22

Nathan stared at the monster. He didn't move. He wasn't sure if he should even breathe.

It stared back at him. It was human-sized and lean, with wet-looking dark, leathery skin and yellow predator eyes sunk slightly into an elongated, narrow head. Its arms were longer than they should have been, ending in equally oversized hands that ended in long fingers that ended in nasty claws. Its mouth was slightly open, revealing a row of sharp teeth.

It stood at the entrance to his little cave and didn't move, as though it was waiting for something.

Waiting for what?

He kept his eyes on the creature while he started reaching for his plasma pistol. Its head shifted slightly, and it hissed at him.

He stopped moving his hand. Did this thing

know what a gun was? If it did, that meant it had some level of intelligence. But where the hell had it come from?

He kept his eyes locked on it. It lowered its head slightly, still watching him.

"What the fuck are you?" Nathan whispered, putting his hand on the EJP, ready to grab the pistol if the monster decided to do something more than stand there.

It hissed again. Then it shifted back slightly. Then it shifted to the left and vanished back into the street.

Nathan picked up the plasma pistol and returned to his feet. He checked his injured hand, and then he moved to the edge of the cave again, looking in the direction the monster had gone. He saw a dark shadow crest the top of a car, leap four meters to the second story of a crumbling building, and climb up and over the edge of the damage.

He shivered, unnerved by the creature. He had never seen anything like it. He had never heard of anything like it. At least it seemed as afraid of him as he was of it. It didn't want any part of him.

Nathan lowered the pistol.

"Now what?" he said quietly, looking out into the street.

Someone had shot down the Explorer. Someone had almost killed him. That meant there was someone alive out here, though it might not be anyone he wanted to meet. What if it was the Trust? They had killed Niobe because she knew something about Earth. Were they here? Had they been waiting for him? There was no way a message from Proxima could have reached the planet ahead of him.

If not the Trust, then who? Why?

He wasn't sure if it mattered.

He also wasn't sure what to do. He couldn't stand there forever. At least if he started walking in the direction the missiles had risen from, maybe he would stumble into something useful.

It seemed as good of an idea as any. He would start walking west and worry about what to do when he hit the water. He was still better off here than he was in some cell on Proxima.

He hoped.

He left the small cave and the EJP behind. He moved out into the street, walking south, and scanning ahead and around him as he did. He was especially vigilant for dark demons like the one he had seen. It had run away instead of attacking, so it didn't seem dangerous.

He had gone about twenty meters when he noticed something sticking out from behind one of the rusty old cars.

Was that a foot?

He started toward it, keeping the pistol up, leading with it as he moved.

The foot moved too, shifting and vanishing behind the vehicle.

What the hell?

He thought about saying something to get the person's attention. He decided against it. He reached the far side of the vehicle, staying close to the rear and creeping across to the other side. When he reached it, he spun out from the back; gun pointed slightly downward.

He froze, heart thumping. The foot was attached to a leg, which was attached to a short pole. A young boy was holding it in one hand. He had a gun in the other.

They stared at one another, both of them motionless, each waiting for the other to react. The boy couldn't have been more than ten. Wiry and small, he wore faded and torn clothes. He kept his gun trained on Nathan. It was a revolver, with a wooden handle and a steel barrel and cylinder. It looked comically large in the kid's small hands.

"Hold up," Nathan said. "I don't want to hurt you."

The boy dropped his makeshift bait, putting a finger to his lips. "Shhhh."

"My name is Nathan. Who..."

His voice trailed off as a dark blur caught his attention. A moment later, it landed almost silently behind the boy.

The creature hissed, reaching out for him.

Nathan's arm shot up, and he squeezed off a round from the pistol. The heavy red bolt sizzled past the boy, hitting the demon in the chest. It screeched and fell back, getting the kid's attention. He looked around, saw the dying creature, and dropped onto his stomach, quickly dragging himself beneath the car.

"Hey, wait," Nathan said, leaning down. "Where are you going?"

The boy looked back at him, eyes wide in terror.

"Come on out, kid," Nathan said. He wished Niobe was with him. She was great with kids. "It's okay. I got it. It won't…"

He trailed off a second time when he heard a soft, rumbling noise from down the street. He paused, turning his head to look back in the direction of the sound.

"You have to be fucking kidding me," he said softly, eyes landing on hundreds of the creatures as they poured out of one of the buildings down the street and started coming his way. He glanced back at the car. There was no way in hell he could fit under there.

He turned south again, ready to run. He caught another dark blur out of the corner of his eye, falling toward him from the building on his left.

He spun, aiming the pistol up at the demon. Too late. It smacked the weapon aside with its long arm, feet hitting Nathan in the chest and knocking him back as they dug into him. He shouted, throwing a hard, heavy punch into the side of the creature's head. He was rewarded with a sharp crack, and the monster fell off him, dead.

His pistol was sitting near the rusted back wheel-well of the car. A small hand was reaching out for it.

"No you don't," Nathan said, diving to the ground and snatching the gun before the boy could take it.

He rolled over when he heard a hiss, firing up into the creature falling toward him and leaving a hole right through its skull. The corpse fell on his foot, and he kicked it away, looking over at the boy hiding beneath the car before getting back to his feet.

He found the demon horde rushing toward him, more of them pouring out of the nearby alleys and leaping down from other buildings. It was like a nightmare, a fucking nightmare. One he didn't know how to wake up from. He turned and ran, sprinting down the street to the south, keeping his eyes peeled for more of the monsters.

An entire group of them came around a corner in front of him, half a dozen strong. They hissed and rushed forward, lunging at him as a group.

He backpedaled, firing his pistol into them, dropping three of them in quick succession. Then his feet got caught on some debris on the ground, and he fell over.

The creatures reached for him, hissing to one another as they did. He kicked one of them in the face, the blow enough to lift it off the ground and throw it backward. He grabbed another by the arm, swinging it almost too easily and pulling it into the third. The creatures were lighter than he expected or imagined. It was as if they had hollow bones.

He got up again. The horde at his back was getting closer and giving chase. He started running again, along the side of the street near the cars. He only risked one look back, finding the boy still under the car, watching as the demons started passing him by unnoticed.

Nathan scanned the street. The monsters were gaining, and now a whole new group of them was emerging from further up ahead, at least one hundred strong. It was too many for him to fight. Way too many. He needed to escape. He needed somewhere to go.

He spotted a dark hole up ahead with a railing on either side, overgrown with vegetation. An old, faded sign announced it as something called a *subway*.

He didn't know what that meant, but none of the creatures were coming out of it. He sprinted toward the entrance, racing to get ahead of the groups threatening to box him in. What the hell were these things, that they were coming after him in such force? He was one man. One human. The only one he had seen other than the boy.

He made it to the subway entrance as the group of creatures ahead of him reached the same space, slowing to vault onto and over the railing. He pointed his pistol at one of them, shooting it point-blank, swinging the weapon to the other side and shooting another one. A third tried to tackle him, and he caught its hand and pulled it down, slamming its head on the railing and breaking its neck. Then he threw himself forward, tumbling down the steps and into the hole, rolling to a stop at the bottom and bouncing to his feet. He turned to face the demons, weapon up and ready to shoot.

The creatures remained at the top of the entrance, yellow eyes looking down at him, the rest of the horde catching up and gathering outside. They had him outnumbered. Why weren't they following?

He started backing up, continuing to watch the demons above. His back slammed into something, and he spun wildly, spinning back when he realized he had smacked into a metal bar across his path. It reminded him of the gate in the loop station.

He grabbed the bar, intending to step over it. It slid aside, groaning loudly. He slipped through the gap, passing behind it, still watching the creatures. But they didn't come down.

Why?

Not that he was complaining. There were hundreds of them out there. Maybe thousands. If they did give chase, he was as good as dead. Still, it was as though they were afraid of something. If they were afraid of whatever was down here, shouldn't he be too?

If there was one alien creature here, there was no guarantee there weren't more.

Who did Earth belong to, anyway?

Chapter 23

Sheriff Hayden Duke stood on top of the tank, right next to the turret. His hat was pulled low over his brow; his head dipped to reduce the glare. One of his smooth metal hands was resting easily on the handle of an ordinary six-shooter. The other was leaning against the vehicle, keeping him steady while it slowly advanced.

A dozen deputies advanced in front of him in a single column. They were all wearing body armor and carrying a mixture of shotguns and more modern personal firearms.

Further ahead, tall grass had split and overgrown what had once been a highway connecting the city of Lavega to the west with parts currently unknown to the east.

Parts unknown. That was the whole reason all of them were out there.

The United States of America had been a big country. At least, that's what Bennett had told him. It had stretched nearly four thousand kilometers across, had been home to millions of people, and had been one of the most powerful nations on Earth.

That was before it had all been destroyed.

That was before it had all been forgotten.

"Sheriff."

The voice rose up from the open hatch of the tank. A young woman's voice, soft and firm.

"What do you have, Latos?" Hayden called back.

His wife, Natalia, had fitted the tank with a sensor array that allowed it to track movement up to half a kilometer away. He had held onto the hope that it would remain silent all day, but they had already cleared the last three kilometers without running into any problems, and good fortune like that wasn't meant to last.

"Looks like there's trouble brewing from that old power station we spotted yesterday," she replied.

Hayden looked up. He could see the silo of the station in the distance. He had hoped to get into it before anything came out of it, but it wasn't meant to be.

He tapped the star-shaped pin on his collar, opening a channel to his deputies.

"This is Sheriff Duke. It looks like we have incoming. Fall back to the tank for cover."

The deputies stopped their forward momentum,

reversing course and raising their weapons. They backpedaled to the safety of the armor, while Hayden reached behind his back and retrieved a plasma rifle. He casually flipped it on.

"Remember," he said. "Everyone behind us is vulnerable, which means nothing gets through. Do you copy?"

"Yes, sir," the deputies replied.

Hayden retreated to the back of the tank. A three-meter tall robot was attached to the rear by a pair of large hooks. He opened a panel on the back of its neck and turned it on. He couldn't see the eyes from behind it, but he knew they would be flashing while it booted up.

"Latos, I'm prepping the Butcher," he shouted. "You have the remote?"

The robot would only take instructions from whoever had possession of the small device.

"Yes, sir," Latos said.

"Can you run it back?"

He heard her boots on the metal of the tank's interior, and then her face appeared below the open hatch. She was the youngest deputy he had, with long golden hair tied back in a pony tail and a sweaty face. She was also the best tank driver they had trained. She held the control device up to him, and he reached down to take it.

"Any sign of Goliaths?" he asked.

"No, sir," she replied.

"Good."

He returned to the front of the tank. He could see the movement in the growth ahead, grass and bushes rattling as something started passing through them. Any day without a Goliath sighting was a good day.

He hoped.

"Two hundred meters," Latos shouted. "Closing fast. They may be evos."

Hayden shook his head. They were coming across more evolved trife than regular ones lately.

"Hold steady," Hayden said to his deputies. "Stay calm. Protect the innocent."

He hopped onto the turret to get a higher vantage point. The Butcher control device turned green in his hand. He smiled and lifted it to his mouth.

"Butcher, dismount and defend."

The device flashed green to confirm.

There wasn't much left of what Hayden had taken to calling Forgotten Earth. War had reduced it to fragments of what it had once been. Broken skylines, crumbling infrastructure, and what sometimes felt like an endless number of rusted and useless cars littering roads like this one was the only evidence that anything better had ever existed. They pointed back at better days, to when humans had subdued the planet and made it their own.

Better days when they had been the dominant species.

"Here they come," Hayden said. He could see the

top of their heads moving through the brush, closing in on the group.

He looked down to see the Butcher starting forward, going out to meet the incoming horde. He brought his rifle up, sighting through the small display mounted on top.

"Remember, stay calm. Watch each other's backs."

He had done his best to train the two-dozen men and women with him on the edge of the Expansion Zone. They were the best of what he had right now, and they had stood strong against the enemy before.

Something in his gut was telling him this one was going to be different. That the demons coming to kill them were more of a threat than the others. He wasn't clairvoyant, but he had the instinct of a third generation Sheriff. The instinct for sniffing trouble was in his bloodline.

He breathed in, the moving brush nearly to the front of the line. If they were coming head-on, it meant they believed they had the numbers to take out the small human force.

One of the Deputies opened fire, a pair of red-brown bolts sizzling through the air and burning through the growth. One of the creatures hissed and collapsed, falling victim to the shot.

The Butcher was only a meter away from the foliage when the demons broke through, a dense mass of them shoving the brush aside and charging toward the humans like a living oil slick. The robot grabbed the closest one by the neck, crushing it, at the same time punching at second and slamming it sideways and into a third.

"Fire at will!" Hayden shouted. He didn't need to aim. Not yet. He fired down into the slick, bolt after bolt finding hard flesh.

Shotgun blasts echoed, plasma bolts sizzled. The tank started releasing rounds from its smaller machine gun, wiping out an entire row of the demons in seconds. At least a hundred of them fell from the first volley, immediately replaced with a second wave.

Latos had been right. The creatures had evolved, their bodies smaller than the others they had encountered. There was a reason humankind had lost the war, and a big part of it was because their enemy adapted fast and reproduced even faster.

Hayden continued shooting, pivoting and firing at the demons who were drawing the closest to his deputies. The enemy line was stalling out, but he could tell by the movement out of view that it wasn't going to last. He had been so careful with the expansion, making sure they didn't try to bite off more than they could chew. The power plant ahead didn't seem big enough to feed so many of the creatures.

That was the evolution, wasn't it? This group had gone smaller to support greater numbers. Were a greater number of weaker soldiers better than fewer stronger ones?

It seemed to be the case. The slick of demons was pooling toward them, two of the creatures replacing every one they killed. Their line was breaking, the enemy getting closer to the tank.

"Butcher, fall back," Hayden said through the robot's control device.

The machine responded instantly, backpedaling as it continued to crush and smash the demons. There was a group of them trying to overpower the robot and bring it down, but their smaller size was making them less effective against it. At least the Butcher would survive the attack.

He wasn't as confident about the rest of them.

A hiss from his left attracted his attention, just as one of the creatures leaped toward him. Its jump matched the height of the tank, taking it over the deputies below. Hayden held his rifle in one hand, batting the monster away with the other. He had lost both of his arms during previous battles, and he had gotten lucky to have them replaced by Centurion augmentations. He hit the demon as if he were swatting a fly, the impact crushing its body and sending its corpse flying back out into the scrum.

He heard a shout on the right side of the tank, and he vaulted the turret, looking down to find one of his deputies on the ground, a demon on top of her. He leaped down, losing his hat as he grabbed the creature and squeezed, its head crushed beneath the force of his grip. Another demon hissed and lunged at him, and he swung his rifle and smashed it in the face.

He turned his head toward the front line. The seemingly endless supply of creatures were breaking through.

He had a fleeting thought of Natalia and their newborn daughter, Hallia. Had the successes of the last six months made him sloppy?

He had no intention of dying today.

"Latos, let her rip," he said into his communicator.

"Roger," Latos replied.

He hated to waste the tank's shells. They had a limited supply. There was no other choice.

The large cannon emitted a deafening roar and a gout of flame, launching the explosive shell out and forward, aimed low to hit the area only fifty meters or so ahead.

Dirt and demons flew into the air, at least a hundred of them killed with the single blast. It was enough to bring new hope to the deputies, and they renewed their effort, still blasting at the closest enemies.

The Butcher reached the tank, grabbing the closest demons and slamming them into the armored sides. Two of the deputies moved closer to it, helping it dispatch the creatures and speeding up its path of destruction.

Hayden made his way forward, firing his rifle until it was out of cells and then switching to his revolver. He fired into the demons, making sure each round led to a kill. Once that gun was empty, he started mimicking the Butcher, using his powerful arms to crush them.

He felt a pair of claws rake the back of his armor. They were sharp and tough, but not sharp and tough enough to pierce the ceramic plates with a single attack. He turned and punched, the force putting his fist into the creature's chest. He yanked it out, ducking as one of them tried to grab his face. It landed on his shoulder, and he threw himself backward, crushing it against the tank.

"Sir, Giles is down," Deputy Yakshin, said. "He's bleeding real bad."

"Where?" Hayden asked.

"Left side, near the tank."

"Keep him covered."

Hayden hurried around the tank, using the plasma rifle as a club. He found three deputies standing over Giles, fighting back against the demons.

"Sheriff, it's not looking good," Latos said. "Sensors are picking up more of them incoming from the plant."

More? How the hell could there be more?

He clenched his jaw. He had to get the deputies out of there.

"Fall back," he said through his comm. "Fall back to the perimeter." He reached the deputies. "Yakshin, Shi, Naples, fall back. I've got him."

None of them looked happy, but they did as he said, pulling back and away from him and the tank.

"Butcher, cover the retreat," he said. The device flashed green twice to confirm.

Six months of victories. Six months expanding the safe zones. They were bound to lose one sooner or later. As long as Hayden could get them out, as long as they could hold the perimeter, he would take what he could get.

He bent over Giles, checking his wounds. The deputy had a deep gash on his neck. His eyes were glassy and blank.

Damn it.

"Latos, back her up," Hayden said. "Cover the retreat."

"Roger, Sheriff," Latos replied.

The tank started slowly rolling backward.

"Give them another shell," Hayden said.

"Roger."

The cannon fired again, a second shell blasting the slick.

Hayden grabbed Giles' rifle, turning away from the dead deputy to face the incoming horde again. He moved forward while the rest of his people moved back, ready to sacrifice himself to get them out. Natalia was going to be pissed if he died, but she was as strong as they came. She would make sure to keep things running smoothly.

He fired into the masses, advancing toward them. The creatures were starting to recognize him as the one who was the most dangerous, and they became more cautious and more eager to take him down. They gathered around him, signaling one another with short hisses, organizing an attack they believed would remove him as an adversary. The whole thing was buying his people precious seconds to retreat, to get back inside the main defensive perimeter. To weather the storm.

At least a hundred of the demons circled him. He stopped shooting, lowering his rifle and turning his head around to look at them. They surrounded him as if he were a stone in the middle of a raging river. One they were eager to remove.

He reached to his chest, to the plastic silver star affixed to the top of his duster. He brought it forward slightly. It was kind of hokey, but if he was going to die, he was going to do it right.

"I'm Sheriff Hayden Duke of the United Western Territories. Vacate this area immediately. I repeat. Vacate this area immediately."

The demons seemed to hesitate, confused by the words.

"Sheriff," Latos said. "Sensors are picking up something airborne. It's big, and it's closing fast."

The creatures attacked before Hayden could respond, all of them rushing toward him like a tide. He flipped a switch on the rifle, adjusting it from a bolt-thrower to a plasma-thrower, and spitting gouts of superheated gas at the demons as he turned in a tight circle. He killed at least a dozen of them before they overtook him. He dropped the weapon, throwing his hands over his head as they piled on. The longer he could stay alive beneath them, the more time he would buy the rest.

He felt their claws scraping at his metal hands and at the armor he was wearing beneath his duster. The creatures shredded through his coat and his communicator in seconds. The armor kept their teeth and claws at bay, slowing them down as they all tried to squeeze in to reach him, their hissing so loud he couldn't hear anything past their noise.

He didn't know how long he was there. Long enough for claws to get through the fabric part of his armor and start cutting into his shoulders and legs. Not deep, at least not at first, but deep enough to hurt. Deep enough for the injuries to bleed. If it weren't for his synthetic arms, they would have shredded his face and torn through his neck straight away.

He wasn't sure when the last one vanished. He could tell their attack was weakening, and as they disappeared and their hisses lessened he found he could hear beyond them, to the intense whine above his head and the sizzle of plasma fire. He moved his arms from his head, peering up and finding the sky blotted out by a mass of dark metal hovering above.

He pushed himself to his feet in time to watch a pair of large projectiles launch from the starship. He followed them as they streaked toward the power plant, vanishing from view. He saw the flash from the site and the detonation. He glanced to his left as a Centurion Spacer appeared beside him in full combat armor.

Together, they watched the power plant vanish beneath a cloud of fire and smoke. A dozen seconds later the ground shook beneath their feet, and they braced themselves against the blast of hot air that washed over them a moment later.

The Spacer next to Hayden grabbed his helmet and lifted it off, turning and smiling.

"Sheriff Duke," Special Officer Austin Bennett said. "Sorry about ruining your chance to sacrifice yourself to the cause, but I need your help."

Chapter 24

The Kiev touched down in an open field nearby. Hayden started following Bennett and the other Spacer soldiers back to it, with the promise of some medical attention when they arrived. He was bleeding from half a dozen places. Not badly enough to be fatal, but that didn't make it any less painful.

"If I remember correctly," Bennett said, "The last thing I said to you before I left was to be careful."

"That's always the last thing you say to me," Hayden replied.

"So why didn't you try doing it?"

"We had the area scouted. We estimated the count based on the size of the plant, just like we discussed. You saw them. They were smaller, which totally threw off the estimates. It normally takes one round to kill one trife, whether there are a hundred or a thousand."

"Bastards keep switching tactics," Bennett agreed. "It's like they can all communicate with one another to plan different experiments. It's like, hey, why don't you guys try going with smaller size and greater numbers, let's see how that does."

"It sure seems that way," Hayden agreed. "But we have no evidence of that happening. Every nest is an island to itself. Hell, they attack one another when they cross paths. In any case, that one won't be any more trouble, thanks to you."

Bennett shook his head. "But you're down a plant. We can't afford to keep taking out reactors if we want to secure more territory."

"I'd rather live with candles than lose my people to the trife."

Bennett laughed. "Roger that, Sheriff."

"Thanks for the assist, by the way. You literally saved my ass. I've got the gash there to prove it."

"I have to say, Hayden, you looked kind of ridiculous standing in the middle of them and holding out your badge. Danethi captured the whole thing on the Kiev's recorders. Fucking legendary."

Hayden allowed himself a quick smile before returning to serious. "I lost at least one deputy. Probably more. I'm not too happy about that."

"I hear you, Sheriff," Bennett said.

"And you aren't supposed to be back here for

another month. And you said you need my help. I can't even begin to imagine why. That's scaring the hell out of me."

"We'll talk about it once we get you cleaned up," Bennett said. "After this, what I'm going to ask for will probably seem like a walk in the damn park. How are Nat and the baby, by the way?"

Thinking about them, and that he would have a chance to see them again, brought a fresh smile to Hayden's face. "They're good. Real good. Nat wanted to come to the Expansion Zone with me, but I convinced her she was better off staying in Sanisco with Hallia."

"I can picture that argument."

"A part of her understands the EEZ is no place for the baby. A part of her thinks this is our life now. This is how it's going to be, so Hallia needs to be prepared to live in this world."

"I'm doing my best to get Proxima Command to stop being such assholes about the situation here. If I keep doing my job, then hopefully your daughter won't have to live in this kind of world."

"I appreciate the help you've provided so far. Don't get me wrong. We had ten billion people on the planet, and we still lost. Even with the help of the Centurions we're fighting an uphill battle."

"How many square kilometers have you added in the last six months?" Bennett asked.

"About four hundred," Hayden replied. "And

we've cleared fifty kilometers of the former interstate out of Lavega. I'm not saying we aren't making progress, but look at what just happened. If you hadn't shown up, we might have just lost half of what we've gained. Not all of the nests are within easy reach of your dropship's missiles."

"I hear you on that too, Hayden. I do. You know you have an open invitation to move to Proxima. I thought you wanted to stay and fight?"

"Until or unless every human still on Earth is invited to Proxima, I'm staying. This is supposed to be our home. Outside, under the open air. Not stuck in a bubble."

"It's a dome, and it's not that bad once you get used to it."

"I grew up in the belly of a starship," Hayden said. "I was okay with it because I thought that was all there was. Now?" He waved at the landscape. "This is worth fighting for. I wish you could get Command to see that."

"I'm trying."

"Sheriff." Deputy Naples was coming over, leading the rest of the surviving deputies to his position. "I'm glad to see you're okay, sir." Naples was one of his oldest deputies at twenty-eight. He had short brown hair and a crooked smile.

"Thank you, Naples," Hayden said.

"Giles, sir?" Naples asked hopefully. Hayden shook his head. Naples spit on the ground and cursed. " Bastards. I heard from Diamont, we lost Patrello, too."

Hayden sighed and lowered his head. Two deputies dead? Damn it.

Naples turned to Bennett. "Thanks for the rescue, sir. I was afraid we were going to end up as trife chew toys."

"I'm glad we got here when we did," Bennett replied.

"Naples, get the others organized and see if you can find Giles and Patrello's bodies so we can give them a proper burial. I'll meet you back at the perimeter."

"Roger that, Sheriff," Naples said.

"If there are any other wounded, send them over to the Kiev," Bennett said, pointing to the dropship. "We've got full medical supplies on board. No sense wasting what you've got."

"Thank you," Hayden said.

"That's what friends are for," Bennett replied. "Believe me; I'm already going to get shit from Command for blasting that reactor." He raised his voice in pitch to sound like a scolding grandmother. "How do you know none of the savages saw it, Special Officer Bennett? No Contact Protocol, remember?"

"The only people Proxima Command hates more than replicas are Earthers," Hayden said.

"Yeah, but they chose to create replicas," Bennett

said. "So how fucked up is that? Anyway, they've started marketing designer replica babies. If that catches on, maybe we can gain some better footing."

"Are you suggesting we start shipping orphaned Earthers up to Proxima?" Hayden asked. "Because I think that might work."

"You know, you might be on to something. I'll bring that up at the next policy meeting. It'll be fun to watch Command all spit out their coffee."

"What's the deal with your starship?" Hayden asked, pointing at the Kiev, still a few dozen meters distant. "It looks like a major downgrade from the Tokyo."

"It's a long story."

"Does it intersect with the reason you're here?"

"It does."

They walked together in silence until they reached the ramp leading up to the Kiev's hold. Hayden stopped there and turned to look back toward the tank and his remaining deputies. Three of them were on their way across the field to join him. They were operating under their own power, which was good, but Hayden could see they had blood stains on their armor.

"I should have brought a doctor with me," Bennett said, seeing them. "I left in kind of a hurry. Danethi, our pilot, has some medical training. I'll have him give them a look and bandage them up, right after he's done with you."

"Thank you again."

"You're welcome again."

Hayden noticed the other Spacers had stopped behind Bennett, all of them coming to stiff attention.

"Come on up," Bennett said to him, using his hands to signal the soldiers to head into the dropship. "We'll get you stapled back together, and then I'll introduce you to my squad."

Hayden nodded, reaching out and putting his hand on Bennett's shoulder, standing with him at the bottom of the ramp. "Austin, what is this all about?"

Bennett smiled. "You're a Sheriff. A lawman. I need to catch a fugitive."

Chapter 25

Bennett led Hayden to the dropship's small medical room. Captain Danethi was already waiting for them there. There was an opened med-kit already on the small table on the side of the room.

"Captain Danethi, this is Sheriff Hayden Duke," Bennett said, introducing them.

"I'm not sure whether to salute or shake your hand, Sheriff," Danethi said. "Either way, it's a pleasure to meet you."

Hayden stuck out his hand. "Let's shake on it, Captain. I'm law, not military. We don't salute. And you can call me Hayden."

"Of course, Hayden," Danethi replied. "Sunil." He looked Hayden over. "You'll need to take that off for me to get a look at you."

"Of course."

Hayden started unclasping the body armor. Bennett lent him a hand, helping him to get it off and leaving him in a bloodstained t-shirt and underwear.

Bennett groaned at the sight of him. "Damn, Sheriff. That looks painful."

"It is," Hayden admitted.

"There's a shower in the head over there," Danethi said. "Wash off, and then have a seat." He motioned to an examination table in the center of the room.

Hayden nodded and walked into the tiny bathroom. He couldn't help but see himself in a small mirror mounted over the sink as he pulled off the rest of his clothes. The prosthetics on his arms went up slightly past his elbows, joining to puckered and scarred flesh that butted up against a pair of lustrous metal rings. The rings were the control systems for the augmentation, the computer brain that translated signals from organic to digital and back, and made the fake limbs feel real. His body was lean and chiseled from the hard labor of life on the forgotten Earth, covered in scars and bruises from his dealings with both the trife and the members of their new society who didn't want a return to order and justice. He always apologized to Natalia for being so ugly, and she would respond that he had always been ugly. The scars just added character.

He stepped into the shower, quickly washing off the blood and sweat and grime. The wounds burned, but he had been in much worse pain. Once he was clean, he dried off and went back out into the medical room. He didn't sit on the table, instead turning his buttocks toward Danethi.

"It might not be efficient for me to sit," he said.

"I see that," the captain replied. "Two on your shoulder. One on your thigh. No, two on your thigh. None of them look deep. Good news for you, we've got patches."

"Patches?"

Danethi took one out, tearing off the paper that surrounded it. It was about eight centimeters long, with a butterfly shape and a gel-coated pad on the bottom. "We use these instead of stitches. No danger in tearing them open, faster healing, no scar."

"No scar? Great. I wouldn't want to ruin my perfect complexion."

Danethi chuckled while he pinched Hayden's skin and applied the first patch.

"I can help with that," Bennett said. "Hand a few over."

Danethi passed him some of the adhesives, and the two of them set about gluing his skin back together. It only took a few minutes. Once they finished, Bennett pointed to a fresh stack of clothes.

"Lucky for you, we're about the same size," he said.

Hayden pulled them on, unaccustomed to the

patches and moving cautiously so he wouldn't disrupt them.

"You ready to meet the team?" Bennett asked.

"Pozz," Hayden replied.

"I assume pozz means yes?" Danethi said.

"Pozz," Bennett said, smiling.

"Got it."

Hayden followed the two Spacers out of the sick bay and up to the next deck. They brought him to a small briefing room, where the rest of the Space Force soldiers were already waiting. They had already discarded their weapons and armor, showered and changed into basic uniforms of their own.

They sat spread out among the dozen seats that faced the front of the room, standing and coming to attention as they entered. Bennett left them that way until Danethi had chosen one of the seats to stand in front of, and both he and Hayden presented in front of the squad.

"At ease," he said. "Let's get a roll call for our guest. Hayden, you already know Captain Danethi."

The soldier nearest the door shifted forward slightly. He was a big, muscular grunt, the largest of the group.

"Private Hafiz Suarez, sir," he said. "Call sign, Happy."

Hayden nodded to him. The private nodded back and then sat.

"Private Harold Furter," the soldier on the other

side of the room said. Hayden realized then they were going in rank order. The man was of average height and build, nothing about him standing out. "Call sign, Frank."

Hayden nodded to him, and he returned the gesture and sat.

"Private First Class Carlos Suarez," the next soldier said. He was the smallest man in the group, stocky, with an olive complexion and handsome features. "Call sign, Animal."

He sat after exchanging greetings.

"Corporal Lin Smith," the first female said. She was tiny, with pale skin and a don't-fuck-with-me look. "Call sign, Neko."

"Sergeant Nancy Illario," the next Spacer said. Another woman, almost as tall as Happy but much leaner, with blonde hair and a hard face. "Call sign, Seventy."

Hayden nodded to her, and she sat down without returning the gesture.

"Judicus Imani Shia," the final woman said.

Hayden looked at her. She stood out from the rest of the soldiers. Her stance was different. Her body language was different. She even had a different title.

"Call sign, Judge," she added.

"Is that what judicus means?" Hayden asked.

"Not exactly, Sheriff," she replied. "Though I do work for the Justice Department. The fugitive was under my care when he escaped."

"Which is why she's here," Bennett said. "She doesn't have to be, but she volunteered."

"Understood," Hayden said.

"You've met the team. Let's talk about our outlaw."

He reached down, activating the control surface of the table in front of them. The wall behind them lit up, displaying the image of Nathan Stacker.

"Captain Nathan Stacker," Bennett said. "Wanted for the murder of his wife, Niobe Rivera Stacker."

"He killed his wife?" Hayden asked. "Why?"

"The motive is still in question," Judicus Shia said. "We suspect they got into an argument over money. Captain Stacker was buying illegal narcotics from a dealer back on Proxima. After he killed his wife, he went after the dealer. We stunned him out before he was able to finish choking him to death."

"Money's a reason to get into a fight. It isn't a reason to kill."

"Stacker is a first-generation replica, Sheriff."

"I don't know what that means."

"He was one of the first replicas produced," Bennett said. "He doesn't look it, but he's over eighty years old."

Hayden looked back at Stacker again. He didn't look a day over forty, at best.

"Are you—" he started to ask Bennett.

"No. After the first generation, it was decided that aging controls should be coded into our genome. It was supposed to help us garner better acceptance among the civilian population."

"Did it work?"

"I've told you how things are," Bennett said. "But I think it helped."

"Are all of you replicas?" Hayden asked, looking at the rest of the Spacers.

"I'm not," Judicus Shia said.

"The rest of us are," Happy said. "Me and Animal are from the same root genome, which is why we have the same last name."

Hayden was surprised. They couldn't have looked much more different.

"They've gotten better at randomizing some of the secondary traits," Bennett said, noticing his expression. "Most replicas are as unique as anyone else."

"Except the first-gens," the judicus said. "They're all very similar. In some cases, identical."

Hayden considered that for a moment. "And you're sure Stacker killed his wife? Not a duplicate version?"

Shia smiled. "Yes. There are only two other Stackers who could have potentially committed the crime. They've both been questioned, polygraphed, alibied, and cleared."

"This isn't about guilt or innocence, Hayden," Bennett said. "We're here to bring him back to Proxima alive."

"It's always about guilt or innocence in one form or another," Hayden said. He watched Bennett's face closely. Something told him the Sergeant wasn't being completely honest with that assessment. "You're telling me you don't have secondary orders to kill him if he doesn't come along willingly?"

Bennett didn't answer, which was the answer.

"Why?" Hayden asked.

"Why what?" Bennett replied.

"Why do you need me if you want to kill him? You've got superior firepower. You've got superior soldiers. You just saved my tail, remember? So why bring me along? Why get me involved?"

"I knew you were going ask me that," Bennett said. "Three reasons. One, I'm hoping that if we work together on this, it will build some equity with Command to get you more resources. Maybe even a platoon deployment or two. Two, because you know how people think down here. You know how they live. That's valuable. Three, because you're a natural leader. People trust you. They want to help you. Stackers are intelligent and adaptive. He'll figure out how to survive, and he'll figure out how to fit in. I need someone I trust who can match that. I need you."

Hayden kept staring at Bennett, glancing out at the other soldiers a few times. There was something else the Spacer wasn't saying. He could still see something in his face.

"Stacker says he's innocent, doesn't he?" Hayden asked.

The question took Bennett off-guard.

"What?" Judicus Shia said. "How can you know that?"

"It's that little twitch in the eye. The tightness in the throat. You're under orders to bring Stacker back or put him down, but there's more to it than that. Tell me what you don't want to tell me, or you can forget about my help."

Bennett was hesitant. His eyes shifted to the other Spacers like he didn't want to say anything in front of them. Finally, he relented.

"I never told you about the Trust," he said.

"Negative," Hayden replied. "Who are they?"

"A myth," Judicus Shia said. "Sir, you can't be suggesting you believe the Trust is real?"

"It doesn't matter if they are or not. What matters is that Stacker believes they are. They're a crime syndicate, Hayden. The largest and most powerful on Proxima."

"You have crime syndicates on Proxima?"

"We're still a human society. Anyway, Nathan Stacker claimed the Trust set him up to take the fall for killing his wife. Which alone isn't very interesting. But CSF-LM tracked the ship Nathan Stacker stole to get to Earth. It was shot down by a pair of ground-to-air missiles. Missiles that shouldn't be on Earth in the first place."

Hayden wasn't sure what to think of that news. "Hold on. You told me you need me to help you catch Stacker, and now you just told me his ship was shot down?"

"That doesn't mean he's dead," Bennett said. "I also told you he's intelligent and adaptive. He could have survived. Even if he didn't, someone firing advanced missiles at passing starships should concern both of us."

"So you want me to come check it out with you? Like a guide?"

"Like an important part of my team, which you would be. You can say no, Hayden. I'm going anyway. I have my orders. But if you come, you can help me, and I can help you."

"I've got a lot of responsibilities here," Hayden said. "You want me to leave the expansion behind to help you catch a suspect who may or may not be alive?"

"Three days, Hayden. I'll have you back here in three days."

Hayden considered it. Life on Earth was hard enough without Proxima dumping more of their dirty laundry down on them. Still, Bennett was his friend, and the thought of having a few platoons of Spacers helping to deal with the trife was tempting as hell.

"I need to stop home first," Hayden said.

"We're in a bit of a hurry," Bennett replied. "Command is worried Stacker is going to compromise the NCP."

"Fuck your NCP, Austin. Seriously."

"Personally, I agree. But I still have orders. If you need to talk to your wife, I can relay a message through the link to Sanisco."

Hayden sighed.

Three days. How much could go wrong in three days?

Chapter 26

Nathan started walking.

He had no idea where he was or where he was going, or even if there was going to be a way off the island. Hell, he barely had enough light to see.

He made his way along one of the tunnels. It was old. Much older than what he had seen above, even though it was in better shape. The vegetation hadn't been as successful breaking through the stone walls, sticking out only in random cracks that pierced the thick surface. It was usually somewhere near colorful, chaotic artwork that someone had left behind a long time ago.

There were metal rails on the ground near his feet, three of them that followed the course of the tunnel. Water dripped from overhead, making splashing noises in small puddles.

The demons hadn't followed him down here. He still didn't know why. An hour of walking had only made him feel alone again, as though he were the only living soul nearby who didn't have black, oily skin. He knew that couldn't be true. He had seen the boy. Where had the kid come from?

There had to be more people somewhere. Maybe down here? He couldn't imagine the demons would be afraid of them, not when they were so numerous.

Still, he couldn't believe what he had crashed into. He had headed to Earth because he thought he would find asylum here. Everyone on Proxima believed Earth was as civilized as they were. As advanced as they were, if not more so. The datastores that had been transferred from the colony ships all backed that assumption up. There was no mention of these creatures. No mention of the apocalypse.

Had it all happened after the ships left?

Did Proxima Command even know?

They had to, didn't they?

The planet's coordinates were pre-programmed into the Explorer's computer. There was no way the Centurions hadn't been back in the last two centuries.

They knew and hadn't told the general population. They knew and hadn't even told most of the CSF.

Who else was aware of this?

Did the Trust know?

He wouldn't have been surprised to find out half of Proxima Command was part of the Trust. That was how deep their connections were rumored to be.

Someone had torn the Explorer out of the sky.

Someone had tried to kill him.

Who? Why?

The thoughts circled in his mind while he walked. He used his gun for light, the small display on the side of the weapon giving off just enough illumination for him to not trip on anything. He reached under his shirt and picked up the chain there. He had found it in the Space Pack with his other things. Niobe's wedding band was dangling from it, the diamond sparkling whenever it caught the light of the pistol. Was this the secret she had died for? Was this what she had learned?

Real love never dies.

That was true. Niobe was dead, but he still loved her. The data chip was important, and he would find a way to read it and to learn what she had learned. Maybe it involved Earth, but it also had to be about more than Earth.

Was it related to her research?

He stopped walking, taking a moment to sit against the side of the tunnel to rest. He was tired. His body ached. His soul ached more. Damn, he missed her. He tried to steady his breathing and relax as much as possible. He wasn't going to give up. He didn't have to convince himself of that.

He closed his eyes, listening to the drips of water sinking through the sediment and winding up in the tunnel. There were three of them striking the ground in an even cadence.

Plip. Pause. Plip. Plip. Pause. Plip. Pause. Plip. Plip.

He found the tempo calming, and he was safe enough down here, wasn't he? The demons wouldn't descend, but there was no sign of anything frightening. Maybe they were afraid of the dark? It seemed silly to him, but they weren't like him. He didn't know anything about them except they weren't friendly.

Plip. Pause. Plip. Plip. Pause. Plip. Pause. Plip. Plip.

He started to drift, his ears attuned to the sound of the water leaks. He lowered his gun to his leg, covering the display. He could sleep down here. He could rest.

Plip. Pause. Plip. Plip. Pause. Plip. Pause. Plip. Pause.
Plip. Pause. Plip. Pause. Plip. Pause. Plip. Pause.

It took Nathan a few rounds before he realized the tempo had suddenly changed, and one of the drips had vanished. His eyes snapped open, his heart rate increasing again. The only reason the sound would have stopped would be if someone, or something, were blocking it.

Plip. Pause. Pause. Plip. Pause. Pause. Plip. Pause. Pause.

Shit. He jumped up, lifting the gun to reveal the display again, spinning it in a tight circle. Its light only stretched a meter or so, and he didn't hear anything else. The dripping water was still wrong, still off its original cadence.

He backed against the wall, at least covering one avenue of attack. His heart was pumping, his body tense.

Plip. Pause. Plip. Plip. Pause. Plip. Pause. Plip. Plip.
Plip. Pause. Plip. Plip. Pause. Plip. Pause. Plip. Plip.

The normal rhythm returned. It didn't make him feel any better. Whatever was out there, it was moving.

It was getting closer.

He still didn't hear anything. No feet. No breathing. No rustling or shaking or any other kind of noise. Was this why the demons were afraid?

Tip. Tap. Tip.

The noise was faint. He probably would never have heard it if his hearing wasn't slightly better than a normal human's. It came from his right side. He turned that way, trying to aim his light, wishing he had more.

Tip. Tap. Tip. Tap.

The noise repeated, slightly louder, still coming in his direction. Fuck, he wished the damn thing would show up already. He pointed the gun in the direction of the sound and took a few steps back, careful not to trip on the rails.

Tip-tap. Tip-tap. Tip-tap-tip-tap-tip-tap.

He watched the area ahead, only able to see out

the length of his arm. He kept the gun close to his chest, ready to aim and fire. He drew his other hand back, in position to grab anything that appeared.

The sound stopped.

Nathan stared into the darkness, squinting his eyes to try to tell if anything changed. It had sounded like the thing was right on top of him, but there had been...

He flipped the gun up to the top of the tunnel, raising his head to the light there.

The creature opened its mouth. It had multiple rows of sharp teeth and a long tongue. He didn't get to see the rest of it. It fell toward him, still almost silent, humanoid hands reaching for him, teeth coming down at his head.

He fired his gun into it, below its head. The bolt lit the area for a split second, and he was able to see the hard, mottled skin that covered it as the gas sank into its flesh.

It still didn't make a sound, though it did lose some of its momentum. Nathan was able to punch it with his other hand, sidestepping as he did. The creature fell to the ground, rolling over and getting back up.

He saw it more clearly now. Two meters tall. Two legs. Two arms. Four ridged fingers on each hand. Wide feet. Its head was oval, and nearly eighty percent mouth. He didn't see any eyes or ears or a nose. He had no clue how the thing had found him, or how it was tracking him. Its chest had a hole in it from the plasma bolt, and some thick blood trickled out. But the burn was less than Nathan would have expected, and it was already starting to heal.

What the fuck?

He fired at it again, but it seemed to be ready for him this time. It jumped sideways, the bolt flashing past and heading down the tunnel, giving him a view of it. He saw an old vehicle up ahead, resting on the tracks.

Then he was under attack, this new creature reaching out with humanoid hands. He slapped one of them away, but the other grabbed his shirt, and when he tried to pull away the material stuck to its fingers. He yanked hard on it, barely getting his face back as the teeth closed in on it, the mouth chomping down in an effort to bite off his nose.

"Fuck you!" he shouted at it, planting another bolt in its abdomen. It let him go, silently falling back. He shot it again, and it dropped onto the floor.

It wasn't dead. It rolled over, climbing up the wall and scrambling into the darkness. How did it know where the darkness was if it couldn't see?

What senses was this thing using?

He didn't know. He didn't even know if the damn thing had retreated. He swung the pistol in the direction it had gone, looking for it.

Something wet landed on his shoulder, burning right through his shirt and into his arm.

It hurt like hell, but that wasn't important at the moment. He dove away, rolling across the ground and to his feet as the creature landed where he had just been standing, its blood dripping off it to the ground, its wounds healing. He brought his pistol up again and fired, four times in rapid succession, slamming it with enough superheated gas to knock it into the wall and down.

It didn't move this time. He walked over to it, pointing the pistol at its head.

"Don't!"

The voice stole his attention, and then something hit his gun hand, knocking his weapon to the ground. A hand touched his chest, shoving him away from the monster.

"If you want the trife to come down here, you'll kill it. If you want to live, come with me."

The woman's voice was sharp below his ear. He glanced out of the corner of his eye. She didn't have any light on her, but she had found him in the darkness. He could see she had goggles over her face.

A tiny beam of light came on, pointing at his pistol.

"Pick up your gun and let's go."

He bent over and grabbed it. The creature was recovering, slowly turning over on its hands and feet.

"What the fuck is it?" Nathan said.

"The reason we're still alive," she replied. "Come on."

She grabbed his hand with hers. It was tiny compared to his, callused and rough. Everything about her seemed rough, but then living in a place like this she probably had to be.

"You have a name?" he asked.

"Not now. It'll heal in a minute, and then it'll be even hungrier. You don't want to be here when it recovers."

"What's it going to eat?"

"This must be your first time in New York. If there are no people and no trife? Rats."

Chapter 27

She led him quickly away, keeping a tight grip on his hand as she broke into a jog. They were headed toward the vehicle he had seen on the tracks, and she squeezed him in beside it, navigating along it. He couldn't believe how big it was, stretching along the tunnel like a giant worm. It was somewhat similar to a loop pod but so much longer and bulkier.

An earlier iteration, maybe?

They cleared the machine, but they didn't stop jogging. Nathan could tell by the woman's grip and her pace she was still worried about the monster. She led him almost blindly through the tunnels, and then finally up into a small alcove on the side where there was a rusted metal door and a short stairwell. They went through the door. She came to a stop.

"One second," she said.

She grabbed the door and lifted it, slowly adjusting it to get it closed without making much noise. Nathan could see bare, lean, muscular arms flexing to shift it into place. She left only a small gap before setting it down.

"Is—"

Her finger pressed against his mouth, shutting him up. She grabbed his hand again, leading him through a series of smaller corridors. They passed through a few more open doorways until finally bringing him to a second stop.

"I'm taking a big risk helping you," she said in a soft whisper before he could speak. Her finger poked into his chest. "Don't you dare be one of those demented assholes that thinks the best thing to do when surrounded by monsters is to rape the first member of the opposite sex who comes along." He felt something else poke into him. The edge of a knife. "Because if you even think about it, I will fucking kill you."

"You make that speech after you let me take back my gun?" he asked, keeping his voice low. "You can take the knife out of my ribs. I have no interest in hurting you. Right now, you're my guardian angel."

She pulled back the blade and her finger. Nathan heard her moving, and then a small light came on between them, letting him see her face.

She had removed the goggles, holding them in the same hand as the light. She looked to be about thirty years old, with short brown hair and a long face. Her nose was flat, her eyes large, with thin lips. She had a scar that ran across her left cheek, deep and ugly. She had a burn on her forehead, giving her a slightly off-kilter hairline. She was wearing a faded dark jacket over a stained shirt and black pants that led down to bare feet. A wide belt crossed her hips, with different items tucked into built-in pockets.

"Captain Nathan Stacker," he said. " Space Force."

"Did you say, Space Force?" She stared at him. "Your accent. You aren't from around here. Where did you come from? How did you get into Manhattan?"

"New York. Manhattan. I don't know what any of that means. Shit, I don't know what any of this means. I came from…"

He trailed off, stopping himself. The people of Proxima didn't know what had happened to Earth. Did the Earthers know anything about Proxima? He wasn't sure he could trust this woman enough to tell her more than he already had.

"Came from where?" she prodded.

He stared at her. How was he going to get the answers he needed without giving any more away?

She spread her hands. "Come on, don't hold out on me. Came from where, Nathan Stacker?"

"The mountains," he said at last. He had seen them before he crashed. He was sure she had never been there. "I was born there. I lived there with my parents. My father, he had an old aircraft in a shed. We worked on it for years. He used to say, son, one day this bitch is going to fly, and then we're going to get out of here." Nathan smiled. "They died last year. I spent all my time making good on his dream, only to fucking crash." He shook his head. "He always wanted me to grow up to be in the Space Force, whatever that is. A pilot. Captain Stacker. He gave me this." He motioned with the pistol. "He said it came from another place and time, when things were better."

"Wow," she said, buying into his story. "Why'd you want to leave the mountains? It sounds like it was safe up there."

"That depends on your definition of safe. Anyway, I managed to survive the crash with minor injuries." He showed her his hand, and then the wound the creature had left on his shoulder for added effect. The damn thing had acid or something in its blood, and it would probably leave a scar. "But I don't know anything about this place, or those oily black demons. I must have had a thousand of them chasing me."

"The trife," she said. "They're the reason the planet went to shit. You don't have trife where you came from?"

He shook his head. "No. I don't know why."

"Mountains," she said. "Probably too cold for them. They like heat and energy."

"Where did they come from?"

"Nobody knows for sure. I've seen some old vid streams. There was a storm, and then a plague. It killed a lot of people. Billions. And then the trife showed up and killed a lot more. They aren't from Earth, I can tell you that much. Were there a lot of people where you lived?"

"No. Not that many."

He fell silent. Not from Earth? These trife had entered the picture after a disease had already left humankind weak? That didn't seem like much of a coincidence.

The thought left him curious. Was there a connection between the trife on Earth and the ships Command had been sending out to explore the galaxy? They said it was to find another habitable planet, but what if they were looking for wherever these things had come from?

Nathan bit his lip. Were they afraid the trife would find Proxima before Proxima found them?

Niobe's research would have given their ships greater range. It would have let them look further out. If his first mental leap was even close to correct, she should have been celebrated for her work, not killed.

What the hell was going on?

"You okay, Nathan?" the woman asked.

He looked at her and nodded. "Yeah. It's been a long day. Sorry if my questions seem stupid, but I've been pretty isolated from all of this. Didn't we try to fight back?"

"Of course. The trife multiply faster than rats as long as they have enough food."

"People?"

"No. The bastards would have died off a long time ago if they ate people. Heat. Energy. Even the Sun is enough to feed them; that's the whole problem. They have a big nest on the other side of the island, on an old navy ship."

"Nest?"

"Yup. I've never seen it, but that's what I've heard. I don't go over there. I try not to go above ground at all, but we all have to take turns hunting. I bet you'd make a great hunter."

"We. There are more of you?"

"There's a few hundred of us living in the tunnels down here. We've been here a long time, trapped on the island with the trife. I don't know if you saw the bridges when you crashed. They were destroyed during the war, to try to keep new trife from coming to the island. They don't like water all that much."

"It didn't work."

"Nope, and before you ask me why not, the answer is I don't know."

"Do you have a guess?"

"There's a collapsed tunnel on the west side. I have a feeling it wasn't always collapsed. Or maybe we just never got rid of all the trife that started here."

"What do you mean, started here?"

"Some people think the trife fell from the sky by the billions."

"What about that other thing? The one that attacked me. Are there more of those, too?"

She shook her head. "Not that I've seen. I don't know where it came from, either. Before he died, my pops said it just showed up in the tunnel one day. Within a few months, all the trife had left. Of course, it got plenty of ours too, before we learned to deal with it. It showing up here was the best thing that ever happened to us. You killing it would have been the worst. It's a good thing I heard you shouting and came running."

"So what now?" Nathan asked.

"We do what we've always done. Hide from the trife, try to survive, eat, sleep, and make merry."

"No," Nathan said. "I don't have time for that."

"What do you mean? Your plane crashed. You're stuck here."

"I need to get off this island. I need to head west."

"Why? You're safe here. Safer than you would be out there. It isn't just the trife. People aren't the same as they used to be. When the survival instinct takes over, it makes us into monsters, in some ways no better than the trife. That's what my grandpa always used to say."

"Safety isn't my top priority right now," Nathan said. It was, but not in the way she thought. "You're telling me there's absolutely no way off the island?"

"I can't say for sure. Why don't you come back to our settlement? We have food and water, and a change of clothes. I can ask Margie if she knows another way out. I mean, I guess you could always swim. Do you know how to swim?"

"A little," Nathan replied.

"Maybe you could swim across, then? Either way, you should come back with me."

He considered her invitation. He wouldn't mind getting out of his wet and torn clothing and having something to eat. She seemed friendly enough.

"I'll come with you," he said. "But then maybe you can lead me to the westernmost exit? The one that will bring me closest to the water and the mainland?"

"Sure," she said. "We can work it out." She smiled. She seemed pleased he had decided to come. "It's Rhonna, by the way."

"What?" Nathan said.

"My name. It's Rhonna. You never asked."

"I'm sorry, Rhonna. It's been a long day."

"It's okay." She grabbed his hand again. "So you don't get lost," she said. Then she turned out her light, casting them back into the darkness. He could hear her moving, putting the goggles on.

She squeezed his hand once, almost affectionately, and then started leading him through the pitch black.

Chapter 28

Nathan did his best to memorize the path they were taking by counting steps and reciting the turns in his head. He lost count somewhere near the twentieth change in direction, and at that point realized he was at Rhonna's mercy.

It wasn't a comfortable feeling. He was being forced to trust her. He started to regret agreeing to go back to her settlement, but the truth was, she could have led him to it either way, and he had already been at her mercy from the moment she stopped him from killing the creature.

She didn't speak the entire time they walked. Nathan wondered if she was overcautious, considering she had said there were only one of the strange creatures in the tunnels. Then again, the beast had moved silently and would have killed him if it hadn't dripped blood on his arm.

She pulled up at a small door, straining to open it. Nathan offered to help her, but she waved him back.

"You'll make too much noise."

She got the door open, and they went out into a tunnel like the first. There was another of the long vehicles directly in front of them.

"Here we are," Rhonna said.

"What do you mean?" Nathan asked.

"The camp." She pointed at the metal snake. "We live on the train. We have for a long time. The trife can't reach us in here. Neither can the Stalker. Come on."

She led him along the side of the train. He noticed all the windows had wooden boards covering them. They were pulled up tight against the openings and probably braced from inside. Only the smallest trickle of light escaped past the edges of the boards, allowing him to see writing on the side of the train, beneath a layer of dust and oily grime.

Amtrak.

It didn't mean anything to him.

They walked all the way to the front. There had been hatches at the regular intervals along the vessel, but she brought him to the one closest to the end of it, which sloped downward into a bullet-shaped nose.

She knocked on the door, three times fast, then twice slow, then five times fast.

A metal bar pierced the center and shifted between the two panels of the hatch until it slid the right panel aside. Light tumbled out of the train, so bright that Nathan was momentarily blinded.

Four hands, all of them larger than Rhonna's and much rougher, grabbed his arms, pulling him up and into the train. He blinked violently, trying to get his eyes to adjust to the light, a pair of men slowly coming into focus.

"What'd you bring us?" one of them said.

"We don't need any more meat right now," the other said, laughing. "Just kidding, bruddah. End of the world joke, you know? Your eyes will adjust in a few seconds."

Nathan forced himself to stay calm. He could have pulled free of the two men if he wanted to, but that was no way to make friends.

"Hey," he heard a small voice say. "I know that guy. I saw him topside when I went up to hunt. That fucker cost us dinner."

Nathan turned his head. His vision was still sharpening, but he could see the boy coming his way. It was the same kid who had nearly stabbed him. The one who had been using a human leg to draw in the trife.

Nathan tensed for a moment before forcing himself to relax. Maybe there was a good explanation for it? Rhonna said nobody ever came to the island. Where would he get a leg from, anyway?

The boy reached him, drawing back and punching him in the stomach.

"Lonnie!" Rhonna hissed. "What the hell is wrong with you?"

"Asshole," Lonnie said, turning and walking away.

"So, you met Lonnie," one of the men said, releasing his arm. "He's a little shit. But he's a good hunter for his age."

"He was using a leg," Nathan said. "A human leg."

The other man laughed again. "Nah. It's fake. A replacement from the days of the war. Looks real as fuck though, I'll give you that, bruddah. Trife can't tell the difference either."

"Prosthetic?" Nathan asked.

"Yup. I'm Kilo, by the way." The man laughed again. He was tall, but not as tall as Nathan. Barrel chested, big face. Same complexion as Rhonna, similar eyes and nose.

"Gary," the other man said. He bore a resemblance to Rhonna, too.

"Are you all related?" Nathan asked.

"Everyone in Amtrak is related," Rhonna replied. "Two hundred years, we've pretty much used up the genetic diversity."

"Incest?"

"So judgmental," Kilo said. "Look, bruddah, it

isn't because we're into kinky shit. We're just trying to keep humanity alive. We can talk about it more, but I bet you're hungry and thirsty?"

"And could use some new, old threads," Gary said. "You look like hell."

"You'll have to tell us where you came from and all that good stuff. We haven't had new blood on the island in at least ten years. Where'd Rhonna find you, anyway? "

"You had someone else make it to the island?" Nathan asked. "If someone can get in, that means there's a way out."

"You want to leave?" Kilo said. "Bruddah, you just got here."

"I told him I would take him to the westernmost exit," Rhonna said.

"I get it," Kilo said, noticing the plasma pistol in Nathan's hand for the first time. "Oh, shit. I've never seen one like that before."

"I found him in the tunnels," Rhonna said. "He was being attacked by the Stalker. He was about to kill it."

Kilo's smile faded, his eyebrow going up. "You can't kill the Stalker, bruddah. What? You think you're a badass?"

"Cut the shit, Kilo," Rhonna said. "He didn't know what it was or why it was there. He didn't even know what trife were."

"Is that even possible?" Gary asked.

"I'm just trying to survive," Nathan said. "Like you."

"I hear you," Kilo said. "Let's cut the tension down a notch, what do you say? Come have some meat, have some water. We just refilled the reserve tanks with water from the cistern. David damn near got his ass bitten off on the way back down."

Gary and Rhonna laughed at that. Rhonna held his hand again. "Come on, Nathan," she said. "You can meet Margie."

Nathan followed her down the aisle of the train. There were seats on either side. Lonnie had spread across two of them, an old, worn picture book in his hands. There were a few other younger kids in the area, each of them staying occupied.

Rhonna reached a door at the end of the corridor and slid it open. Nathan realized the train was composed of separate cars, with a covered joint in between, like an airlock. She opened the next door, bringing him into a different type of car.

He could smell the meat as soon as they entered. The car had tables on both sides, and a few people were there, already eating. They looked up at him as he walked down the aisle, curious but silent. They had plates in front of them, with bits of dark, stringy meat on top that they picked at with their fingers. They didn't look like they were enjoying it, but right now it seemed good enough to eat.

"Gary, have Sean prep a plate for Nathan, will you?" Rhonna said.

"Sure," Gary replied. He walked over to the kitchen in the corner of the car and disappeared through a narrow door.

"Good thing the Stalker can't smell," Kilo said. "Or he'd come running for some delicious trife meat."

"Trife meat?" Nathan said. "You eat them?"

"What else are we going to eat, bruddah? Each other?"

"It doesn't taste that good, but you get used to it," Rhonna said. "At least it's edible and somewhat nutritious. There isn't much else to eat around here."

"We've got a small garden on top of one of the buildings, over on thirty-fourth," Kilo said. "We've got a couple of weeks before the crops will be ready, so you're shit out of luck unless you decide to stick around."

"That's not an option," Nathan said.

"Why not?" Kilo replied. "We're good people, I promise. In a world of shitty ones."

"How do you know what other people are like? You're isolated here, as much as I was isolated where I'm from."

"Where was that?"

"The mountains."

"Which ones?"

"Does it matter?" Rhonna said, sparing him. "We

have vid streams and old newspapers from during the war. Before all of that stuff shut down."

"Looting, murder, chaos," Kilo said. "It was fucked up, bruddah. You think those survivors out there aren't the same? They're probably worse."

"If there are any survivors out there besides Tinker," Rhonna said.

"There was Kate."

"Who's Kate?" Nathan asked.

"She turned up in the tunnels one day. Kind of like the Stalker. Batshit crazy. We took her in. She was with us for six years, had a couple of kids. Then she snuck out one day and fed herself to the beast."

"She committed suicide?"

"Yup. Sad. I figure anyone out there is probably just as nuts as she was, or they made her that nuts. That's good enough for me to want to stay where I am."

"You said she had kids?"

"Gary's kids. They had a thing."

Gary emerged from the kitchen, holding a plate of the trife meat. "You can eat it in front of Margie, it's fine." He handed it to Nathan, who took the plate and brought it up to his nose.

"Not bad," he said.

"It smells better than it tastes," Rhonna said.

She led him through the next two cars, first-class sleepers, she explained. The doors to them were all closed, so he didn't see what they looked like. The fourth car seemed to be a lounge area. That's where most of the residents had gathered.

That's where he met Margie.

Rhonna's mother was at least fifty years old. Thin, frail-looking, with short white hair and a face that was either amused or pissed, he couldn't quite tell.

"Rhonna," she said when her daughter entered. "You catch anything?"

"Trife? No. A man? Yes. Margie, this is Nathan. Nathan, my mother, Margie."

"A man is better than a trife," Margie said, eyeing him like he was the meat in the room.

She was sitting alone in the center of a long sofa, two dozen or so other members of the group scattered around the floor and a pair of armchairs. She patted the cushion next to her.

"Come sit, Nathan," she said. "I see Rhonna's already taking care of you?"

"Nice to meet you, Margie," Nathan said, picking up the trife meat and putting it near his lips. "Thank you for the food, and for the hospitality."

"You don't have to thank me. It's all fair exchange. Barter system. It works fine for us all."

Nathan dropped the meat onto the plate. "Barter?" he said.

"Margie, Nathan is a pilot. He came here in an aircraft. It crashed earlier."

"I saw it," Lonnie said, coming up behind them.

"Big thing. It was on fire. It hit the old Chrysler Building."

"Damn," Margie said. "How'd you survive that?"

"I had an emergency jump pack," Nathan said. "It let me bail before the crash. I'm sorry, I'm not familiar with the barter system? My parents and me, we had everything we needed at our place in the mountains."

Margie cackled roughly. "Okay, Mr. Innocent, I'll tell you what. The first meal is free. So is a shower and some replacement threads. We'll start keeping score after that, okay?"

"Sure," Nathan said, not sure of what she meant. "I'm not planning on staying long. I need to get off the island."

She cackled again. "Okay. We'll see about that."

Nathan lowered the food again. "Is that a threat?"

Every pair of eyes in the room looked up at him. He had a feeling these people would turn on him in an instant if he said the wrong thing in the wrong way.

Margie laughed a third time. "Not at all, Nathan. Just, maybe by the time you're ready to leave, you won't want to leave. That's all. It's happened before. Eat your meat."

Rhonna rubbed Nathan's back affectionately. He glanced over at her. The touching seemed innocent enough. He took a bite of the trife meat. It was as chewy as he expected and didn't taste good at all.

He managed to get the first swallow down.

Kilo went to the corner of the car, to a display attached to the wall. He turned it on and then adjusted something in a cabinet beside it.

"You were asking about how we know what we know," Kilo said.

The display changed, showing a man talking toward the device recording him. Behind him was a scene of devastation, fire red and smoke black. People were running through the streets. As he spoke, two of them got into an argument. One produced a gun and shot the other in the face. Then he noticed the reporter and turned the gun on them.

Nathan looked away before the fatal shot. He took another bite of the meat, not because he wanted it but because he wasn't sure how Margie might react if he didn't eat it.

"They nuked most of the biggest cities," Kilo said. "Killed millions of the fuckers. Killed plenty of our own, too. That stream is what happened once the police were gone. Once the soldiers were gone."

"We read a couple of stories about the government building ships to take us off Earth, to settle in the stars," Rhonna said. "Can you believe that?"

"Bullshit propaganda to keep our hopes up," Margie said. "That's all it was."

Nathan took another bite of meat. He almost spit it out when she said that.

So the colony ships had left after all this had

started? Someone on Proxima must have known about this. Someone must have hidden it from the people.

Someone stole the truth from them. Made them forget.

"You okay, bruddah?" Kilo said.

Nathan shook his head. He had probably gone pale. "I don't think I'm used to this meat."

"You don't have to eat it all," Rhonna said. "I'll finish it as my ration for today."

Nathan handed it to her.

"Gary, why don't you show Nathan where he can get cleaned up?" Margie said.

"Okay," Gary said. "Follow me."

Nathan followed, still a little shell-shocked from what he had just learned. How could Command do this? They had left Earth a mess and done nothing about it over the last two centuries?

Gary led him back to the first-class sleeper cars. He took out a ring of keys and used one to unlock the door and open it. Nathan was surprised to see the room. It was in great shape, with nicer stuff than he had back on Proxima.

"Bathroom and shower are in there," Gary said, pointing to a small secondary room. "Have you ever used a shower before?"

Nathan nodded.

"Lucky for you, we've got the Amtrak hooked up to a portable generator, and there's plenty of fuel around. You should have hot water, too. I'll be right back with some fresh clothes. We must have some extra large around."

"Thank you."

"No problem. Remember, Nathan. Just enjoy it."

Gary left the room. Nathan's heart skipped when he heard the door lock, but then he realized he could unlock it from the inside. He supposed it was for his privacy.

He stripped out of his clothes and went into the bathroom. He figured out how to turn on the shower and stepped in.

His body shook when he stood under the cold water. It didn't settle even as the water got warm. Everything that had happened over the last week was catching up to him, and his mind could barely take it. The doctors had given him treatment for the Stacker instability, and they thought it had worked.

He knew for a fact it hadn't.

He also knew how it felt when he was losing control, and all of this was putting him on edge.

He heard the door to the room unlock and open. He figured it was Gary dropping off the clothes. He waited a few seconds and heard it lock again.

He closed his eyes, letting the water run off him, trying to calm his breathing and relax.

Something touched his back.

He spun around, his other hand coming up and grabbing at whatever had touched him.

Rhonna cried out in pain, her wrist crushed in his grip.

He let go, backing into the wall of the shower. She was standing in front of him, completely naked, her eyes wide with fear.

Chapter 29

"What the hell is this?" Nathan said, grabbing the shower head to keep from losing his temper.

She came toward him again, putting her hand on his chest. "Margie told me to come. She told me I need to do my duty for the family." She stepped closer, reaching out with her other hand.

Nathan took it before it could touch him. "What do you think you're doing?"

"You don't like me, Nathan?" she asked. "You don't think I'm pretty enough?" She turned her head slightly, making her scar and burn less obvious. "I know I'm damaged. Do you think I'm ugly?"

He hadn't noticed one way or another and didn't care. "Rhonna, I can't do this."

"I know, you grew up in the mountains. You've

probably never been with anyone before, have you? If it helps, I haven't either."

Nathan couldn't believe this was happening. "It isn't like that. I just can't."

Her eyes landed on the ring around his neck. "Oh. Is that a wedding ring? I've never seen one like that before." She reached for it.

He turned away. "Don't touch it. I understand genetics. I understand that your group wants more diversity. But I can't give you what you want."

"Yes, you can. Lie down with me, Nathan. Help me help my family, and I can get you whatever you need. Food, clothes, weapons. Anything."

"Is this what Margie meant by barter?"

She nodded. "Please, Nathan. I have a responsibility to my people. I'm twenty-two, and I haven't had a child yet. I've put it off as long as I can because I don't want to be with Kilo. He puts on a good show, but he isn't right."

She sounded desperate. That desperation helped him calm slightly. He let go of the shower head, putting his hands on her shoulders, using his strength to help hold her arms back and keep her away from his body.

"Rhonna, listen to me. I can't help you. Even if I have sex with you, I can't help you. I can't have children. I'm sterile. I'm sorry."

Rhonna's expression was one of horror. She reacted as if he had just punched her in the face.

"Sterile?" Her voice was weak. She stepped back, out of the stream of water and away from his grip. Her right hand fell between her legs, and her left across her breasts to cover herself.

"I'm sorry," he repeated.

"Nathan," she said. "You don't understand." She shook her head. "Of all the damn things to happen."

"It's fine," he said, turning the water off. "I'll keep my old clothes. I'll go. No harm done. Just show me the way out."

She laughed sardonically. "You think it's that easy? We just forget the whole thing, and you leave? Margie isn't going to like this. At all. She's going to be pissed at me, and she's going to be pissed at you."

"I can take care of myself."

"Damn it; there are over a hundred of us on this train. You're one man."

"She would kill me over this?" Nathan asked. "After all of Kilo's talk about being good people?"

"We didn't expect you to say no. How many men would refuse a safe place to live, food to eat, a family, and the pick of any woman in the group whenever they wanted them?"

"I thought—"

"Not just me. Margie said it seemed like you liked me. You could have a different one of us every night if you wanted. There are thirty-two women of age here. We need fresh genes, like you said. Margie's whole line about the first meal being free and all that? It was bullshit built on the assumption that you'd be happy to stay with us once you learned how it would be."

Nathan shook his head. "And what about Kate?" he asked. "The girl who came here. She was new blood. Did she even have a choice?"

Rhonna looked at the floor. She shook her head, just enough he could tell what the answer was.

"You should have told me what the expectation was. I would never have come here."

He moved past her, into the other part of the room. Fresh clothes were laying there. An old black t-shirt, blue pants, underwear, and socks. His old clothes were gone, and they hadn't given him new shoes.

The plasma pistol was gone, too.

"What are you doing?" Rhonna asked as Nathan started angrily pulling on his clothes.

"I'm leaving. I can't stay here. I'm useless to you, anyway."

"Nathan, you can't go," she said. "Margie will kill me if I let you go."

Nathan froze, looking back at her. She was so afraid she had forgotten about covering herself. Her arms were at her sides, her entire body shaking.

"I was never going to stay," Nathan said. "Even if I could give you what you wanted. It was a stupid assumption to make. I have to go west."

"Why?" she said, almost pleading with him.

"I have unfinished business. That's where I was heading before I crashed."

"Nathan, please. Don't leave." She reached out for him, taking his arm in her hands. "I was supposed to be pregnant by now. I've already tested Margie's patience and pushed her to the limit. If she at least thinks you had sex with me, that'll buy me a few months while she waits to see if it takes. Please. We can just sit here. I won't say anything."

He stared at her. He wanted to get the hell out of there. These people were dangerous. His instinct had been right. If they didn't get what they wanted, they were ready to kill over it. They had already driven some poor, innocent woman to kill herself.

And they had taken his gun.

He had to be smart about this. They both had something to lose.

"Can you get me my gun back?" he asked.

She nodded. "And other weapons, if you want them. If you say you'll stay, they'll give you whatever you need."

"I can't stay.'

"They don't have to know that yet. I have an idea."

Nathan didn't move. "How do I know I can trust you? You could say I attacked you. You could kill me in my sleep."

"Margie's smarter than to believe that." She was shaking less now that he was considering helping her lie to her mother. "Please, Nathan. We can be together anyway if you want to."

"I don't want to," Nathan said.

"Because of your wife?" she said. "I didn't think people still got married. Where is she?"

Nathan felt his eyes immediately begin to tear up. He tried to blink them away, and then he wiped at them. Damn it. He couldn't help himself.

"She was lucky to have someone love her so much," Rhonna said.

"No," Nathan said. "I was the lucky one."

Rhonna smiled sadly. "I'm sorry for your loss, Nathan." She crossed the floor, grabbing her clothes from the bed and putting them back on. "I'll help you get to the west side in the morning. Right now, get some rest. If you're going to try to escape the island, no matter how you do it, you're going to need it."

Chapter 30

Natalia was waiting when the Kiev landed, two hour's drive out from Sanisco where it could set down unnoticed.

Hayden descended the ramp from the dropship ahead of Bennett and the others, crossing the small field to where she was sitting on the hood of a car.

She hopped off as he approached, falling into his loving embrace. "Hayden. When I got the message through the link, I was hoping you were joking."

"I'm afraid not," Hayden replied before kissing her forehead. He looked past her. "You came alone?"

"I've got a car full of guards a kilometer back, on the other side of the hill. I figured you wanted to keep things quiet."

"Who's watching Hallia?"

"Malcolm."

"Isn't he a little busy?"

She laughed. "The Governor had some free time on his schedule."

"Did you bring everything I asked for?"

"You know I did."

Hayden smiled. As much as Bennett had wanted to get on Stacker's tail immediately, they weren't going to get very far with their no contact protocol dressed like soldiers from another planet. They needed supplies. Earth supplies. And this was the easiest and fastest way to get them.

Besides, it gave him time to see his wife again before they left.

"Nat," Bennett said, coming up behind Hayden. Natalia smiled, walking over to him and giving him a warm hug. He grinned back at her. "I was worried you might slug me."

"Because you want Hayden to help you catch a dangerous fugitive? I thought about it, but that is sort of his job. How's Rico?"

"I don't even know. I got turned around and sent back here so fast, I saw her for about five minutes."

"Maybe you can bring her down next time?"

"If we take care of business, then Command might give me anything I ask for."

"Speaking of which…"

Natalia led them around to the back of the car. It was a big vehicle, with a long front and rear modified with steel plates, some of which had spikes welded across them. The windows had bars, and the back half of the roof had been cut to allow two people to stand and shoot from the relative safety of the vehicle. The body itself was somewhat rusted, dented, and aged, but the engine had been reconditioned and was as good as new.

She reached under the trunk, hitting the release and then pushing it open. Bundles of cloth filled the top level, tied off with twine. She looked over at Bennett. He was wearing a dark navy Spacer uniform, too crisp, clean, and well-tailored to be from this planet.

"Yeah, this is definitely going to be better than that," she said, smiling. She lifted one of the bundles out and handed it to him. "One of these for each of your crew. Sorry, we can't spare a change of clothes, so don't wear them unless you're in the field."

"Pozz," Bennett said.

Moving the bundle had made a crate visible beneath. Natalia opened the top of it, revealing the hint of gunmetal amidst some straw that Hayden knew would be a mix of revolvers, shotguns, and ammunition. They were able to manufacture simple firearms at the moment, and they were working on tooling for more complex weaponry. Until then, they were dependent on what they could scavenge and what little help Proxima was willing to provide for more advanced firepower.

"These were delivered to Sanisco yesterday,"

Natalia said. "Just in time, I suppose." She put the cover back on as the other Spacers approached.

"Natalia Duke," Bennett said. "This is my team. Team, Natalia Duke."

"A pleasure," Natalia said. "Make sure you don't let my husband get himself killed."

They laughed.

"Yes, ma'am," Seventy said.

"Grab the equipment and bring it on board," Bennett ordered. "We'll be on our way in ten minutes."

"Yes, sir," they said.

The three of them moved aside to let the soldiers grab the bundles and the crates.

"Let's walk," Hayden said, taking Natalia's hand and leading her away from the scene. "Three days, Nat. Bennett promised."

She nodded. "I'd say I'm not worried about you, but it comes with the territory. What do you think about all of this?"

"I think I don't want to get involved. Bennett's a good man, but his bosses?" He shrugged. "They don't give two shits about Earth. You know that. They're using him, and they're using us. He thinks my help will show his leaders we're worth helping, but considering what they've provided so far and why, it's all lip service."

He paused. "Still, he said Stacker's ship was shot down, and that worries me. He thinks some crime syndicate on Proxima may be involved, and that worries me too. We don't need their dirty laundry. And we don't need their dirty businesses coming here."

"I think it's more likely their dirty businesses have been running here for a while," Natalia said. "If you can help him do something about that, it'll make our lives easier in the long run."

Hayden nodded. "Which is why I'm going."

"How are you going to find him?"

"Stacker? They tracked him on the way down, so they know where the ship crashed. It's got a shielded box that can survive pretty much anything and automatically sends out a beacon in the event of an emergency. That'll get us close. From there, if Stacker's still alive they can try to ping his identification chip, but they have to get within half a klick of him to do it."

"That's a pretty small needle."

"It is, which is why the Spacers need to blend in. I don't think we'll be able to straight-out grab Stacker. We'll have to ask around a little bit." He paused, turning her and looking into her eyes. "Things got a little crazy at the Expansion Zone. If Bennett hadn't shown up when he did, I don't know if I'd be standing here right now. I got sloppy."

She reached up, cupping his face in her hand. "Every minute out here is a risk, Hayden. You're trying to make life better for everyone, and I respect you and love you for it. And I know you're doing your best. Bennett did show up, and you are still here. We have to be grateful for that, and we have to keep going."

"I don't want to leave Hallia without a father."

"You can't always control that. It would be stupid and naive for either of us to expect we can. So many people here don't have fathers or mothers. But they survive. If there's one thing we'll teach Hallia, it'll be to survive."

Hayden returned her gesture, taking her face in his hand. "I thought she was going to be an Engineer, like her mom?"

"She'll be the best of both of us like it should be."

"Sheriff, time to go!" Bennett shouted, back near the car.

"Pozz that!" Hayden shouted back.

"Be as careful as you can," Natalia said. "Be as strong as you can. If you don't make it back, know that I love you and I'm proud of you, and I'll make sure Hallia knows what kind of man her father was." She paused, her eyes glistening. "But make it back."

He embraced her again, holding her tight for a moment. Then he kissed her a few times, promising himself he would remember this moment and hold onto it. He wasn't expecting serious trouble, but out here, you could never be sure of anything.

"I love you," she said.

"I love you, too," he replied.

They walked back to the car together. They said goodbye a second time. Hayden started back to the dropship with Bennett. He heard the car's engine roar to life, and he turned his head to watch it pull away.

"I know the feeling," Bennett said.

"Let's find this guy so I can get back home."

Chapter 31

The Kiev rose from the field, staying low as it maneuvered out toward the sea, taking a southerly route to avoid the few scattered human settlements nearby. Proxima's No Contact Protocol was more of a Low Contact Protocol because it was impossible to know how many people were hiding in the remains of the old world, struggling to survive amidst the constant threat of the trife. A cabin here, an old storefront there. The basement of a house, the top of a half-fallen skyscraper. The first ninety percent of humanity had been relatively easy to destroy, initially with a virus and then with the trife.

Hayden knew the last ten were proving much more resilient than either the unseen enemy who had launched the attack or the pilgrims who had escaped it ever imagined. It both inspired him and worried him.

What if the enemy was getting tired of waiting for the trife to finish off humankind?

What if they decided to come back?

He knew the Centurions were searching for them, trying to find them before they returned, to learn their identity and learn to fight back. At least the people on Proxima were good for that. But if the enemy did return to Earth, he knew there would be no help coming. They would be on their own.

They had to be ready.

Sometimes it seemed like an impossible task. He had expressed his frustration to Natalia on more than one occasion. She was a pragmatist, and her response was always the same. "We do the best we can, one day at a time. One minute at a time. That's the only thing we can control."

Worrying wasn't going to change the world.

The Kiev reached the ocean and started to ascend, rising vertically from the planet's surface. Hayden was belted into one of the seats on the bridge, with Bennett beside him, Judicus Shia on his left, and Captain Danethi piloting up front. He stared at the rear display as they rose, heart thumping in wonder at the sight of the planet from so high above. He had been in a dropship once before, and it had gone pretty high to avoid being seen.

But not this high.

They headed into a low orbit, far enough from Earth that he could see the entire thing beyond the displays, in all of its external beauty.

"Pretty amazing, isn't it?" Bennett asked.

"Pozz," Hayden replied. "How does it compare to Proxima?"

"Proxima is ugly from the outside," Bennett replied. "A brown rock split by rivers and covered in domes. But there are no trife."

"Sir," Captain Danethi said. "We've reached orbital sync."

"Roger," Bennett replied. "Scan for the beacon."

"Yes, sir. Scanning." Danethi tapped the control surface a few times.

Bennett looked at Hayden. "We know the ship was crossing what used to be North America when it was hit. It should only take a few minutes to get a lock."

"What happens when you get the position?" Hayden asked.

"That depends on where it is. We might have to do a HALD jump."

"HALD?"

"High-altitude, low-deceleration. The Kiev is a dropship. Pretty self-explanatory there. The basic armor's good for low-altitude jumps like we did back at the expansion zone, but we've also got high-altitude jump packs on board."

"You want to jump out of the ship from up here?" Hayden said. "And what? Fall back to the surface?"

"Pretty much. We drop in at night, so nobody sees us. The jump packs use compressed gas to slow the fall, making us nearly invisible from the ground. It'll help keep us from spooking Stacker, if he's still alive."

"I don't know how to do a HALD jump. And I sure as hell don't want to, either."

Bennett laughed. "It's not so bad. You'll be strapped to me, which means you'll do just fine."

Hayden tried to calm his nerves. Would he have agreed to this if he had known he would have to jump from a starship?

"Come on, Sheriff, where's your sense of adventure?"

"I've never had a sense of adventure. Only a desire to help protect the innocent."

"A noble sentiment that I appreciate and admire, especially because I know you're sincere. You'll be fine. I promise. Trust me."

"Okay," Hayden said. He did trust Bennett. "How will we know if Stacker's alive or not, once we find whatever's left of the Explorer?"

"We'll have to do a sweep of the area and look for his identification chip. It's shielded the same as the Explorer's Black Box, so even if he got his limbs blown off, we can track it."

"He could lose the chip and still be alive."

"And wounded. Sure. That's when we have to

start the deep search. I never guaranteed this would be easy."

"You told me three days."

"That's my optimistic timeline. Believe me, Hayden, I want to get back to Rico as much as you want to get back to Natalia. But we have to play it smart, or we're all going to end up dead."

"Pozz that."

They waited another minute in silence.

"Got it," Captain Danethi said. "Pulling it up."

He switched one of the displays to a map of Earth. A tiny beacon became visible on the east coast of the former United States.

"Can you zoom in?" Bennett asked.

The display zipped downward toward the beacon, zooming in on it until the landscape surrounding it became more clear.

"Do we have visual data we can overlay with the map?" Bennett asked.

"Yes, sir," Danethi replied. It appeared a few seconds later, a top-down view of the remains of a city.

"Where is that?" Hayden asked.

"According to the database, it was called Manhattan," Danethi said. "Also known as New York City, in the United States territory of New York."

"It's a small island," Bennett said.

Hayden examined the imagery. "It looks like all of the bridges were blown out."

"That it does, Sheriff. The good news is, we found our ship and its on an island, so it won't be easy for our fugitive to have gotten too far too fast. He's naturally contained."

"What's the bad news?" Hayden asked, even though he had a feeling he already knew.

"Even if we wanted to bring the Kiev down nearby, we can't. There's nowhere to land."

Hayden pointed to a green patch on the south side of the island, not too far from the beacon. "What about there?"

"It's too overgrown," Danethi said. "I can bring her down there in an emergency, but I don't recommend it otherwise."

Hayden blew out a long sigh. "Damn it."

"Sorry, Sheriff," Bennett said. "HALD it is."

Chapter 32

Hayden assembled in the briefing room with the rest of Bennett's team, taking a seat in the front row close to Animal while Bennett headed to the front to explain the situation.

"Hola, Sheriff," Animal said. "How are you enjoying the ride so far?"

"I'd prefer to keep riding," he replied, drawing a laugh from the man.

"We'll take care of you."

"Spacers," Bennett said. "If I can have your attention."

The soldiers all snapped to attention in their seats. The same map Hayden had seen twenty minutes earlier appeared on the screen behind the Sergeant.

"This is the position of the Explorer's beacon,"

Bennett said. "The ship crashed on an island, which is both good and bad."

"Are we going in HALD, sir?" Happy asked.

"Affirmative, Private," Bennett replied.

Hayden hated how happy Happy seemed to be about making the jump.

"We'll be dropping from fifteen kilometers. Full HALD apparatus. Earther clothes with bodysuits beneath. Spacer weaponry."

Hayden opened his mouth to object.

"I know," Bennett said before he could. "But we don't have any proof there's anyone alive on the island, and we also don't have a count of trife. I'm hedging my bets that we'll need the increased ordnance loads of non-solid ammunition."

"You don't have any drones on board?" Hayden asked.

"Negative. The Kiev is usually a museum piece. We had to pull her into service because Stacker damaged our space port's airlock. We can't get any ships in or out of the main facility until it's repaired." Bennett waited a few seconds for Hayden to continue the argument. He didn't. "We'll touch down here." Bennett pointed to an area a few streets over from the beacon. "We find somewhere to stash the jump packs and set them to destruct. Then we cross over to the site, standard wedge, eyes and ears open. If we're lucky, we get a reading on Stacker's chip, and find enough of him we can verify that he's dead."

"If we aren't lucky, sir?" Neko asked.

"It's going to be a long night. We'll try to estimate where he might have gone based on the environment."

"It'll be faster if we split up, sir," Animal said.

"Negative," Bennett replied. "You had your first contact with the trife on your way in, and that was with the support of the Kiev and during the day. The bastards are more active at night. We survive by sticking together. I know it'll take longer that way, but that's my call."

"Sir," Judicus Shia said. "No offense, but didn't you tell us on the way here that the Earthers had an entire army that went up against the trife and lost?"

"Multiple armies, but yes."

"And the seven of us are supposed to land in the middle of an island that may be crawling with them?"

"Your hesitation is understandable, Judge. Our orders are to find Stacker and get him under control. I didn't see anywhere Command made it optional based on the number of trife in the area. You're all supposed to be the best Proxima has to offer, hand-picked by Colonel Bard for this mission. You've done the sims, you've gotten high marks across the board. We have a better chance in an urban environment because we can bottleneck the fuckers and block them out if needed. Besides, that's worst case. An island like this isn't going to have a lot of energy pouring in, which is going to limit how many of them can survive."

"Understood, sir," Shia said.

"You scared, Judge?" Happy asked.

"You should be," Hayden said. "You'll live longer that way."

"I'd take the Sheriff's advice if I were you," Bennett said. "He lives in this shit every day."

"Yes, sir," the Spacers said.

"We've got twenty minutes to prep. Let's get moving."

"Yes, sir."

The Spacers filed out of the room ahead of Hayden and Bennett.

"This is getting worse with every word that comes out of your mouth, Sergeant," Hayden said.

"I'm sorry, Hayden. I really am. You can stay here if you want. Hell, I would if I had a choice."

Hayden remembered what Natalia had said. If they were going to represent Earth, they had a responsibility to put their lives on the line to help protect it.

"And abandon my friend? I wasn't made that way."

Bennett clasped him on the shoulder. "You and me both."

They made their way to the armory. The other Spacers were already there, shrugging out of their utilities and into their bodysuits. The tight material was the same steel silk that sat beneath the ceramic plates on the combat armor, though its slightly thinner weave offered less weight and more range of motion to go along with less protection. It was enough to stop an indirect hit from a trife claw or keep a smaller caliber bullet from piercing it, depending on range, but it wasn't a substitute for the full deal.

"Maybe we should go full armor?" Hayden said quietly, seeing them. "Blending in isn't worth dying for."

"Bodysuits will keep us more nimble," Bennett replied. "To be honest, I think that'll be more valuable if we get in trouble. Combat armor is worthless if there are enough trife to overwhelm us, and if there aren't, we should be able to handle them anyway."

"Pozz that."

"You're right about one thing, Hayden," Bennett added. "We're going in dark; we should stay dark." He whistled, getting the attention of the Spacers. "Change of plans. Bodysuits and all-blacks."

"Yes, sir," they replied.

"Sheriff, we've got a suit for you here," Seventy said, holding it up.

He quickly stripped out of his overclothes and took it from her, sitting to tug it over his feet. He shrugged it past his arms and up, zipping it in the front.

"You have a lot of scars, Sheriff," Neko said, noticing his body while he changed. "All from the trife?"

"Not all," Hayden said. "A lot of them."

"What about your arms?" Frank asked.

"No. The arms aren't because of the trife. Let's just say there have been some good people doing bad things out here."

He didn't want to say any more about it. This wasn't the time or the place for those memories.

The Spacers opened a different cabinet to pull out a rack of black fatigues. They were lighter and more fitted than the standard utilities, with spaces for ammo and equipment sewn into or clipped onto the material. Each of the Spacers grabbed their appropriate size, quickly pulling the uniforms on. The fatigues also came with facemasks which they pulled over their heads, leaving only their eyes visible beneath.

Hayden did the same, winding up covered head to toe in black cloth.

They finished prepping by grabbing an ear communicator, night vision goggles, a plasma rifle, and a laser pistol from the proper rack and bins in the armory, checking the charges and grabbing extra cells for each weapon. Hayden also dug out one of the revolvers and a black ammo belt from the crates Natalia had given them. It seemed appropriate, especially since they were forgoing the rest of the equipment he had requested.

"You sure you want that, Sheriff?" Animal asked when he saw the gun and belt.

"I'm a better shot with this than I am with a blaster," Hayden replied. "Just in case."

"Suit yourself," Animal said, smiling.

The Spacers filtered out of the armory, redirecting down into the ship's hold. Bennett opened the storage compartment containing the jump packs. Each one was about a meter long and half a meter wide and deep, with four nozzles poking out of the bottom and a pair of semi-flexible arms with joysticks attached. A helmet was resting on top of each one, connected to the left side of the pack by a hose and wire.

"Seventy," Bennett said. "We need to double mine up. I'm going tandem with the Sheriff."

"It's going to be a drag on your fuel supply, sir," Neko said. "I'm the lightest. I should take him."

Bennett looked at Hayden. "You good with that, Sheriff?"

Hayden nodded.

"Okay. Let's add a fuel extension to Neko's pack, and get a Y-split and another tube."

"Yes, sir," Seventy said.

She opened another storage space beside the jump packs, locating the additions. She pulled one of the packs out and quickly made the modifications.

"Ready, Sarge," she said when she finished.

"Good work, Seventy," Bennett said. He raised his voice. "Line 'em up!"

The Spacers each took a pack. Neko shrugged into a harness and then motioned for Hayden. "Back up toward me."

He did, backing up until he pressed against her. She reached past his chest, wrapping a trio of straps around him.

"Pull against me to check it," she said.

He did, trying to break loose of the harness. Neko gave him a thumbs up when it didn't budge.

"Ready, sir," she said.

"The rest of you Spacers ready?" Bennett asked. He picked up his pack, slipping it onto his back.

"Yes, sir!" they shouted.

"Helmets!" Bennett said.

The Spacers slipped their helmets on. Hayden lifted his over his head and pulled it down. The foam on the bottom gave way to his head and then expanded to sit snugly at the base of his neck. Oxygen fed into it through the tube, and a digital overlay on the mask provided him with all kinds of data he didn't know what to do with.

"Don't worry about a thing, Sheriff," Neko said, her voice loud and clear in his earpiece.

That was easy for her to say. Hayden controlled his breathing, refusing to lose his cool. He had been through worse than this.

"All right Centurions," Bennett said. "Give me comms check."

"Animal, check."

"Frank, check."

"Happy, check."

"Neko, check."

"Seventy, check."

"Judge, check."

"Sheriff, check," Hayden said.

"Sarge, check," Bennett said. "Here we go. Danethi, seal the deck and drop the ramp."

"Roger," Danethi said.

The doors to the hold locked, secondary shields sliding down ahead of them. Hayden couldn't feel the space depressurizing, but he could tell the air was getting colder despite the bodysuit.

A few seconds later, a red strobe started flashing near the ramp. It thunked and hissed and began to open, a blast of frigid air washing in.

Hayden looked out through the slowly descending ramp. He could see the curve of the planet from this height. How the hell were they going to drop on target?

His heart started racing, his adrenaline pumping.

"Don't hyperventilate on me, Sheriff," Neko said. "You could kill us both."

Hayden did his best to relax. "How many times have you done this?" he asked.

"On Proxima? About fifty," she said. "Earth's

gravity is a little heavier, but not enough to make a difference."

"Ready," Bennett said, pausing. "Steady." He paused again, raising his hand and holding it out to them. Another pause.

His hand curled into a fist. "Go!" he shouted. "Go, go, go, go, go."

The Centurion Spacers ran to the edge of the ramp and jumped.

"Let's go, Sheriff," Neko said, pushing him lightly.

His legs started moving, carrying him closer and closer to the ramp, and the long fall that came once he ran out of hard surface. He nearly pulled up at the last second, but Neko seemed to sense his hesitation and gave him a tougher shove, which carried them both out of the dropship.

Then he was falling.

Chapter 33

The air at fifteen kilometers was cold enough to get through the bodysuit, ripping into his flesh and giving him an almost immediate chill. It wasn't enough that it would kill him, but it also wasn't very comfortable.

Otherwise, the drop, at least the beginning of it, was almost fun. The Spacers tumbled through the air, all seven of them in a line, slightly spread out but visible through the infrared display of the jump helmets. The data in front of Hayden's eyes changed in a hurry, and he was able to figure out which of them was altitude and which was velocity.

The second one was static after about seventeen seconds, while the change in the first became steady.

At that point, there wasn't much to do but fall, looking down at the planet as they drew closer to their landing point.

Three minutes passed. Earth grew beneath them, the group remaining silent on the ride down. Hayden turned his head from side to side, trying to take in as much as he could. He had been afraid of the HALD jump before he had done it. He was less afraid now, but he didn't think he would ever do it again.

He stopped moving his head when he noticed a red flash in the distance, somewhere down below. He didn't think much of it.

Maybe he didn't think enough of it.

His helmet was suddenly flashing, a yellow reticle around something coming from the same direction and closing fast.

"Shit," Bennett said through the comm. "Evasive maneuvers!"

What?

Hayden's stomach clenched as Neko fired the thrusters on the jump pack, throwing them into a hard right turn. He could see the other Spacers beneath them, taking their own route out of the path of the approaching object.

Something split the group, diving through the center of where they had been a moment earlier. Hayden tried to turn his head to follow it, but he lost sight as they continued to roll and move.

He noticed another flash down below. Not near their target, but to the west.

He heard a rumble above, and the sky illuminated at his back.

"Heads down, Spacers!" Bennett shouted. "Move!"

The jump pack fired, rotating Hayden and Neko until their heads aimed toward the ground. The jump pack continued to fire, thrust pushing against resistance and getting the velocity counter in his helmet increasing again. They accelerated, shooting groundward while more projectiles exploded above them.

"What the hell is this?" Animal said. "Sarge, you said Earthers don't have advanced tech."

"They don't," Bennett replied harshly. He was pissed. "Keep evasive going and watch your fuel indicators. Especially you, Neko."

"Yes, sir," Neko replied.

Another round of red flashes from their right, slightly larger at lower altitude.

"Target vector is below us, sir!" Seventy shouted through the comm.

"Fuck!" Bennett said. "Pull up or blow through. Neko, you need to blow through."

"Roger," Neko said. "Hang on, Sheriff."

Most of the Spacers flipped their feet downward, firing their jump packs to slow the descent. Neko kept them pointing down, adding a little more thrust. "We're too heavy to pull back," she said. He had guessed as much.

His helmet showed the projectiles incoming; small dark slivers carried toward them by the same invisible exhaust the jump packs were using. He clenched his teeth. They weren't going to make it.

"Damn it," Neko said, realizing the same thing. "Sarge!"

She swung them over as the missile exploded a few meters away, sending shrapnel through the sky. He heard pieces of it hit the jump pack. He heard Neko groan. Then the thrust cut out and she fell limp behind him.

He wasn't supposed to die before he made it to the ground.

He continued to fall, suddenly on his own. The jump pack must have had some kind of balancing mechanism in it because it allowed him to shift direction without letting him roll out of control. He flattened out, going belly down.

"Bennett," he said. "Neko's out."

"Roger," Bennett replied. "Stay calm; I'm coming to you."

Hayden noticed the counters on his screen. One of them had reached thirty and was ticking down. A timer? He noticed a few more flashes out of the corner of his eye.

Who the fuck was shooting at them?

The whole thing started again. His helmet flashing warnings and locking on the projectiles while the Spacers tried to avoid the missiles and the shrapnel they produced. He was a big fat target among them, falling even and flat.

He saw a dark shape rocket past him, dropping fifty meters below and then rolling over, putting the pack toward the ground. Bennett spread his arms, a thin film expanding beneath them and between his legs, catching him and slowing the fall. Hayden dropped right into him, and Bennett grabbed his harness and held tight.

"This is going to suck a bit, Sheriff," Bennett said. "Stay calm."

Hayden noticed the timer had reached ten. "What's the countdown?"

"Never mind that."

The last round of missiles exploded behind them.

"I'm hit," Frank cried out, "Ahh. Damn it. Fuck it hurts."

"Son of a bitch," Bennett muttered. "Okay, Hayden, give me your hands."

Hayden offered them, and Bennett took them, moving them to the clasps keeping him connected to Neko.

"When I say release, you release. I'll catch you, okay?"

Hayden didn't like the sound of that, but it was probably better to risk dying than to die for sure. "Pozz."

Bennett held the harness, using it to swing around to the back of the jump pack.

The timer was past zero and into negative numbers.

Hayden couldn't see what Bennet was doing. All he could see was the ground coming up fast. He could make out the old buildings, already way too close. He had lost sight of the area to the west where the projectiles had launched. He didn't have a good feeling.

"Release!" Bennett shouted.

Hayden didn't hesitate. He pressed on the clasps, and the harness opened. He felt Neko and the jump pack shifting away behind him.

He was still falling. Unencumbered. With no way to slow down.

And the buildings were coming hard and fast.

He didn't panic. Bennett said to trust him, and Hayden was going to trust him. He kept his arms and legs out, falling toward his death. He...

Strong arms wrapped under and around his, legs shifting and hooking his ankles. He was yanked hard upright, and then he heard the hiss of the jump pack's thrusters firing full-bore.

"Got you!" Bennett said. "Now let's hope this bitch has enough juice to keep us from being flattened."

They held on, the ground approaching in a hurry. The jump pack changed direction, angling them away from the buildings but also away from the other Spacers.

"This is going to hurt," Bennett said, as they sank in between two of the damaged skyscrapers. They were headed toward a street filled with old and rusted cars, with only a single, small clearing ahead.

The jump pack thrusters seemed to find another level, the hiss rising to a whistling whine that was going to bring the trife running if there were any nearby. Hayden was yanked back, the momentum slowing, and then Bennett rolled him over like Neko had done, getting them on their backs and letting the jump pack hit the ground first. It offered a minimum of protection as they touched down, bouncing and sliding. Bennett grunted. Hayden lost his breath. They slid across the small clearing and slammed into an old wreck.

"Damn that hurts," Bennett said, pinned between Hayden and the jump pack.

Hayden rolled forward onto the ground, trying to get some air. Bennett stayed down behind him, testing his arms and legs to make sure nothing was broken.

"Any landing you can walk away from," Bennett said.

Hayden grabbed his helmet, pulling it off and throwing it on the ground. He coughed a couple of times, leaning over on his hands and knees.

"I never, ever want to do that again," he proclaimed.

"You and me both, Sheriff."

"Sarge, this is Seventy. Do you copy?"

Her voice was less crisp through the ear communicator than it had been in the helmet.

Bennett shifted his jaw, activating the comm. "Roger that, Seventy. I hear you."

"How's Sheriff Duke?"

"I'm okay," Hayden said. "A little banged up, but still alive."

"What about Frank?" Bennett asked.

"He didn't make it. Died on the way down."

"Fuck. Neko, too."

"Damn, Sarge," Animal said. "What the fuck is going on out here?"

"I don't know. Nobody on Earth should have ballistics like that. Hell, I've never seen anything like that on Proxima, either." He picked himself up.

"Someone saw us coming," Hayden said. He didn't like hearing they were attacked by a weapon neither of them could identify. "Not only that, but they were ready to attack. How can that be?"

"We'll have to work on that little mystery, but first order of business is to regroup. Seventy, what's your position?"

"Tall buildings, lots of old cars."

"Us too. Fire a plasma bolt into the air for me; I'll see if I can track it."

"Roger, sir," Seventy said. "Standby."

Hayden turned around to face Bennett. He froze. "I think we should be the ones to fire the plasma."

Chapter 34

Nathan didn't go to sleep, despite Rhonna's suggestion.

He laid on the bed.

He closed his eyes.

He listened.

Rhonna spent fifteen minutes perched near the door to the room, likely listening for her family to make sure they weren't eavesdropping on what they expected to be happening in the room. Once she was satisfied, she sat on the bed beside him. Even with his eyes closed, he could tell she was looking at him. Examining him. He was strange to her, wasn't he? He had experienced so many things she wanted but would never have the chance to do. Travel. Fall in love. Get married. He didn't blame her. Despite everything, he wouldn't trade his life for hers.

After a while, she let herself relax, and she

slipped under the threadbare blankets beside him. She put her hand on his chest, and then thought better of it, removing it and tucking it in.

Nathan kept his eyes closed until she began to snore lightly.

He looked over at her, watching her for a few seconds. Then he slid off the bed, the way he had done with Niobe so many times. He was good at being quiet. In this case, not having any shoes helped.

He went over to the door, listening for a moment. It was silent on the train, now that it was late. He had heard the members of the family going through the aisle earlier. He had heard doors closing, toilets flushing. He was impressed they had kept all of that in working order for all these years. Hell, he was still impressed they had managed to live down here like this, even if they had resorted to inbreeding to survive.

It didn't mean he wanted to stay. He didn't doubt Rhonna was telling the truth about Margie. She was the matriarch, and if she told her family to kill him, they would do it.

He reached the door, slowly flipping the lock. He glanced back at Rhonna. Would Margie punish her for his escape? He hoped not, but he couldn't take responsibility for her. He had his own problems. He would have preferred to let her guide him west, but it was better if he snuck away.

He opened the door, taking his time. If she woke and saw him leaving, he could handle it. He wouldn't even lie. Nothing to lose. That's where he was right now.

She didn't wake. Her snoring got a little louder. He closed the door behind him, glancing both ways along the length of the car. He was alone in the hallway. Only dim lights on the floor allowed him to see enough to navigate.

He looked toward the front of the train. Dining car, passenger car, exit. It was an easy escape from here. Except he had no shoes and no gun. If he went out like that, he was as good as dead.

He hesitated a moment, and then went back the other way. He needed a chance to survive as much as he needed to get out. He reached the rear airlock, carefully opening the door as quietly as possible and then closing it behind him. He repeated the process to get into the next car.

There were two Amtraks sleeping on the couch where Margie had been earlier. A boy and a girl at opposite ends, a single blanket passed over them. Their mouths were open, light snoring coming from both. He watched them as he crossed the car. Where did they keep the supplies?

He went through that car to another passenger cab, and then another sleeper. He heard movement in one of the rooms as he moved through that one, and he waited for it to settle. A third passenger car. The one after that was the one he wanted.

It was a storage car, with racks on either side loaded with all sorts of supplies. There were piles of clothes and shoes, boxes filled with cans of food, old electronics, and finally a rack filled with both wooden and metal spears, a large locker beside it. His boots were with the other clothes, and he grabbed them and a pair of worn socks and slipped them on. Then he went to the locker. It had a combination padlock on it, securing it.

He stared at it for a moment. He wanted to be quiet, but he also wanted his gun. He glanced over at the spears. They were handmade, whittled down or pounded. They looked sharp. A couple of them had cloth wrapped around them for a thicker handle and better grip. He grabbed one of the metal ones, slipping the end through the loop of the padlock. He got it properly leveraged.

Then he pulled.

The locker groaned under the force. Nathan kept his eyes on the door at the end of the car while he kept pushing, trying to leverage the lock and force it to snap. His muscles flexed with the effort, the door of the locked denting inward from the strain.

"Come on, damn it," he muttered, shifting his eyes back to the lock. He pushed harder, and he could see it starting to stretch.

The overhead lights in the train turned on all at once, momentarily hurting his eyes.

Had Rhonna told them he was missing?

He quickly turned the spear the other way, shoving as hard as he could, putting more pressure on the lock. It finally gave way, a sharp crack sounding as the metal bent and released. It hung on the spear for a second before sliding off and clanging on the ground.

He pulled the door open. There were weapons inside. Most of them looked old and ordinary, like black rectangles with triggers. There was one larger rifle with a long magazine that hung down in front of the trigger, also black. A few pairs of night-vision goggles sat on the top shelf. Magazines for the guns rested on the bottom.

His plasma pistol wasn't there.

He heard voices now, coming in his direction. He looked back to the end of the car. He could see shapes through the two windows that separated them from him.

He grabbed a pair of goggles and pulled them onto his head, keeping them up and off his eyes. He also took two of the handguns, shoving one of them in the back of his pants. Then he reached down and claimed four magazines as well, shoving them quickly in his pockets. He turned back to face the incoming Amtraks, aiming the pistol. It felt heavy and odd in his hand. He had never been a big fan of projectile weapons.

The airlock opened. Kilo made his way through. He was pulling Rhonna with him.

"There you are, bruddah," he said. He dragged Rhonna to his side. He had a long knife in his free hand, and he put it up to his sister's throat. "You know, it isn't nice to steal. And when people do things that aren't nice, innocent people get hurt."

"How did you know I was here?" Nathan asked.

"She told me you were missing," he said, shaking her slightly. "It didn't take a genius to figure out where you would go, especially since we took your gun. I've never seen a piece like it before."

"What did you just say about stealing?" Nathan replied.

Kilo smiled. "You got me there, bruddah. I guess it's all fair. Nobody needs to get hurt here. You know, we don't have to have a problem at all. We aren't bad people. We just need to survive, you know?"

Nathan could see more of the Amtraks were coming, closing off his escape.

"What do you want from me?" he asked. "I can't stay with you. I can't stay on this island."

"We're reasonable people," Kilo said. "You do what you need to do, and we'll let you walk. You can take one of the guns and a few mags. No problem."

"What about my gun?"

"Barter. Since you aren't sticking around."

The other family members were staying back in the other car. Nathan could make out Margie's gray hair and stone face through the glass, watching them.

Nathan looked at Rhonna. She was terrified and shaking harder than she had been before. She had a fresh welt near her eye, close to the burns. She had told Kilo where he was, but had she done it willingly?

He lowered the gun. "Fine," he said. "Pass her over."

Kilo laughed. "And let you shoot me? I'm not an idiot, bruddah. I know you aren't a monster. You could have done whatever you wanted to Ronnie here, and you didn't touch her. That's all beside the point." He turned Rhonna in his arms, keeping the knife against her throat. "No, you come over here, and you do what you need to do. It's called leverage."

Nathan clenched his jaw. Rhonna whimpered, shifting uncomfortably in Kilo's grip.

"I can't believe you would do this to your own sister," Nathan said.

"Yeah, well I understand priorities a hell of a lot better than she does. We die off, that's giving up. After all these years, we can't give up. Otherwise, what was it all for? What do you say?"

Nathan closed his eyes. He had settled somewhat while he had been resting and waiting, but the pressure was pouring back, the rage returning. Whatever

Rhonna was, however she had been raised, she didn't deserve this. Nobody deserved this.

His body tingled, a chill running over his skin. His finger shifted on the gun, moving to the trigger unnoticed.

"I'm not who I said I was," he said.

"What do you mean?" Kilo asked, genuinely curious when he should have been afraid.

Nathan's hand snapped up, rising and firing in one smooth motion. He hated projectile weapons.

That didn't mean he couldn't use them.

The round caught Kilo right in the mouth, blasting through his teeth and into the back of his head. He dropped the knife, trying to scream in pain from the sudden wound, and letting Rhonna go.

"What did you do?" Rhonna said, turning back to Kilo. "Damn it, Nathan."

Her voice was accusing. Hadn't he just saved her life?

The gunshot put the other Amtraks in motion. They started for the car, coming after him.

Rhonna picked up Kilo's knife. She started toward him. Not for protection. Was she planning to use it?

"Rhonna, what the hell?"

"They'll kill me. Don't you get that?"

"Come with me. I'm getting out of here."

"How?" she asked. "Through them? All of them? We'll both die."

He pointed the gun at her head. He hated Earth and everything on it. This whole thing was a nightmare.

"You can stay if you want," he said. "I'm leaving."

He looked to his left. There had been doors on every other car, at the front and the rear. This one was no different. The exit was boarded over and hidden behind a rack of supplies, but it was there.

He grabbed the edge of the shelf.

"Make your decision," he said.

Her eyes suggested she wanted to come with him. They were sad and jealous, fearful and pleading.

She didn't move.

He could imagine what they were going to do to her. It wasn't his problem. She made her choice.

He shouted as he pulled on the shelf. The door behind Rhonna opened. Gary was the first Amtrak through, and he was holding Nathan's pistol.

Gary aimed and fired just as Nathan got the shelf to start toppling. The plasma bolt hit some of the electronics, turning them to slag.

"Whoa!" he heard Gary say, amazed at what the weapon could do.

The shelf hit the opposite side of the car while everything on it toppled off. It was enough to block the Amtraks' path.

Nathan used the spear to lever the wooden board, pushing against it and breaking it free of the screws holding it. He stopped when Gary neared the barrier, firing the pistol without aiming and forcing the man to retreat. A second hard pull brought the wood off completely, and he shoved the spear between the two panels of the door, giving one more push to get it open.

He jumped out of the train an instant before a second plasma bolt hit the wall behind his head. He hit the ground, rolling to his feet and looking back. They would have to move the shelf before they could follow.

He lowered the goggles onto his eyes, blinding himself. There had to be a switch or something. He dropped the spear to feel the sides of the device until he found a small toggle. He flipped it on, hearing a soft click. Then the world became visible ahead of him.

He picked up the spear and ran.

Chapter 35

Nathan didn't know where he was going. He was pissed at Rhonna for leaving him on his own, especially after he tried to help her. He was pissed at Niobe for dying, and not even telling him what she was doing. He was pissed at Yamaguchi and the fucking Trust. He was pissed at whoever the fucker was who blew him out of the fucking sky and left him stranded on this fucking island.

He ran along the same tunnel the train was resting in because it seemed like as good a place to run as any. He knew the platforms were along the main tunnels, and if he could get to a platform maybe he could go back to the surface.

He'd rather deal with the trife than the Amtraks.

He kept running for a dozen minutes or more, covering a fair distance. He spotted an opening up ahead, which he hoped meant a platform. The Amtraks had given chase at first, but he had outpaced them almost too easily, his overall strength and fitness and angry resolve carrying him away.

He slowed as he came out of the tunnel and into the station. He scanned the platform. No trife. No humans. No Stalker. He would take it.

He went to the edge of the platform and tossed the spear onto it before pulling himself up. He found the stairs at the rear of the station, and he rushed over to them.

He looked up toward the surface and then shook his head angrily. There was no surface. The top of the stairwell was buried under tons of stone.

He turned around, heading back to the tunnel. He would have to go for the next one.

He heard a crack, and a bullet hit the platform in front of him. Not close, but close enough. He backed up, finding a column to duck behind as another volley came his way, bullets slapping the ground and the ceiling and the column.

At least their aim was shit.

"Just let me be!" he shouted. "I don't want to hurt you."

"You killed Kilo, asshole," Gary said. "We can't let that be."

Nathan was glad to hear Gary's voice. The fucker still had his pistol. If the Amtraks weren't going to back off, then at least he was going to get his gun back.

He leaned out from the column, leaving his head exposed for a few seconds while he found the Earthers. They were huddled together, half a dozen strong. They thought six of them could take him out? They probably still believed his story about being raised in the mountains. They probably thought his shot on Kilo was a lucky one or an accident.

Idiots.

"Seriously," he said, his voice echoing across the space. "I will kill every last one of you if you don't back the fuck off."

They responded by shooting at him again. He moved back behind the column, deciding on the best approach.

He took a few breaths, trying to calm himself. It wasn't working. Not now. He growled softly, spinning out from behind the column. He charged toward the group, leaping down from the platform as he fired.

Two of them dropped before he hit the ground, multiple holes in their chests. He hid beside the third rail, tucking his shoulder and rolling while bullets whipped above his head. He popped up, shooting a third Amtrak.

A plasma bolt lit the tunnel, causing a flash in his night-vision goggles that nearly blinded him. He found his next victim through it, sending two more rounds into that man's stomach while more plasma bolts sizzled past. Gary was only a few meters away, with one other Amtrak beside him.

Then the remaining man broke rank, turning to run.

Nathan's lip curled in a feral snarl. He squeezed his trigger.

It clicked. Empty.

Gary's lips parted. He smiled in surprise victory, adjusting his aim and getting a bead on Nathan with the plasma pistol.

The smile vanished when the spear crossed the distance, sinking deep into his chest, the force of the impact knocking him back and sending the plasma bolt into the ceiling.

Nathan reached the stricken man, looking down at him with disdain. Gary's breathing was shallow, blood rushing from the wound.

"I would have let you keep the gun," Nathan said, bending down to pick up the pistol. "And your life. You should have listened to me."

"You aren't from the mountains," Gary complained, his voice barely audible.

"No. I'm a soldier, asshole. A Centurion."

"Centurion? Like the ones that helped Tinker build Edenrise?"

"What?" Nathan said, dropping to his knees to get closer to Gary's face. "What the hell did you just say?"

Gary didn't answer. He also didn't move.

Nathan stood up. The narrative had shifted, surprising him again. He remembered that Rhonna had dropped the name Tinker. Who were they talking about?

He dropped the projectile handgun and replaced it with the plasma pistol, checking the charge. Thirty shots left. Then he grabbed the spear, yanking it back out of Gary's corpse.

He turned and ran again, heading into the next tunnel. He hadn't wanted to kill any of the Amtraks. At the same time, it had given him some raw relief.

He ran until he reached the next station. Again, he climbed onto the platform and made his way to the stairs leading to the surface. His luck was better this time. He smiled when he saw the night sky behind the damaged buildings. Now all he had to do was head west.

He ascended to the surface, turning a full circle to scan the street. He was clear. He breathed a sigh of relief, grateful for the moment alone, without someone or something coming at him.

He shuddered when he heard the loud crack above and the flash of light that followed. He looked up in time to see a second flash, small and dense. It looked like an explosion.

Who would be launching missiles out here? Tinker?

He hadn't been able to tell where they were coming from or what they were being launched to hit. He stared skyward for a few seconds but didn't see anything.

Was it a coincidence the explosions were here, now? Someone had shot the Explorer out of the sky. Did they know he had crashed here? The projectiles were going up. They wouldn't be firing them if there wasn't something there, would they? But what could be up there?

He stared for a few more seconds. Had Proxima Command sent someone after him? Did they want him that badly? If they did, they would be able to track the Explorer. Its black box was designed to survive anything, and it would emit an emergency beacon when it detected a problem.

But how could he be worth that much to them? He hadn't killed another Spacer. He had allegedly killed his wife.

His hand dropped to his shirt, pressing against the ring around his neck. Did the Trust know what Niobe had done? Had they come looking for the prize?

They weren't going to get it. Gary had associated the Centurions with someone named Tinker. He was going to find them, whoever they were. He was going to get some damned answers.

First, he had to get off this fucking island.

He started turning another circle, trying to determine which direction was west. He knew the Explorer had been headed east when it was hit, and the sun had been behind him. But it was nighttime. There was no sun to follow. Could he afford to wait until it rose to get moving? He wished he knew what time it was.

At least it had stopped raining.

He was nervous about picking a direction. What if he headed east? Then he would have more ground to cover. If he stayed close to the station, the Amtraks might show. Then there was whoever the missiles had targeted. If Command had sent Space Force soldiers after him, they would probably do a HALD jump into the city. They would find the beacon, and then they would start searching for him.

He glanced down at his wrist. If they got close enough, they would be able to track his chip.

He had to make sure they didn't get close enough.

Decision made, he picked the nearest cross-street and started running again. He stayed on the sidewalk, using the rusted and overgrown vehicles and the walls of the buildings to keep his flanks covered. As long as he remained quiet, and as long as nothing came off the rooftops or through a broken window, he should be safe.

He covered two blocks, keeping his body crouched to stay below the level of most of the vehicles, careful to slow and sweep the alleys on his left as he passed them. The night-vision goggles gave him added confidence, allowing him to see much further than he would have otherwise. The stars were providing some light, but the eye wear gave him clarity and resolution.

Thankfully, he didn't see any trife.

He rounded the corner of an alley, aiming his plasma pistol down it and quickly scanning for activity. Clear. He turned back, staying low and moving in front of an old building. It had a rusted metal grate slung over its face, where broken windows revealed the remains of a storefront that had been picked clean years ago.

He heard a high-pitched whine to his right and he turned and raised his pistol, the sudden noise reaching through him and causing an immediate reaction. He saw the two Spacers at once, coming down together on one jump pack, their vector and velocity all wrong for a clean landing.

He ducked behind the nearest car, watching them. The noise was deafening, the sound enough to bring any trife anywhere in the city running. He stayed there a moment, cycling through his options. He had to run. He knew that much. But in what direction?

He would rather deal with the Stalkers and the Amtraks than the horde of demons that were going to descend on this spot.

He took one step back the way he had come.

A trife slipped out from the dark alley he had passed. It was also low, crawling on all fours, watching the Spacers' descent.

Had it been there the whole time, and he just hadn't seen it?

There was a loud crunch, and when Nathan looked back to the street, he saw the Spacers had hit the ground, landing belly-up with the pack absorbing the brunt of the impact. It was a smart move, a hard move. Whoever was guiding the landing was no rookie.

The pack kicked up sparks as it slid, approaching Nathan's position in a hurry. The trife was watching, but as the Spacers moved forward, its head swiveled, and it found Nathan crouching there.

Its mouth opened slightly in a silent hiss.

The pack hit the car in front of Nathan, pushing it back toward him in an echoing crash. He threw himself backward, his shoulder hitting the rusted metal as he ducked low, watching the vehicle slide toward him.

It came to a stop less than a meter away. Nathan spun in the direction of the trife.

It was gone.

The Spacers were moving. One was coughing. "I never, ever want to do that again," Nathan heard the man say.

"You and me both, Sheriff," the other one replied.

Sheriff? He wasn't familiar with the term. Was it some kind of Centurion Special Agent, or simply the man's call sign? He turned toward the Spacers, staying out of sight.

"I'm okay. A little banged up, but still alive."

Sheriff was keeping his voice low. He must have been talking through a communicator. That meant there were more Spacers in the area.

"What about Frank? Fuck. Neko, too. I don't know. Nobody on Earth should have ballistics like that. Hell, I've never seen anything like that on Proxima, either."

Nathan pressed against the other side of the car. It sounded like they knew as much about that as he did, and they were from Proxima. If Command was working with Earthers, wouldn't they know about it?

Then again, if they were on the same side, they wouldn't have taken fire. It sounded like they had lost two soldiers on the way down.

"Someone saw us coming. Not only that, they were ready to attack. How can that be?"

"We'll have to work on that little mystery, but the first order of business is to regroup. Seventy, what's your position?"

Nathan had to make a decision, and he didn't have time to think about it. The Centurions had come for him; he was sure of that. Two of them were already dead, and right now they were still disorganized. These two had been separated from the group. A Spacer squad was between five and ten soldiers. If he killed them now, forty percent of their group would be out of commission before they had a chance to start searching for him.

He liked those odds.

"Us too," the first soldier said to whoever was on the other end of the comm. "Fire a plasma bolt into the air for me; I'll see if I can track it."

Nathan popped up.

One of the Spacers had their back to him.

The other one was looking right at him.

Chapter 36

Hayden stared at the man on the other side of the old car. He recognized the face immediately and could hardly believe it.

Was this the best fucking luck he had ever had, or the worst?

Nathan Stacker stared back at him. The fugitive had a gun, and it was resting on the top of the car, pointed directly at him.

"Captain Nathan Stacker?" Hayden said. He recognized the plasma pistol. At this range, a bolt from it would pass right through the bodysuit.

"Who the hell are you?" Nathan said.

Bennett's eyes met Hayden's for a moment, and then he started to turn around.

"Don't," Stacker said, gun shifting to Bennett's back. "Don't fucking move. Who are you? Did Command send you? Or the Trust?"

"Captain Stacker," Bennett said. "I know you haven't been here long. We just made enough noise to wake the dead. That's about a hundred times more noise than we needed to make to get something from your nightmares headed this way in numbers that will make your head spin. None of us have time to stand here like a bunch of lollies, so if you're going to shoot me in the back, then shoot me in the back."

Hayden watched Stacker. The man looked conflicted. Like he wanted to shoot Bennett, but not like that. He wasn't a killer, then. A killer wouldn't hesitate no matter the situation.

Hayden caught a hint of motion to Stacker's left. A trife, rushing the fugitive.

"Stacker!" he said, reaching for his gun. The man looked at him, pistol shifting in his direction.

Hayden fell to his right, grabbing his revolver and extending his arm as he landed hard on one knee. The plasma bolt whizzed past his ear, so close he could feel the burn and hear it sizzle. He pulled the trigger, the round hitting the trife in the shoulder and throwing it off-balance.

It hissed and crashed into the fugitive, who rolled with it and vanished behind the car.

Hayden popped up as Bennett spun around. Something rose from behind the car, and Hayden aimed at it.

The trife's lifeless body came up, sliding across

the roof and falling in front of them. A dark form sprinted away from behind the vehicle, heading west.

Bennett grabbed his rifle from his back, flipping it to his shoulder and taking aim.

Hayden seized the end of the weapon, shoving it down.

Stacker vanished around a corner.

"What the fuck are you doing, Sheriff?" Bennett shouted. "I had him."

"He didn't shoot you in the back," Hayden said. "You owe him one."

Bennett bit his lip, holding back whatever initial response he was considering. He nodded. "There's never only one trife." He turned away from the direction Stacker had gone, and to the direction the trife had arrived.

Hayden swapped the revolver for his plasma rifle. His shoulder hurt when he reached for the weapon, sore from the ordeal of surviving the HALD jump. He saw more trife appearing at the mouth of the alley.

"This isn't going to go well," he said.

"We could have been done already," Bennett replied. "I had him."

"If we don't have honor, if we don't have justice, we're worse than them," Hayden said, motioning to the trife.

They had shown him both before. Despite their desire to kill nearly every human they found, they still had a sense of honor, fairness, and respect a lot of people he had met were lacking.

Bennett responded by firing into the trife, killing three of them before they started pouring out of the alley toward them.

"Seventy, what's your location?" Bennett asked, standing firm for the moment. Hayden joined him in the defense, firing plasma bolts into the oncoming demons.

"I shot the plasma into the air, sir," Seventy replied. "Didn't you see it?"

"I was a little busy," Bennett replied. "We've got incoming and could use some backup. Follow the flashes."

"Yes, sir. On our way."

Bennett scanned the area. "That way," he said, motioning toward another storefront.

"You don't want to chase Stacker?" Hayden asked.

Bennett raised his wrist, looking down at a bracelet wrapped around it. "He's still on the move, and heading out of range in a hurry." He glanced back at the trife. "Let's see how we do once backup shows."

They kept shooting, retreating toward the storefront. It had a metal gate in front of it, hanging open on bent hinges. The smaller entry would force the trife to either bunch up or give up.

"Watch your shots," Bennett said. "We don't have any more ammo than what we're carrying."

"Pozz," Hayden said, firing again. The trife were gaining, spreading apart to get around their flanks. He wouldn't have kept shooting, but he wanted to make sure Seventy and the other Spacers found them.

Bennett and Hayden continued to retreat, nearing the storefront. They were almost directly in front of it when Hayden heard the hiss behind them. He grabbed Bennett and pulled him roughly away from the entrance as a trife pounced from the shadows. Its claws just barely caught the Spacer on the arm, a glancing blow that cut the black fatigues but not the bodysuit beneath.

The trife landed and turned, throwing itself at them. Hayden let go of Bennett and sent his augmented hand into it, the force crushing its head and throwing it sideways.

Bennett hopped up, taking a few wild shots with his plasma rifle as the mass of trife closed in, the short break in fire giving the aliens a chance to gain ground. Two more of the creatures fell, but the two humans were getting overwhelmed in a hurry.

Hayden turned back toward the storefront. More trife had appeared there, rushing for the opening. Only two could make it through at a time, and Hayden shot the first few before they could clear the gate, slowing the egress of the rest

"Seventy, any fucking day now," Bennett said angrily.

He motioned to their right, to an alley that was clear of trife. Hayden followed him, taking a few more shots with the plasma rifle and dropping a few more aliens.

"I've got visual on you, sir," Seventy replied.

Hayden scanned the street. At least a hundred trife were bearing down on them. He could see dark shapes moving behind the cars and along the walls of the nearby buildings. There were likely more of them on the rooftops, following the action and trying to take them by surprise.

He found the other Spacers coming out of a cross-street. They started firing into the back of the enemy, cutting them down as they caught them unaware.

The monsters began to scramble like insects, rushing out of the street and seeking cover, leaping up and over the cars in powerful jumps, landing behind them and vanishing. The Spacers stopped shooting, fanning out and watching the flanks as they started to cross the distance.

"Clear," Seventy said.

"Seventy, hold," Hayden said.

"The bastards are on the run."

"If the Sheriff says hold, you hold, Sergeant," Bennett said.

The Spacers stopped moving.

Hayden watched the street. It was suddenly deathly quiet. The trife had vanished along the sides of the road, moving into alleys or staying low behind the vehicles. The rest of the Spacer squad was straight ahead, a hundred meters separating them.

"Now what?" Seventy asked.

"It's a trap," Hayden said. "As soon as you get to the center, all hell breaks loose. We don't have enough soldiers to counter that."

"What do you want us to do, Sheriff?"

"Head south. Two blocks. We'll do the same. They're going to rush you as you reach the corner. Be ready."

"Why two blocks, then?" Animal asked.

"They'll already be closing from there, waiting in reserve. Move faster than they do. You need to get past them before they can surround you."

"Shit. I thought these things were like bugs," Happy said.

"Bugs that are smarter than a lot of people," Hayden replied. "Go. Now!"

The Spacers across the street turned and ran.

He glanced at Bennett, and then they did the same.

Chapter 37

Hayden and Bennett rushed down the alley. The trife nearer to them followed, many remaining back and out of sight, a few coming into the open. It was intentional. They were trying to herd the two of them, to force them to move in the direction they wanted.

When Hayden had first encountered the trife, he had thought they were mindless predators. Monsters who killed for food. Then he had learned they didn't eat people. They killed because that's what they had been programmed to do. By who or what? Nobody knew. He had also seen them attack for revenge. He had seen them stop an attack out of respect. He had seen them plan and organize.

Now it seemed more like they hunted for sport.

At least, some of them did. Every nest of trife was different. They were often competitors, and with so few humans left on the planet, there was little argument that they were the dominant species. They attacked one another as often as they attacked people. It was one of the only things that kept humankind from being completely overrun.

That and lots of firepower. They had cleared a large swath of land from Sanisco to Lavega, and even some territory north toward Ports and south into the wilderness. They had proven that with the right tools and the right tactics and the right weapons, they could make some gains against the trife and maybe start rebuilding Earth's civilization.

Or maybe they would hit a wall of the things they couldn't pass. A massive nest too big to clear. He had heard rumors from travelers that such things existed, though he hadn't stumbled across any yet. Then again, his part of the world was minuscule compared to what used to be under their control. For all of his work and gains, it was nothing when matched against the whole.

He tried not to think about that. It was easier to do when dozens of trife were chasing him, hissing at his back and throwing themselves at him and Bennett. Hayden was careful not to waste charges from the plasma rifle, doing his best to ensure one shot equaled one kill. Bennett did the same beside him, covering the front while he covered the rear.

The trife hunted for sport, but it still wasn't much sport, at least not to Hayden. The individuals were willing to sacrifice themselves for the success of the group, and they worked in numbers often exceeding ten to one, putting the odds as high in their favor as they could. It was like shooting an unarmed man with a rifle point-blank and calling it a sport.

But then, they were aliens. They didn't think like people did. They had their own motivations and goals. He knew what the top three were. Protect the nest, reproduce, kill humans. All of them made his life that much harder.

"We're getting swamped, Sheriff," Bennett said, firing another shot from his rifle. A trife in front of him hissed and fell, replaced by a fresh one the moment it cleared the path. He shot that one, too. "I think they want to take us in the alley."

They were nearing the next street, covering the first block of their semi-retreat. The goal of the HALD had been to land silently and unnoticed, and they had failed miserably at that. Whoever had fired at them probably knew what would happen. They had likely guessed that if their missiles didn't connect, the trife would help them out.

It would never make sense to Hayden how people could still spend so much time fighting with one another when there was a clear and obvious enemy in their midst. A common danger. He knew why they did it, but he still couldn't come to grips with that part of the reality. So many had given up hope; they fought over the scraps they had instead of focusing on the real problem. He wasn't made that way.

He could never be that way.

He fired three quick rounds, knocking three trife away from him. Bennett was right. They were starting to mass near the end of the alley. He had told the other portion of the Spacer squad they needed to move fast, but he wasn't moving fast enough himself.

"We need to pick up the pace," he said.

"Easier said than done," Bennett replied, taking out a couple more of the demons. "I've got ten charges left."

Hayden checked the counter on the side of his rifle. "Fifteen."

They both had fresh cells in their pockets, but they would have to pause to reload, and the timing for that was bad.

Movement from above caught Hayden's attention. He looked up as a half-dozen trife came over the corner of the building on his right, climbing face-first down an old metal staircase there. He swung his eyes to the left side, finding a similar scene there, too.

"We have to make a break for it," he said, swinging the rifle onto his back. It locked over his clothes, held by special magnets built into the bodysuit. He grabbed his revolver and sprinted forward, passing Bennett. "Come on, Sergeant."

Bennett followed, losing the rifle and switching to a laser pistol. The weapon was relatively effective against the trife as long as the shooter's aim was good. Its small area of effect meant hitting something vital was, well, vital.

The Centurion Spacer added speed, his genetically enhanced legs carrying him forward and getting him back in line with Hayden. The trife recognized the two of them were trying to break through their closing trap, and they accelerated as well. The demons on the fire escapes jumped from their positions, trying to tackle the pair. Hayden felt their claws scrape along his back. One of them caught his rifle with enough force to yank it off its mooring, causing him to lose it.

"Too close," he said, firing his revolver into a trife in front of him. At this range the round went straight through, hitting a second and knocking it down too.

Bennett lashed out with tight, invisible beams that burned through the demon's skulls, killing one after another.

It seemed like a lot. It wasn't nearly enough.

"Sir," Seventy said. "We're in a bad spot. There's too many of them."

"You don't give up, Spacer," Bennett growled into the comm. "Remember your training. This is what it was all for."

"Yes, sir."

Bennett had told Hayden none of his troops had ever actually seen combat before. None of them even knew the condition Earth was in before they were on their way to the planet, and they were sworn to keep the truth secret. It was the worst part about dealing with Proxima. Knowing they kept their populace in the dark about the humans back on their homeworld. It was something both he and Bennett were hoping they could change.

They still had to survive long enough to do it.

They reached the end of the alley. The streets all seemed the same to Hayden. Tall buildings damaged by bombings and riots and looting. Rusted out wrecks of cars along the sides of the streets. Vegetation that had managed to find its way through the cracks and had become overgrown over the years. It was similar to Sanisco, though they had managed to clean up some of the roads and all the old wrecks had been cleared and repurposed into effective walls. King had been responsible for a lot of that effort. It was probably the only good thing the despot had ever accomplished.

Dozens of trife poured toward them. Hayden's revolver clicked empty. He grabbed one of the speed loaders from his ammo belt, and snapped open the cylinder, sliding them in and clapping it closed. He fired a round into a trife's head only moments before it reached him, kicking it away and back into the others.

"Should have brought some fucking grenades," Bennett said beside him, grabbing a trife by the arm and swinging it into another before shooting a third.

It was fortunate for them the trife were relatively fragile. They did their damage with numbers, not with brute strength.

They seemed to have more than enough numbers.

They pushed through the thick mass of trife, breaking free. Dozens of demons were rushing at their backs and giving chase. Humans could outrun the creatures at a full run, but that kind of pace was hard to maintain, and the trife could hold their pace for miles. It was only a matter of time before they were surrounded again.

Would they catch up to the others by that point? Would they find somewhere to hole up that was more readily defensible? If they could keep the trife back, they could stall them until morning.

The creatures needed to feed, and they did that by retreating closer to the nest and soaking in the rays of the sun or the radiation of whatever power supply they were sourcing. Depending on how many had been killed, some might be invited to reproduce with the queen and her consorts.

A few humans weren't as important to them as that.

"Seventy, what's your position?" Bennett barked.

He and Hayden sprinted across the suddenly open street, heading for the next block over where they would rejoin the others. A few trife were emerging from an alley ahead, but not in the same numbers that were behind them.

"Closing in on the rendezvous point, sir," Seventy said. "But we've got a mess of demons on our asses."

"Roger that," Bennett replied. "Once you get there, see if you can scout somewhere to hunker down and ride out the storm. These fuckers will disperse once the sun comes up."

"Roger."

Bennett glanced over at Hayden."We having fun yet, Sheriff?"

"Loads," Hayden replied.

The trife swarmed behind them, merging from their different attack vectors into an inky black pool at their backs, undulated toward them as one massive whole. Hayden and Bennett had broken through the main choke point, and now the demons were intent on overwhelming them, getting to them and cutting their throats before they could find any suitable cover.

They fired into the trife ahead, knocking down one creature after another. Hayden grabbed another speed loader from his belt and slapped the rounds into his revolver, smacking it closed and firing judiciously into the approaching enemy. Bennett did the same, burning holes into the trife and bringing them to the ground.

They were going to cross paths. There was no way around it, and no way to kill all of the demons before they did. They couldn't afford to slow down. Any misstep would bring the horde piling on top of them, dozens of pairs of claws ripping and tearing.

Hayden slipped his revolver into its holster, flexing the fingers on his hands. Bennett saw him out of the corner of his eye, and the soldier slowed to let Hayden get in front.

The trife leaped at Hayden as they came into range. Hayden raised his arms, using them as both weapon and shield. He let the trife claws smack against his wrists. He let them tear through the fatigues and into the bodysuit to the alloy below. The replacements had been new eight months ago, but they were already scratched and scuffed from similar use.

He didn't slow, barreling through the trife, smacking them with elbows and fists, careful to protect his legs and keep them from tripping him up. When one lunged for his legs, it was halted by a plasma bolt from behind, one of the few Bennett had remaining in his rifle.

It felt like hours, but it all happened in seconds. Hayden crossed through the mess of demons, leaving a gap for Bennett to follow along behind. Then they were through the enemy, sprinting out the other side like they were running from the flames of a fire.

"Seventy, tell me you've got something," Bennett shouted into his comm as they raced for the second block over.

Hayden could see more trife up ahead, coming up from further west to cut off their escape route. How many of them were in this city? It was too many to be sustained only by solar radiation. There had to be a power supply here, somewhere. A nuclear reactor was most likely.

"Working on it, Sarge," Seventy replied. There was a short pause. "I think I've got something. It looks like a small opening under some of the debris. As long as it's big enough for all of us, it should do."

Bennett hesitated for a moment. Hayden knew the Spacer would need to make the judgment call. If it wasn't big enough for all of them, someone was going to die.

"Go," Bennett said. "Animal, duck in there and scout it."

Hayden met Bennett's glance again. They both knew this was a risk, but they had to take it.

"Going in, sir," Animal said.

Hayden's heart was already pumping hard from the run, but it found another level, the anticipation causing a spike of anxiety. He looked back at the trife chasing them. They were falling further behind, but that wouldn't last for long.

The trife ahead of them were closing in, still a couple of streets away. They reached the corner and broke left, finding the rest of the Spacer squad standing a third of the way down the block, near one of the buildings. Hayden could see the large pile of rubble behind them.

"Jackpot, sir," Animal said, his breathing hard but excited. "We've got enough room for everybody. In fact, it looks like somebody else used to live here."

"Roger that," Bennett said. "Haul ass."

Hayden saw the other Spacers vanish around the side of the debris. Having an escape route gave him a second wind, and he found a little more energy to speed up that much more. Bennett did the same, keeping pace as they covered the distance.

The bastard didn't even look winded.

They reached the rubble at the same time as a smaller group of trife. Hayden grabbed his revolver, ready to fire, but a stream of plasma tore into them from nearby, cutting them down like paper targets. He saw Judge crouched near the hole as they reached it. Her face was sweaty, but she was smiling.

"Welcome to Hotel Neverdie," she said, motioning to the hole.

Bennett pulled up, turning back to the trife. "Judge, Sheriff, you first."

Hayden waited for Judge to drop in. He hurried to follow, turning back to aim his revolver out of the hole. Bennett slipped in through the small opening, coming down next to him. The first trife that tried to sink in got its head blown off. So did the second.

Then Animal produced a metal plate with hooks on one side, which snapped perfectly onto screws driven into the stone around the hole. They heard the trife bang against it for a few seconds, and they all stood with their weapons drawn and ready, just in case.

Then the scraping subsided. They could almost feel the trife moving away, giving the chase up for lost.

"Do you think we just locked out whoever made that?" Happy asked.

"Who the fuck cares," Animal replied. "It's keeping us alive."

They were safe.

For now.

Chapter 38

Nathan rounded the corner, risking a glance back as he did, just in time to see the one called Sheriff push the muzzle of the other Spacer's rifle down and ruin his shot.

He was surprised by the action, but he didn't have time to give it too much thought. Not right now. He had to get away from the area and away from the demons he knew were coming.

The Centurion had known they were coming, too. Which meant he already knew about Earth, and about the aliens who had overrun it. For him, it was more proof that Proxima Command was aware of everything happening here, and purposely keeping it quiet.

Not that he needed more proof.

He rushed along the street, trying to stay against the sides of the buildings. He could see trife moving more toward the center of the city, rushing to the soldiers and not paying him any mind. He was grateful for that much.

It was also proof that Command had sent this team of soldiers to retrieve or kill him. He wasn't that valuable on his own. Did it mean the Trust knew about the ring and the data chip, and that they also believed he had it? What was on the thing that was so valuable they had sent soldiers after him?

He was even more eager than ever to find out what information he was carrying, though he had no idea how he would do it from here.

He had to get off this damn island and headed west. He had to find some way to read the contents of the chip. Would he be able to use it to expose the Trust? Would it help him figure out which members of Command could be working with the syndicate? Or would it unveil something much more valuable, and possibly something much more sinister?

If he was going to find out, he had to survive.

He made it to the corner of a building, turning left. He was going to circle back to the tunnels, back to the station where he had emerged on the surface. He didn't like the idea of going back underground and dealing with the Amtraks and possibly the Stalker, but his above ground route had been determined by moving silently and avoiding detection. The Spacers had made that impossible.

If he could take the tunnel route a few more

stops, he could hopefully come out somewhere quieter. He could find someplace to wait for the rest of the night, and in the morning he would know which direction was west, and he would head to the river and find some way across.

Hell, he would swim if that was the only way.

He started back down the street. He had the spear in hand; his guns tucked in the back of his pants. At least the spear was silent and dark, even if it did mean letting the enemy get closer to him.

He stayed to the side, eyes sweeping the path ahead and every so often glancing behind. He could hear the trife in the distance, the sheer number of them causing a soft rumble in the air. Would the Spacers be able to survive the assault? He didn't think so. They had come prepared, but their firepower was limited by the HALD approach. Even if they killed three trife for every round they fired, there would still be too many of the creatures to kill them all.

Part of him felt sorry for the soldiers. He didn't have any animosity toward them. They were just doing their job. Following orders. They probably didn't know anything about the Trust's involvement. It wasn't like Command would be honest with them. It wasn't right that they should lose their lives chasing an innocent man.

But there was nothing he could do about it. He had to take care of himself. He would rather have them dead than on his tail, shooting at him. That didn't mean he had to like it. Every possible outcome was bad.

He pulled to a stop as he neared the middle of the block. A soft crack ahead put him on alert. He crouched slightly, raising the spear and pressing himself tighter against the nearest building, lowering his profile. He watched the area ahead of him, black and white through the night-vision goggles. A figure moved out from behind another building.

Rhonna?

Someone had stripped her to her underwear and written something on the flesh across her abdomen before forcing her into the street. She shuffled into the open, hands clenching the grip of a handgun, her eyes darting back and forth.

What the hell?

He watched her for a few seconds. She was an open target for the trife. An easy kill. Had Margie done this? Had she really sent her daughter out into the street because he had gotten away?

Rhonna kept walking, taking slow steps and looking back a couple of times, to where she had come into view. There had to be more of the Amtraks there, watching her. Did they know what was happening out here? Had they heard the explosions? Seen the soldiers? Noticed the trife gathering? Or were they oblivious to everything but their twisted sense of justice?

One of the demons moved out from the shadows. It had blended in perfectly, invisible to Nathan even with the goggles until it moved laterally to Rhonna, watching her.

Two more appeared nearby as if responding to a silent call. Another moved into view a moment after that.

Rhonna had noticed them by then too. She started looking back at her so-called family more often.

Nathan began moving toward her, staying in the shadows as he closed in on the woman. He couldn't believe these people would sacrifice one of their own so readily, especially a young woman who could bear them children. If she had told Margie about his refusal to have sex with her right away, maybe she wouldn't be out there now?

Then again, if he had been forced to choose between letting her get him killed and killing her, he knew what he would have done.

It didn't matter now. This was where they had ended up. Nathan couldn't stand by and watch the trife kill her. He didn't want her blood on his hands. Not when he was right there and able to do something about it.

He followed the trife, slowly closing on Rhonna. She hadn't seen him yet. He could hear the gunfire in the distance. The Spacers making their stand. The

Amtraks had to hear it too. Didn't they care? It seemed strange to him that they wouldn't.

Hadn't they said nobody ever came to the island? Hadn't they said there was no easy way out?

The trife spread out around Rhonna, putting a few meters of distance between each other and using a few old vehicles for cover. He knew what was going to happen next.

One of them broke rank, leaping over the car and rushing her. She cried out, raising the gun and pulling the trigger.

Nothing happened.

Nathan was already on the move, charging the trife nearest him, cutting horizontally across the field. He noticed her action and the gun clicking without effect. They had sent her out there with an unloaded firearm.

They had sent her out there to be slaughtered.

The trife turned suddenly, realizing he was there. Too late. He jammed the spear into its chest, shoving it straight through, lifting and flipping it over and into the street near Rhonna. That got the attention of the demon nearest her, and it turned and hissed, searching for the culprit.

The next trife in line sprang sideways, landing against the side of a wall and pouncing toward him, at the same time a third came in low. The attack was perfectly coordinated, but he jumped in at the building, causing the airborne demon to come in too high, and swinging the metal spear at the ground-based enemy, the weapon hitting its head so hard its skull collapsed under the force.

The miss put the second trife off-balance, and Nathan shoved his spear into its back, killing it.

The other trife scattered, their numbers too few to continue the attack with confidence. Nathan found Rhonna, and then the Amtraks behind her, three men he didn't recognize along with the boy Lonnie.

They looked surprised by his sudden appearance, and they fumbled for their guns, the spears they were carrying becoming a hindrance to their efforts.

He vaulted the car between him and Rhonna, grabbing his handgun with his free hand as he ran toward her. He could see the writing on her stomach now.

Murderer.

Had she killed someone?

He would figure that out later. Rhonna looked at him fearfully, turning to run back to her group even after they had just tried to kill her. He rushed right past her, shooting at the Amtraks, his anger peaking. All three of the men went down before they could get their guns in hand, so poorly trained they were still fumbling to make the exchange. He came to a stop right in front of Lonnie, pointing his gun at the boy but holding his fire.

Lonnie looked up at him defiantly. "I wish you'd never come here." He was putting on a brave face, but Nathan could see the fear and pain behind it.

"Go home, Lonnie," Nathan said. "And tell Margie to stop sending people after me unless she wants her whole community dead. I'm taking Rhonna, and we're leaving."

Lonnie remained static for a few seconds. Then he turned and ran.

Nathan spun back toward Rhonna. She was walking toward him, and now he could see they had taped the gun to her hand so she wouldn't be able to drop it. Would the trife refuse to attack an unarmed human? It didn't seem likely, but he didn't know them that well.

He scanned the area for trife. They were in the clear for the moment, the majority of the group busy with the spacers. The gunshots might bring them running, so they had to be quick.

He walked over to Rhonna, using the edge of the spear to cut the tape from the gun. It fell to the ground.

She opened her mouth to say something.

"Not now," he said. "Not until we're somewhere safe."

She nodded, then moved to one of the dead men and started pulling off his clothes. It was a dangerous waste of time, but Nathan didn't argue. He kept an eye out for the trife for the thirty seconds it took her to dress.

"I'm ready," she said.

He turned back to her. She looked awful, but at the same time, he could see a glimmer of hope in her eyes that hadn't been there before.

"Thanks for coming back for me."

He wasn't going to tell her he hadn't come back for her. If she needed to believe that, then let her believe it. It would make her a more eager guide.

"You're welcome," he said. "Now let's move."

Chapter 39

Nathan led Rhonna away from the station he had intended to return to, and away from the Spacers who wanted him dead.

They didn't speak to one another, other than when Rhonna pointed out which direction was west and gave him quick instructions to the next closest subway entrance.

The number of trife were light at first. A few scattered here and there, scouts maybe, none of them courageous enough to confront the two of them. As they moved, the demons began to grow denser, trailing conspicuously back from the south.

Back from where the Spacers had gone.

Had they finished the job and killed his pursuers? Or had the Centurions managed to escape? He wished he knew one way or another. He would have preferred to know which enemies he had to still worry about. He was painfully aware of the identification chip in his wrist and their ability to track him through it. He needed to assume they were still alive, and stay as far from them as he could.

They reached the entrance to the next station, descending the steps together.

"I haven't been to this one in a long time," Rhonna said quietly as they navigated down a once-automated staircase. It had weeds growing out of its cracks, and pieces missing from the surface that they hopped over or around. "This section of the tunnel doesn't connect directly to ours." She paused. "You have to go around and switch tracks."

"Does it head to the water?" Nathan asked, pushing aside a spider web.

"Not directly, but yes, it goes west. You can't get to the riverbank without going above ground for some of the distance."

"It would be better to do it during the day then, right?" Nathan asked.

"If possible."

They reached the bottom of the staircase and made their way into the tunnel. There was more debris down here than he was expecting. There were piles of clothing, garbage, and plastic jugs in one corner. A few old tents sat vacant along the platform.

"Somebody used to live here?" Nathan said.

"Yes. There used to be a few separate camps here, but that was a long time ago. We were one of them."

"What happened to them?" he asked.

"What happened to most of humanity? When the trife didn't kill us, we ended up killing one another."

"What for?"

"You really did live an isolated life, didn't you, Nathan?" She paused, shaking her head. "Who are you really? Not some naive traveler from the mountains. You fight like the soldiers in the vids we collected. Actually, you fight better than those soldiers. Where did you come from?"

Nathan hesitated a moment, trying to decide how much to say. Did it even matter now? "What do you know about Centurions?"

Her eyebrows raised slightly. "Do you know Tinker?"

He wasn't all that surprised to hear the name again. "No. Do you?"

"Not personally. He's the leader of a community somewhere on the other side of the river. I don't know exactly where. He broadcasts on old radio frequencies. I don't know if he thinks anyone is listening or not. We have an old radio, and once in a while, he comes on and just starts talking. Not about anything specific. Sometimes he rants nonstop for hours. Other times he plays music. He's mentioned Centurions a few times."

"Edenrise?" Nathan asked.

"Where did you hear about that?"

"Gary mentioned it before he died."

"That's the name of his community, I think. He said the Centurions helped him build it."

"Someone was firing missiles over the city. Could it be Tinker?"

"Could be. Why are you asking about him?"

"I'm a Centurion," Nathan said. "A soldier. A replica."

"Replica?"

"I was…" He paused, not sure how to explain to someone who had little knowledge of technology. "Made. Not born. Grown in a vat of liquid, from an embryo to a full adult in about three months."

Her face paled. She took a step back from him. Was she going to treat him like an outsider now too? He wondered if he had made a mistake to admit it. She would never have known the difference otherwise.

"I was made to be a soldier," he said. "I was made to fight the trife. I'm faster than a normal human. Stronger. More healthy."

"And you were married?"

"Yes."

"Did you?" She paused. "Can you… you know?"

"Yes. I'm a human in every other sense. The only reason I'm sterile is because they made me that way on purpose. Where I come from, replicas like me are valued for our ability as soldiers. But we're looked down on for not being the real thing."

"How sad."

"My wife, she accepted me for what I was. She didn't care. She loved me anyway." He could feel his eyes tearing up again. He wiped at them. "I can't even talk about her without getting emotional."

"Then I take it you aren't from the mountains," Rhonna said.

He laughed. "I'm not even from this planet."

Rhonna froze again. "I... I guess I don't understand."

"The stuff you saw about colony ships leaving Earth? It wasn't propaganda. It was all true. The ships landed on a planet called Proxima B, in the Proxima Centauri star system, about four and a half light years from here."

"Light years?"

"It's very far away. Anyway, the humans who escaped built a colony, and we've been living there since."

"And you don't have trife there?"

"No."

She considered that for a moment. "You have soldiers. And you have spaceships. Yours crashed."

"It was shot down."

"What?"

"Someone here on Earth shot it down. Look, on Proxima, they don't tell the general population about Earth. As far as our people know, Earth is just fine, but you don't like us, and we don't like you. If I weren't already a wanted fugitive, I'm pretty sure my telling you this would get me locked up for treason."

"You're going too fast for me now, Nathan," Rhonna said. "This is all too much. Are you making this up?"

"I wish. It's a long story." He dug under his shirt and pulled out his wedding ring. "My wife, Niobe. She left me this. There's a data chip under the stone. Information. They killed her because of it, and then they framed me for the murder."

"I think I saw something like that on an episode of Hawaii Five-O."

"On what?"

"It was an old television show. We found vids of it. Kilo loved it. That's why he always said bruddah this and bruddah that." She shook her head, smiling fondly. "His name wasn't really Kilo; he just thought it sounded Hawaiian."

"Your brother held a knife to your throat, and you can still think of him kindly?"

"It was complicated. I heard you sneak out. I waited for you to go, and then I went to him and woke him up. I told him everything. About you refusing me, about you claiming you were sterile. We thought if we threatened you, that would be enough to get the truth."

"That was the truth."

"I didn't know you were a soldier. I didn't expect you to shoot him. Everything just got so fucked up after that. Margie sent Gary and the others out, and when they didn't come back, she blamed me. She said I wasn't aggressive enough. If I had done a better job, you would have been interested, and you wouldn't have left. She said Kilo's blood was on my hands, and if Gary and the others were dead, that was my fault too. She sent me to walk the streets."

"What about all that crap about you having an idea to help me escape?"

She looked at the ground, biting her lip. "I didn't have an idea. I was going to tell Kilo everything in the morning, and he would have been ready for you." She looked up again, tears in her eyes. "I wanted to betray Margie, but I couldn't do it. She's my mother. They would have locked you up, and you wouldn't have had a choice."

"Like Kate?"

She nodded. "At least in the beginning. But once you changed your mind..."

"I wouldn't have changed my mind. And you wouldn't have become pregnant. Not from me. Not ever. It's impossible."

"Then why did you come back for me?"

He almost told her the truth. He had suspected she had lied to him, but now he knew for sure. He wanted to be angry, but he needed her help more than he needed personal justice.

"Centurion Spacers don't leave their own behind," he said.

"I'm yours?" she replied. She sounded hopeful.

He nodded. "We're both on the run, and you know the city better than I ever will. We need one another. As long as you don't turn on me again."

"I'm sorry, Nathan," she said. "I didn't know what else to do."

"That part's over now. Proxima Command, the people in charge of the military on Proxima, they sent soldiers to capture or kill me. The trife attacked, and they might be dead. They also might not. I have a small device implanted in my wrist that will help them track me. If they're still alive, they're probably searching for me right now."

"Why don't you take it out?" she asked.

"What?"

"If they can track you with something under your skin, why don't you take it out of you? Let them track you somewhere you aren't."

He looked at her. "I'm not cutting off my hand."

"If it's a small device, maybe you can remove it a little more easily than that?"

"I don't have any tools fine enough to do that sort of work."

She pointed down the tunnel to the north. "I know where you can get some."

Chapter 40

"What I don't understand," Rhonna said as they walked the subway tunnel, "is if you have soldiers and weapons and ships on your planet, why don't you come back to Earth and help us? I mean, we're struggling down here."

"I don't know," Nathan replied. "I didn't know Earth was like this when I left Proxima. I thought I would come here and ask Earth's government for asylum, for protection against the Trust and the members of Command who are under their thumb."

"The Trust?"

"They're a crime syndicate. On Proxima, they sell weapons and drugs and work to undermine the authority of the Civil Council and Centurion Command. They try to bend things in their favor, through whatever means necessary."

"Why?

"I guess because the more you give someone who already has everything, the more they seem to want. I don't really know why."

"It must be nice to have so much comfort there's time to be greedy."

"I don't know if it's greed. Sometimes, I think it's human nature to always strive for more, whatever that more happens to be. For some people, maybe it's power. For others, money. For others, drugs or alcohol or sex. Even food."

"Maybe you're right."

"Anyway, if it were up to me, we would be doing something, but I'm hardly in a position to go to Command to ask them about it."

"Why do they think you killed your wife?"

"I told you I'm a replica. I'm called a first-gen. One of the originals. In the beginning, when they invented the process to make us, we all had very similar DNA, and we all looked very similar. The Trust used another replica who looked like me to kill her, and then they gave that replica a tight alibi."

"I know what an alibi is."

"From Hawaii Five-O, right?" He grinned.

She nodded.

"As far as the authorities are concerned, it has to be me. The judicus assigned to my case, I think she may have even believed me when I said I didn't do it, but without any way to prove otherwise?" He threw his hands up. "I don't blame her for doing what she thought was right. I don't blame any of the authorities. They're going with what the Trust is feeding them." He sighed again. "The truth is, the Trust plays with our lives, and they don't give a shit what kind of damage they do."

"It sounds familiar. Maybe on a larger scale, but..." She trailed off.

"Are you talking about your mother?" Nathan asked.

"Margie is a hard woman. She would always say she had to be, that everyone has to be now. After the war, when we were first trying to survive despite the trife, there was so much violence. And it was stupid because after all of that we wound up with our one small community, isolated from everything."

"You never tried to get across the water?"

"A few of us did. They swore they would come back if they made it, but they never came back. I don't know if they made it. The rest of us were too afraid to go. Better to live together the way we have for all these years than to die out there for no reason." She shrugged. "I should have gone before this. I was never like Kilo or Gary. I never wanted this life. I thought about killing myself to escape, especially after what happened to Kate. And then the way I turned on you because of Margie." She shook her head. "I'm a mess. I'm so sorry, Nathan."

"I already forgave you, remember?" Nathan said.

"It doesn't matter now. What matters is moving forward. I can't change the decisions I made that brought me to Earth any more than you can change the decisions you made that brought you here. Carpe diem."

"What?"

"Carpe diem. It's Latin. An old Earth language. It means 'seize the day.' Niobe used to say it to me all the time, whenever I would get down about Lieutenant Davis, and about working for the Trust."

"Who's Lieutenant Davis?"

Nathan winced. He hadn't told her about the man he had murdered. "He was a friend of mine. We got into a fight, and I accidentally killed him. I went to prison for a long time because of it. I still regret it. Every day."

Rhonna put her hand on his back. "Carpe diem, right?"

He nodded. "Yeah."

They reached an opening in the tunnel. Another station.

"This is it," Rhonna said, going over to the platform and climbing up. Nathan followed her.

"Where are we going?" he asked.

"There's a place nearby. A hospital. The military tried to stay away from it during the war, so it's still in pretty good shape. Looters took a lot of the supplies, but not all of them. I used to go there to be alone. If you're going to get the thing out of your wrist, that's the best place to do it."

They crossed the platform and climbed the stairs to the street. Nathan took the lead, moving cautiously until he could confirm the area was clear of both trife and soldiers. He didn't expect the Spacers to have made it this far even if they had survived, but he was learning to be more careful.

"We're clear," he said, looking back at Rhonna. She climbed the rest of the steps to the surface. "Which way?"

"Right over there," she replied, pointing to a relative low-slung building that was in surprisingly good condition. All of the buildings here were fairly undamaged.

It was only a few hundred meters away. They started down the street, moving quickly and speaking quietly. There was no sign of trife nearby. It was blissfully silent.

"You said the military attacked the city?" Nathan said.

"We have old vids of some of the newscasts," Rhonna replied. "They were trying to get rid of the trife. They tried everything short of nukes here, including napalm." Her face wrinkled in disgust. "They got so desperate; they didn't care if they killed people too." She laughed. "Well, they cared enough not to blow up all the hospitals. I guess that's something. Too bad it didn't work."

Nathan didn't know what napalm was, but he imagined it was pretty horrible considering her reaction.

"I guess the same thing happened everywhere," he said.

"They used nukes in some places. They killed hundreds of thousands of people. They also killed a lot of trife, but not all of them, and they feed on radiation. In the end, it made them stronger. They were right to send people away from Earth. It wasn't right that they never came back."

They reached the front of the hospital. The glass that had once adorned the face had broken a long time ago and the lobby was a filthy mess. It was obvious people had taken shelter in the building. Old food packaging, clothes, and other signs of life spilled across the cracked and dirty floor.

"I wish I had a light," Nathan said. "So you could see where you're going."

He was able to make out the room with the night-vision goggles, but Rhonna wasn't similarly equipped.

"The emergency lighting should kick in once we get further inside," she said. "It's on a backup battery, and it's so low power it'll last at least a thousand years."

"Only eight hundred to go," Nathan joked. It fell flat for both of them.

They moved into the hospital. As they neared the

front desk, the emergency lighting came on the way Rhonna had said. The dim LEDs lining the ceilings provided just enough light to see. Nathan removed the goggles, staring out into the night. He didn't think the light was strong enough for the trife to notice, but what about the Spacers?

He would have to take his chances. If they were already that close, they would be tracking him anyway.

"This way," Rhonna said. She led him to the stairs, pausing before opening the door. "I have to warn you; there are a few bodies still in here. They're pretty old, but it can be shocking the first time."

"Noted," Nathan said. "I'm not squeamish."

She smiled. "I figured as much."

She drew her gun before pushing open the door, keeping it ready. Nathan assumed that meant he should do the same.

"Have you encountered trife here before?" he asked.

"Only once, but it was enough." She turned back to him, pointing at the scar on her face. "It gave me this before I speared it."

"What about the burn?"

She reached up and put her fingers on the damaged flesh, her expression changing.

"Never mind," Nathan said, realizing she didn't want to talk about it. Whatever had caused the wound; the memory was painful.

They started climbing, passing the first body on the second floor. The soft tissue had all disintegrated, leaving a clothed skeleton at an awkward position in the corner. It didn't look like the person had died that way. It was more like someone had pushed it aside, or maybe thrown it down the steps. He felt a twinge of sadness for whoever they had been.

They exited on the third floor, passing another body. This one had broken bones and was resting in the center of a stain of very old blood. Killed violently. By a trife or another human?

"You come here a lot?" Nathan said.

"A couple of times a week. After a hunt."

"I should give this to you," Nathan said, holding out the spear.

She took it. "You seem to do well enough with your fists."

"I'm stronger than an average human, even one with similar muscle mass. Mine doesn't degrade with age."

"How old are you?"

"Eighty years."

She stopped and stared at him. "That's impossible."

"It is nowadays. Newer replicas age like regular humans, but they get a shorter lifespan because they start as adults. It's a curse, to be honest. I already outlived Niobe, and unless something kills me?" He shrugged. "I don't know how long I might live. A hundred years? Two hundred? I don't think anybody knows yet."

They walked to the end of the corridor. Rhonna approached one of the doors and pushed it open. Nathan followed her through, into a room filled with old medical equipment. It was all relatively intact, the machines too big to move. Some of the drawers were open, and some stuff had been thrown around the floor. There was a seat in the center, surrounded by lights. An examination room. Hospitals on Proxima weren't that much different despite the passage of time.

She looked at the debris there, and then walked over to something and picked it up. A pair of glasses with something attached to them.

"These will magnify whatever you're looking at," she said.

He took them and put them on. The world zoomed in, so close he couldn't focus. He looked down at his arm. "I can't see anything."

She walked over to him and reached up, adjusting something on the glasses. "Turn this to focus."

He put his hand over hers, finding the dial. He moved it, and then his hand came into sharp focus, close enough he could almost see the individual cells that composed his flesh.

Rhonna turned away, opening some of the closed drawers until she found what she was looking for.

"I used to bring these back to the train," she said, holding up a few small packets. "You can use them to clean the area before and after to prevent it from getting infected." She handed him the disinfectant packets. "I'll be right back."

Then she left the room. Nathan sat in the chair, waiting a minute for her to return. She had something small in her hand when she did.

"This one still has some battery power left," she said. She flicked it on and pointed it at the ground. A small hole began to burn into it.

"A laser scalpel," he said.

"Yes. Too weak to hurt the trife with, or they would have all been taken. Have you used one before?"

He shook his head. "No, but I get the general idea."

She handed it to him and went back into the drawers, finding a few cloths pads there. "I'll help control the bleeding while you get the chip."

"We'll need something to close the wound," he said, wishing he had brought the stitches from the EJP.

"You're right. I forgot." She searched the room again, finding a needle and thread. "Do they still use stitches on Proxima?"

"Not in hospitals." He showed her his hand again, reminding her of his earlier injury. "But ours are probably stronger." Even with all the action, the work had remained intact. "I can do the stitching myself."

"I think we're ready to go, then," Rhonna said.

She grabbed one of the packets and tore it open, pouring it into her hands and rubbing them vigorously together. He did the same and then used the third packet on his wrist. He wasn't excited about the prospect of cutting himself open to remove the chip. At the same time, he had to do it. Even if the trife killed all of the Spacers, he would never be able to go back to Proxima with the chip telling everyone around him who he was.

He put his hand out on the arm of the chair, turning it over. He took the laser scalpel in his other hand, putting it on the lowest setting. He didn't need to burn straight through his skin to the other side. He just needed to cut the flesh enough to get beneath it.

He held the device over his wrist. He glanced at Rhonna. She had the cloth ready to soak up the blood they both knew was going to come.

Then he activated the scalpel. It burned into him, and he gritted his teeth against the pain, forcing himself to stay focused. The beam was tight, keeping the burned area tight, but it still hurt. He made a six-centimeter line across his wrist, knowing when he was through by the amount of blood that bubbled out.

Rhonna kept dabbing at it, helping him keep it

clean. He handed her the scalpel and then jammed his finger beneath the skin. That part hurt the most, but he fished inside for the tiny chip, finding it a moment later. He got his finger beneath it and pulled it to the surface, sliding it along the underside of his skin until he got it out.

It was the size of a grain of rice, black and smooth. He handed it to Rhonna. She took it and put it on the table beside them, and then handed him the needle.

"Not so bad, was it?" she asked.

"No. Thank you for bringing me here." He breathed through the pain while he stuck the needle into the wound and began to close it.

A loud crash from somewhere in the building interrupted him. His head whipped toward the door to the room, while Rhonna reached for her gun.

"I don't think we're alone in here," he said.

Chapter 41

"Hell, Sarge," Animal said, slumping back against the rubble. "You told us things were hairy down here, and that shit with the trife back west was one thing. I think you undersold these bastards."

"Seconded," Happy said. "Can someone please confirm that I still have all of my body parts?" He turned a circle.

"At least we're alive," Seventy said. "Unlike Frank and Neko."

The other Spacers quieted at that.

"We had positive ID on Stacker," Bennett said. "He's alive, and he looked unhurt."

"Damn," Animal said. "I wonder how he survived the crash?"

"He's a Stacker," Bennett said. "You know the soldier they named him after, don't you?"

"Colonel James Stacker," Judge said. "He came to Proxima on the Dove. I've read his bio and seen the documentary, but I came away from it feeling less than satisfied. The whole thing was fluff; it hardly talked about why he was such a hero besides getting some of the best simulator scores ever recorded."

"Because everything he did that made him who he was got deep-sixed by Command," Animal said. "Didn't it, Sarge? Just like everything else about Earth that's actually true."

"Remember your duty," Bennett said. "You don't have to like it, but you do have to follow it. Most Spacers who get assigned to Earth start to feel like the Earthers are getting a raw deal. Command sees the people here as savages because of the way they handled the aftermath of the war."

"It's still like that now," Hayden said. "But not because the people are savage. In part, because they were abandoned. How do you think Proxima would fare if the trife were infesting your cities?"

"Preaching to the choir, Sheriff," Bennett said. "You know I'm on your side in this. Anyway, the trife got on board the Dove before she launched. Stacker organized the force that cleaned them out."

"You mean he didn't have the best sim scores ever recorded?" Animal said.

"He probably did," Bennett replied. "I don't know."

"So what do we do now?" Judge asked. She was

looking at the device on her wrist. "Stacker's out of range."

"He could be long gone if we wait until sun up," Animal said.

"You want to go back out there?" Seventy asked.

"I didn't say that."

"At ease, Spacers," Bennett said. He made them quiet down. The trife were still scratching against the door, trying to get in. "Hear that? As long as you do, we aren't going anywhere."

"Roger that," Animal said.

"This whole thing is already a monumental disaster," Happy said. "Sarge, we should radio the Kiev and have Danethi blast the area."

"We used the only heavy weapons we had taking out the reactor back west. The techs didn't have time to do a full load before we left."

"Shit."

"Cool your thrusters, Happy," Seventy said. "You thought this was going to be easy?"

"I'm just a little averse to being killed, that's all."

"Then you shouldn't have signed up to be a Spacer," Animal said.

"Who the fuck signed up?"

They all laughed except for Hayden and Judicus Shia. Hayden knew these Spacers were all replicas, and the replicas didn't have a choice in whether or not they joined the Space Force. Most of them didn't mind, but a few did. That was enough for him to think of it as a kind of indentured servitude.

"Okay, okay," Bennett said, silencing them again. "Let's try to figure out what Stacker might do next. Try to get into his head. Sheriff, this is your area of expertise, so feel free to take point in this exercise."

Hayden nodded. "Let's go over what we know about Stacker. For one, he's still out there. He survived the crash, and he's survived the trife so far." He paused, going back to those few seconds of time where the two men were facing off. "He was wearing night-vision gear and Earther clothes. Where did he get them?"

"You got close enough to see what he was wearing?" Seventy asked.

"Pozz," Hayden replied. He thought Bennett might say something about the episode, but the soldier stayed silent. "The trife interrupted, or we might have had him already. Anyway, gear like that suggests there's a community here somewhere, and he found someone who belongs to it."

"Or they found him," Judge said.

"Or they found him," Hayden agreed.

"He might have killed them and taken their gear," Animal said.

"I don't think so," Hayden replied.

"Why not?"

"He might have murdered his wife. That's still open for debate. But he isn't a straight-up killer."

"You know this how?" Happy asked.

"He had me dead to rights," Bennett said. "My ass was right in his reticle. He wouldn't shoot me in the back."

"Wait a second," Animal said. "We know he's here, but he also knows we're here? Fuck."

"Hold that thought," Hayden said. "It's an important point, but we aren't there yet."

"Okay, so Stacker met some Earthers, and he managed to get a pair of night-vision goggles," Judge said. "And a change of clothes. Then there are two new questions. One, where can we find these Earthers and two—"

"Why the hell is he out here at night?" Bennett said.

"Exactly," Hayden said. "If he found a community that's safe from the trife, why would he leave it when the trife are most active?"

"Unless he killed them and took their gear," Animal repeated.

"Let's assume he did," Hayden said. "It still begs the question of why he's out here at night. He knew about the trife. He had to know it wasn't safe."

"You think he has a destination in mind that isn't anywhere but here?" Happy asked.

Hayden nodded. "And he's in a hurry to reach it. He didn't want to wait until morning. Remember, he was out there when we got here. Unless he assumed Command would send a unit after him?"

"I don't think so," Bennett said. "He didn't know what he was coming to Earth to find. He probably thought he would cut a deal with the government here and be free and clear of prosecution."

"Then how can he have a destination in mind?" Animal said. "We were warned about Earth before we got here, and let me tell you the real thing is worse than you made it sound, Sarge. He should be pissing in his tights like we are."

"Speak for yourself," Happy said.

"The point is, he should be laying low and trying to get acclimated to this place. Not storming off to who the hell knows where."

"Agreed," Hayden said. "Put yourself in his shoes. If you decided to take action instead of laying low, what would you do?"

"I'd try to find the assholes that shot me down," Bennett said.

"Who are probably the same assholes that killed Frank and Neko," Animal said.

"And if you're going to do that, you need to get off the island," Hayden said. "Which means he'll have to head west."

"I saw the island coming in," Seventy said. "It isn't that wide. He may be near the river already, trying to find a way across."

"All the bridges were blown out," Happy said. "And I saw some big old rusted pieces of shit docked along it, but no little boats."

"He could swim across," Bennett said. "It isn't that wide."

"He probably wouldn't risk it at night," Hayden said. "Let's circle back to Animal's earlier statement. Stacker knows we're here."

"He's former CSF," Bennett said. "He knows we can track his chip."

Hayden held up his hand, tapping his wrist. "He's going to want to get rid of it."

"If he does we'll never find him," Judge said. "Especially if he gets off the island."

"Which means Animal was right about something else," Bennett said.

"What's that, Sarge?" Animal asked.

"We can't afford to wait here until morning."

Chapter 42

They waited another hour for the trife to give up on trying to reach them. Each of the soldiers spent the time in different ways. Happy and Seventy went to sleep. Animal cleaned his rifle and sang old songs. Judge and Bennett and Hayden spent some time discussing the missile attack that had led to Frank and Neko's deaths, and the failed HALD insertion that had brought the trife down on them.

They didn't go so far as to mention the Trust, but during the conversation, Hayden could sense that Bennett was insinuating the group had something to do with the attack, while Judicus Shia kept hinting that she didn't believe the Trust even existed. It was an interesting interplay between the two Centurions, though it didn't lead to any conclusions. The one fact Bennett couldn't resolve for his argument was that messages between Proxima and Earth traveled with the ships that moved between the planets. There was no way anyone here could have been informed of either Stacker or their impending arrival ahead of time. It was a technological impossibility.

There was one thing they could all agree on. All of them wanted to know who was responsible for the assault and why they had done it, especially taking the Trust and any pre-cognition of the Spacer's arrival and purpose out of the equation. It seemed so random, and yet so prepared.

There was something to it. Hayden was sure of that much. Even if it was the work of another despot, they had gotten the munitions from somewhere. There were a number of old military depots scattered across the globe, plenty of which had either been buried, hidden, or forgotten over the course of time. If the wrong person stumbled onto an experimental weapons facility, research and development site, or secret cache, they could cause a lot of trouble in the region. If they grew powerful enough, it wasn't out of the question that their reach could extend back to the western front. Maybe not immediately, but by the time his daughter reached adulthood.

He was willing to do anything to ensure Hallia lived a long, healthy, and happy life.

"I think they're gone," Bennett said, breaking the silence they had enacted to listen for the trife.

"It's about time," Animal said. "My rifle is so

clean I could use it to take my appendix out and not get an infection."

"Seventy, Happy, hop to," Bennett barked, waking the two napping Spacers.

Their eyes snapped open, and they jumped to their feet. "Yes, sir," they said.

"Sheriff, do you want to do the honors?" Bennett asked.

Hayden nodded. He didn't want preferential treatment, and he wasn't getting it.

"Animal, move the door. Everyone else, be ready."

The other Spacers raised their weapons. Hayden kept his guns holstered. If there were any trife out there, it would be better to keep the noise to a minimum.

"Don't shoot unless I say so," Hayden said. "Quiet is better."

"Yes, sir," the Spacers replied, keeping their voices low.

Animal moved to the small entry, unhooking the metal plate from the mounts. He held it in place for a moment, and then slowly lowered it to the side.

Hayden peered out into the night, his eyes and goggles adjusting to the starlight. He didn't hear or see any trife. He planted his hands on the edges of the hole and pulled himself up, just enough so he could peer further out. He still didn't see anything. He rose the rest of the way out and turned back to the others.

"Clear."

Bennett came next, followed by Judge, Seventy, Happy, and finally Animal. They gathered near the hole, scanning the streets. The trife had gone back to wherever they had come from.

"There may still be scouts around," Hayden said, whispering into his comm. "Keep a sharp eye out for them. We need to take them out before they can tell the group we're here."

"Yes, sir," they replied.

"Wedge formation," Bennett said. "Let's head back to where we found Stacker. If there's a community hiding nearby, we need to try to locate it. Even if we don't, if we follow the streets to the river we might get lucky and get him back in sensor range."

"Yes, sir."

They started back the way they had come, using the route Bennett and Hayden had taken. Dead trife littered the area around them, broken and battered, their blood slick on the streets.

"Are you sure it was just the two of you that came this way, sir?" Animal asked, viewing the swath of destruction.

"I had the Sheriff with me," Bennett replied. "He's probably the most experienced trife-killer on the planet."

"Not by desire," Hayden said. "I'd rather the trife weren't here at all."

"You and me both," Animal said.

They retraced their steps to the discarded jump pack. Hayden walked around to the back of the car, where they had seen Stacker for the first time. He surveyed the area, deciding he had to have come from the east. The trife had been in the nearest alley, and it hadn't jumped him on the way through. While the creatures liked to attack in groups, they would often take a chance if they could catch someone by surprise.

"I think he came from that direction," Hayden said, pointing east.

"Makes sense," Bennett said. "Especially if he wants to go that direction." He pointed west.

"If we want to catch up to him, we should keep going west," Judge said. "Maybe we can get him in tracking range if we keep a quick pace."

"It could be whoever he met here is back that way," Hayden said. "If we can talk to them, there's a chance they can point us to a more precise location. A boatyard, a safehouse, that sort of thing."

"The community could be anywhere," Bennett stated. "We could spend hours and come up empty."

"True. I'm not recommending hours, but it may be worth a few minutes at least. We can jog a few blocks and see if there's any evidence of the people living here."

"Sir, I don't think we should waste time," Judge said. "We know he's going that way. Once we hit the water, we can split up and cover both directions along the shore."

"We shouldn't split up," Hayden argued. "We got separated by circumstance, and look what almost happened."

Bennett was silent for a few seconds while he considered the options. "We said before we think Stacker is going to be holed up for the night. It's about zero two hundred hours right now. We scout east for thirty minutes. We see any trife, we turn around and break west. We don't engage unless we have to. Understood?"

"Yes, sir," the Spacers said.

"If we do happen across the Earthers, we let the Sheriff do all the talking. Sheriff, you're the lead."

Hayden broke into a cautious jog, the Spacers forming up behind him. He still kept his eyes peeled for signs of trife, but he was more interested in signs of humans. His head swiveled from one direction to the other, scanning the ground for recent debris or potential places for them to hide, similar to the small cave they had found respite in.

The first ten minutes didn't turn up anything of note. They covered eight blocks, four east, and two north. At that point they turned around, heading back west but also zig-zagging to go north two more blocks and not cover the same ground.

That was when they found the bodies.

Chapter 43

Hayden noticed them from the opposite street corner. There were three of them, all grouped together. A dead trife was near the center of the street on its back, far enough away that he doubted the creature had killed them.

He ran over to the corpses, slowing when the smell finally reached him. The deaths were recent and judging by the wet blood on the cracked pavement, not more than an hour or two old.

He looked down on them, taking quick note of the spacing of the wounds.

"Gunshots," Bennett said, coming up behind him. "The target pattern is consistent with Space Force training."

"Stacker?" Hayden said.

"That's my guess."

"See," Animal said. "He killed them all and took

their shit."

"He may be right," Bennett said.

"Not completely. Look." Hayden pointed to the ground. There was a footprint in the blood, too small to belong to any of the dead. A child's footprint. Hayden followed it a half dozen steps north before it faded away.

"A kid?" Seventy said.

"It seems that way," Hayden replied. "He let the kid go."

"Why is this one missing his shirt and pants?" Happy asked, poking one of the bodies with the end of his rifle. "You said Stacker had clothes."

"He did," Hayden said. "I don't know why he would stop and take more."

"You saw what he was wearing." Animal said. "Maybe he just wants to change his look."

"Maybe, but it seems like a waste of time," Hayden said. "If I were him, I would think there was a good chance the trife killed us, and I would be too eager to get the hell out of here to worry about what I was wearing. Anyway, the child was going that way. We should scout it out."

"They may not be all that friendly, considering Stacker is killing them," Seventy said.

"And we're still burning time we could be using heading in the direction we think he went," Judge said. "If these people were still alive that would be one thing. But they aren't."

"I'd just like to add," Happy said. "Our wanted-for-murder fugitive who isn't a killer seems to be pretty fucking efficient at killing people."

"Noted," Bennett said. "We'll go north two blocks. We don't see anything, we head west, no more delays."

"Yes, sir," the Spacers replied.

Hayden noticed a piece of tape on the ground near the three men. He leaned over, picking it up.

"What's that?" Bennett asked.

"Tape. It looks like someone cut it." He turned it over. "There are hairs stuck to the adhesive. Fine hairs. Probably a woman's."

"Stacker took one of them?" Animal said.

"No," Hayden said. "He didn't have anyone with him when we saw him. And the bonds were cut over here, next to the bodies. It's more likely he freed someone."

"Maybe our locals aren't very friendly," Happy said. "What was it you were saying about savages?"

"Don't be too quick to judge," Hayden said. "Good people can do bad things when they get desperate enough."

"Okay," Bennett said. "Sorry, Sheriff, but we don't need the complication of dealing with anyone who's going to bind a woman's hands and bring her out into the city at night. I can only guess what their intentions were. We're heading west. We'll walk the riverfront and hope we get in range."

"You know there's a good chance Stacker's removed his chip by now, don't you?" Hayden said.

Bennett nodded. "What else can we do? We have our orders, we follow them to the best of our ability."

Hayden dropped the tape back on the ground. He crouched over, and then saw a light rise from the ground, along the side of the street a few hundred meters away.

"What the hell?" Bennett said.

Hayden stood and turned toward the light. Multiple flashlights were pouring from the ground. There must have been a hole there, a tunnel or something. A small mob of people were headed their way, armed with spears and guns.

The Spacers brought their rifles up at the group. Hayden moved, getting himself in front of them.

"Hold your fire," Bennett barked. "Let the Sheriff handle this."

The Spacers relaxed slightly. They didn't let their guard down.

An older woman broke through the mass to take the lead. She was probably in her sixties. Short, spiked white hair and a weathered face. There was no hint of fear in her.

The woman's eyes landed on the corpses at their feet. Would she think they were responsible? She turned and leaned down to a small boy beside her, saying something to him. He shook his head. That had to be the boy Stacker had let go.

Hayden raised his hand in greeting, turning so the Earthers could see he was armed. The mob came to a stop a few meters back, the woman coming forward. Hayden did the same, meeting her between the two groups.

"I'm Sheriff Hayden Duke," Hayden said, putting out his hand.

The woman looked at it a moment and then took it. She had a firm handshake.

"Margie Gold," she said. She waved to the people behind her. "That there is my family." She paused. "Sheriff. Like the lawmen of the old west? You look more like a Navy SEAL to me."

"And the new west," Hayden said. He patted his uniform. "I don't know what a Navy SEAL is, but this is a uniform. We're looking for someone. A fugitive."

"Big guy?" Margie said, raising her hand well over her head. Nobody behind her was within a head's height of Stacker.

Hayden nodded. "These your people?" he asked, motioning to the corpses.

She returned the nod. "We came searching for them. That man you're looking for, he's a demon in disguise. He already killed six of mine. Nine now." She shook her head, but she didn't look all that upset about the losses. "He said he came from the mountains, but that's bullshit. Who the fuck is he?"

"He's wanted for murder," Hayden said.

"He sure is," Margie replied. "You with Tinker?"

Hayden almost asked her who Tinker was. He stopped himself. "What makes you say that?" he asked instead.

"Your uniforms have the same logo on them that he talks about all the time." She took on a deep, masculine voice. "The eagle stands for pride. It stands for freedom. Come to Edenrise. Join the Liberators today." She smirked. "He jabbers on the radio sometimes."

Hayden made sure to file that bit of intel away. He didn't give her a definitive answer to her question, changing the subject instead. "What can you tell me about the fugitive? Do you have any idea where he's headed?"

"What do you have to barter?" Margie asked, looking him over.

"This man killed nine of yours. We intend to capture him and bring him to justice. I think that's a fair trade."

Margie laughed. "Ha! Unless you just stepped out of a time machine, you know what justice is in this world, Sheriff. I'd like to string that son of a bitch up and take a hot poker to his genitals. You want answers; you give me something we can use."

"I'll tell you what. If you answer all of my questions accurately and honestly, I'll give you my rifle."

"Sheriff," Bennett said behind him.

Hayden looked back, giving the Sergeant his best glare. Bennett submitted. For now, at least.

"What kind of rifle is it?" Margie asked, intrigued.

"Plasma. It has a full charge. Three firing modes. Rare as all hell."

Margie hesitated for a second, considering. "Deal."

Hayden bent down and picked up the tape again. "Who was this used on, and why?"

Margie stared at him. She licked her lips.

"Accurately and honestly," Hayden said. "I'm a Sheriff. I'll know if you're lying."

"My daughter, Rhonna," she said. "She helped your fugitive escape our camp, which led to some of the killings. These three were taking her out for execution."

"You punish crimes by feeding people to the trife? Your own daughter?" He tried to keep his emotions in check. It wouldn't help get the information they wanted to attach his personal judgment to his words.

"She betrayed us," Margie said. "She lied to us. What else can we do?" She waved her hand back at the boy, standing at the front of the group behind her. "These kids like Lonnie here, they learn from us. We don't set a good example; then they don't survive. You should know how that is, Sheriff."

Hayden nodded again. He knew that's how survivors thought it had to be. "I do. So you're saying Rhonna helped the fugitive escape, but he didn't take her with him? And then what? He came back for her?"

"I suppose that's what happened. Nathan left her behind. Maybe he had a change of heart?"

She was lying. Hayden was sure of it.

"When you said the fugitive escaped from your group, why was he being held captive in the first place?"

"I never said he was a captive," Margie shot back defensively.

"You used the word escape. That would suggest you considered him a prisoner."

"I... I... I just used the wrong word. That's all. Rhonna brought him to us. He got lost in the tunnels, and the Stalker almost took him."

"Stalker?"

"It lives in the tunnels. It keeps us safe from the trife."

It was another interesting fact he filed away. "So you're saying he didn't escape?"

"Well... I..."

"Either you were holding him prisoner, or you weren't. Only one of those can be true."

Her face hardened. "What the fuck does it matter to you? It's our business, Sheriff. You have no right to come here and tell me what we did is wrong. The point is, he got away, and he took Rhonna with him."

"Took her where?"

"How the fuck should I know?"

He had gotten her angry and confused enough to speak without thinking about what she was revealing. She was upset enough the group behind her might step in, if only to get him to stop pissing her off.

"If the fugitive was injured, where would she take him?" Hayden asked. "Is there somewhere they might go?"

"I don't know!" Margie shouted. Her voice was dry. She looked like she wanted to rip his face off with her bare hands.

"Come on, Margie," Hayden said, pushing. "Do you want the rifle or not? I know you aren't telling me everything. What are you trying to hide?"

She lowered her head and started moaning and talking to herself.

"Stop it," Lonnie said, rushing forward. He took the woman's hand. "It's okay grandma. You asshole. Why can't you leave her alone? If Nathan's hurt, my bitch sister would have taken him to the hospital. There's one over on the west side, not that far from here. She likes to go there to be alone. Sometimes she brings back supplies from there. I followed her a few times."

"Lonnie!" Margie said, trying to shut him up.

Hayden tried to come up with a reason why she was trying to withhold the information. He could only think of one. She wanted to find Stacker and kill him herself.

"We're done, Sheriff," Margie said. "Give me the rifle."

"I'm not done," Hayden replied.

"Yes, you are. I did what you asked. Now give me the damned rifle. You promised. Barter fair and square."

"Sheriff," Animal said, his voice low through the comm. "We've got incoming."

Hayden looked up, past Margie. Of course, all her shouting had started drawing the wrong kind of attention.

Margie noticed him, and she craned her head back to look. The trife were approaching from the north side, a few scouts moving near some old wrecks on the side of the road.

"It's us versus them, Sheriff," Margie said, her entire demeanor shifting. She wasn't worried about who he was or what he wanted. She was worried about staying alive. "Get to the tunnels. We'll finish talking there."

Her group was already turning and making a break for the hole behind them. The Spacers had all shifted their aim and were taking long-distance shots at the trife scouts.

Hayden followed her, the Spacers right behind him. Bennett still didn't look happy about his promise to trade them a plasma rifle. No Contact Protocol meant not giving the savages advanced Centurion weaponry.

They ran for the tunnels, the trife closing fast, sensing they were going to try to escape. Hayden fired his rifle as he ran, sending bolts sizzling over the Earthers' heads and into the oncoming swarm.

A light hum on either side of them revealed the ambush. Hundreds of trife appeared on the top sides of the nearby buildings, crawling down them in a mass that had been gathering long before Hayden and the others had arrived.

"Stupid woman," Bennett said through the comm. "She must go out to get all of her dead and the damn things know it."

They had been waiting for her to lead her people out into the street to collect the bodies. Hayden cursed himself for not realizing this wasn't the first time.

The Earthers started firing their guns into the swarm, unable to miss in the density of the slick. Trife stumbled and fell, crushed by the others behind them who barely slowed in their pursuit. A sea of black was closing on three sides ahead of them.

"Shit," Happy said. "We aren't getting out to the south."

Hayden flipped his head around to see. More trife were behind them, closing in on every side.

They had to make the tunnel, or they were all going to die.

Chapter 44

Hayden switched his plasma rifle to stream mode. He hated to use it because it wasted a lot of charge in a hurry, but with the number of trife bearing down on them they needed the extra spread.

He held his fire, moving to the outside of the Earthers and sprinting ahead, at once both regretful and thankful for the hard life that had molded him into a high level of fitness. The Earthers looked over at him as he reached their side, aiming his rifle toward the trife, which were barreling at them from the flanks.

He squeezed the trigger, a jet of superheated gas launching out from the weapon like a flamethrower, bathing dozens of the creatures and burning through their flesh. They hissed and fell, immediately replaced with more.

He kept the trigger depressed, washing back and forth with the rifle and watching the charge counter on the display quickly decrease: 100... 90... 80... 70... 60. It only took five seconds to lose half the charge, though nearly a hundred trife had already fallen to the spray.

There were screams up ahead — the Earthers caught by the trife at the front before they could reach the tunnel. The whole thing started slowing the momentum of the fleeing group, which would cause more of them to fall to the demons.

"Keep going!" he shouted. "Break through!"

He pushed harder, getting ahead of the suddenly slowing group. The trife's ambush was successful, and the people were panicking. He got closer to the front, unleashing another spew of plasma that halved his charge and killed dozens of the creatures.

"Sarge, we need support," Seventy said. "Call in the Kiev."

"Negative," Bennett replied. "It's too tight down here. Danethi would kill us, too."

"Bennett, switch to stream," Hayden said. "We can save them."

"Ammo's tight, Sheriff," Bennett replied. "We still have a mission of our own."

What?

Hayden clenched his teeth to keep from cursing at his friend. "They're going to be slaughtered, damn it!"

"Sorry, Sheriff," Bennett said. "We can't save them all. Not this time."

His tone of voice told Hayden he knew he was making the wrong call, but he was making it anyway. Damn it.

Hayden reached the front of the line. The tunnel was close, and some of the Earthers had already made it, practically throwing themselves into the dark opening. He was amazed to see that the trife pulled up when they reached it, refusing to go down in pursuit despite their massive numerical advantage.

What the hell was the Stalker, that it frightened the creatures that much?

He didn't have any more time to think about it. He switched the plasma rifle to burst mode, substituting a flamethrower spread for automatic bolt fire. The weapon was steady in his hands as it cut down another dozen trife.

Hayden glanced down at the charge counter. Six rounds. He snapped it onto his back, switching to the revolver.

A trife came up on his left. He turned and fired, the round knocking its head backward and dropping it, carrying through to another creature behind it. He pivoted, firing into a trife that was chasing a woman toward the tunnel, hitting in the back and knocking it down. He found Bennett and the other Spacers, coming up from the right side and nearly at the tunnel.

The squad started to descend. Bennett stopped, turning back and finding Hayden. The Sergeant shouldered his rifle, firing into the trife around Hayden, giving him a clear path to the hole.

More screams echoed in the night, more Earthers being killed the same way they had been for the last two hundred years. The sound was painful to him. He wanted to save everybody, and while he knew it was impossible, that didn't make it any less frustrating.

"Sheriff!"

He heard the cry behind him and turned. He found Margie with a trife on her back, its teeth already buried in her neck. She had Lonnie cradled beneath her, trying to protect him from the demons.

"Hayden!" Bennett shouted into the comm, trying to get him to retreat.

Hayden didn't hesitate. He charged back into the fight, starting by blasting the trife off Margie's back. She tried to stand, making it a few steps before falling over again.

Lonnie wiggled out from under her, breaking for the tunnel. Hayden grabbed a trife as it lunged for the boy, crushing its neck with his powerful hand. He shot another, and then turned and retreated with the other Earthers.

Bennett was still at the entrance. He fired bolt

after bolt into the trife, his unerring replica aim shattering the enemy line closest the Earthers. They stumbled and ran into the stairwell, hurrying down to the bottom.

Hayden spun back a second time when he reached the entrance, quickly scanning for people and finding none who were still trying to escape.

"Can we go now?" Bennett said.

Hayden nodded, and they descended into the tunnel together.

They reached the bottom. A large, underground station opened up ahead of them. A transit system, like the one in Haven. The Earthers were still on the move ahead of them, pushing past a broken old turnstile and out to the platform, and then jumping down onto the tracks.

The Spacers stayed on the platform, waiting for Bennett and Hayden.

Hayden turned on the Sergeant, reaching out to grab the collar of his uniform. Bennett moved aside, expertly ducking the grab and slamming Hayden in the gut, getting around behind him and putting him in a choke-hold.

"Cool it, Sheriff," Bennett said, holding Hayden while he struggled to break free.

"We could have saved them," Hayden said. "Damn it, Austin. We could have helped them. They didn't have to die."

Bennett kept holding him, putting his face near

Hayden's ear. "People die here Hayden; you know that. We can't save everybody."

"I thought you were on my side," Hayden said.

"We have orders," Bennett said. "And I have a responsibility to my people first, these people second."

Hayden stopped struggling. He exhaled harshly. "That wasn't always true," he said. "You helped me once regardless of your orders."

"I know. And you got me to see the bigger picture. I'm still looking at the bigger picture, Sheriff. I know it's in your blood, but you need to step back a second too. I can't do shit to help you with Command if we don't bring Stacker back. Pozz?"

"Pozz," Hayden said, realizing Bennett was right. "You can let me go."

Bennett released him from the hold. Hayden stood, looking back at the entrance to the tunnel. Not a single trife had come down after them.

The Earthers were assembled along the tracks, regrouping in sullen silence. Hayden walked over to them, jumping down. They had started with close to sixty people. That number looked to have been cut in half.

"How are we going to survive this?" he heard someone say.

"Lonnie," Hayden said, looking for the boy. "Lonnie!"

He found Lonnie off to the side, away from the others.

"What the hell do you want?" the boy asked when he approached.

"I'm sorry about your grandmother," Hayden replied. "I—"

"She would still be alive if you hadn't shown up. You and Nathan. We can't survive this. After all these years, we're done in one day."

Tears streamed from his eyes. He was a kid, but he had already seen so much. Too much.

"I can help you and your people," Hayden said. "I can get you out of here. Give you a better life. But I need you to help me, first."

He was making a promise he wasn't sure he could keep. Would Bennett be able to transport these people back west? If it got him Stacker, he was pretty sure he would.

"Why would you do that?" Lonnie said. "You don't know anything about us. You don't know what we've done."

"It doesn't matter what you did in the past," Hayden said. "It matters how you react to the future."

"You don't sound like you're with Tinker," Lonnie said. "He always talks about cleansing the Earth and the will of the others. He can keep talking for hours."

"The others?"

"I don't know. That's what he says."

"We aren't with Tinker. I don't know who Tinker is. But it's safe where I come from. I can take you and your people back there. However you used to live, you won't need to live that way. But you have to help me."

Lonnie stared at Hayden for a few seconds. Then he shrugged. "I don't know who the fuck you are mister, or if we can trust you or not. But if you want me to help you catch that asshole, I'll do it for nothing. This is all his fault. Everything was fine before he showed up. Tell me what you want me to do."

Chapter 45

"You did what?" Bennett asked.

"I promised I would take them back west if they helped us find Stacker," Hayden replied.

"Shit, Sheriff. I don't know if I can get Command to agree to that."

"For one, Command doesn't have to know. For another, if they want Stacker, that's the price."

"These people could be dangerous, Hayden. You don't know anything about them."

"Give me a break, Bennett. Give people some hope, and they fall in line. How many times do you have to see it before you believe it?"

Bennett glared but didn't reply right away. His jaw muscles flexed. "Fine. I'll make it work."

Hayden smiled. "I knew I could count on you."

They walked back to where the other Spacers

were waiting with Lonnie. The rest of the Earthers had regrouped and retreated, heading back toward their camp deeper inside the network of underground tunnels. Lonnie had called it the subway system.

"You ready?" Lonnie asked.

"We're ready," Hayden said.

"You're going to kill him, right?"

"We'll see."

"I'll kill him myself."

"Are you sure about this, Sarge?" Happy asked.

"No," Bennett replied. "But things have been going so well this far; I figure we've got nothing to lose."

"Roger that," Animal said.

"Lead the way," Hayden said to Lonnie.

The boy flicked on his flashlight. "We don't usually use light down here. Not unless there are a lot of us. Otherwise, it attracts the Stalker." He looked back. "I think I'm safe with you?"

"As safe as you'll ever be," Seventy said.

Lonnie stared at her. "I've never seen such a tall woman before. My brother Kilo would say you have legs that go on forever."

Seventy's face flushed. The other Spacers laughed. Lonnie smiled, proud of himself, and started walking again.

"Kids these days, eh Seventy?" Animal joked.

"Shut up," she replied.

"So, what's this Stalker thing?" Happy asked a few minutes later.

Lonnie was keeping a brisk pace through the tunnels, seemingly eager to help them find Stacker. He also seemed to know exactly where the fugitive might be.

"It appeared in the tunnels one day. It looks kind of like a person, but with lots of teeth and stuff. It can't see, and it can't hear, but it doesn't matter. If you're in here and it's hungry, it'll still find you. If you're a trife, it'll find you even if it isn't hungry."

"It can't see, but light attracts it?" Hayden asked.

"Yup. Don't ask me how. I'm not a fucking scientist."

"Such a pleasant young man," Animal whispered in the comm. "So mild-mannered."

The other Spacers smiled.

"The trife are afraid of it," Hayden stated.

"They should be. They can't fit enough of them in the tunnels at once to kill it. It heals like this." He snapped his fingers, the noise echoing in the tunnel. "Especially when it eats."

"If the trife won't go into the tunnels, it must go up to the surface after them," Seventy said.

"I guess so, gorgeous," Lonnie said. "I'm not its mother."

Seventy looked annoyed. The other Spacers laughed again, amused by the boy's personality.

"You said it showed up in the tunnels one day," Bennett said. "Where did it come from?"

"I just said I'm not its mother," Lonnie said. "Who the hell knows."

"Charming," Animal whispered. "If I had a daughter…"

They spent a few more minutes walking in silence when Hayden decided to try his luck with Lonnie again.

"You said your sister brought the fugitive to your camp?" he said.

"Yeah. She likes to take in strays. Dogs, cats, men she wants. Nobody in the family is good enough for her."

"What does that mean?" Happy asked.

"You don't know what sex is?" Lonnie said. "I can draw you a diagram."

"Not that. The family part."

"We've been stuck on this island for two hundred years, what the hell do you think it means?"

"Uh…" Happy trailed off, not sure what to say.

"Go ahead and judge. There was one visitor on the island in the last hundred years. It's either that or die out completely."

"Maybe that would be better?" Animal suggested.

"Screw you," Lonnie snapped. "I wouldn't be here, jackass."

"We saw the bridges are out," Hayden said,

changing the subject. "What about boats? Nobody tries to cross the river?"

"Of course they do. Or did. There aren't any more boats. Everyone who made it never came back. I wonder why?" He said it sarcastically.

"What, you aren't happy here?" Animal asked.

"It's fucking paradise," Lonnie said. "Why wouldn't I be happy? Anyway, it's been a long time since anyone left. After Christopher left, Margie wouldn't have it. Anyone who talked about getting off the island was dealt with."

"Dealt with how?" Bennett asked.

"The punishment fits the crime, that's all I'm going to say. Most gave up trying to get away. The few who didn't, they got branded and thrown outside or left for the Stalker."

"Sounds harsh," Seventy said.

"In case you haven't noticed, this isn't Hawaii."

"Hawaii?"

"It was a part of the United States," Bennett said. "A series of tropical islands."

"That's a real paradise," Lonnie said. "I saw it on Hawaii Five-O. Kilo loved watching those vids."

"The trife are in Hawaii, too," Hayden said. "It's probably not a paradise anymore."

"The more direct sunlight would let them increase their colony density," Bennett added. "It definitely isn't a paradise."

"Well, fuck," Lonnie said. "There goes that wet dream."

They rounded a turn in the tunnel, coming out into another station. Lonnie pointed at the platform.

"We'll go up there. The hospital is right down the street. You can't miss it."

Bennett raised his wrist, checking the tracker. He nodded. "He's in there. Or at least his identification chip is."

"Maybe you should stay behind?" Hayden suggested, looking at Lonnie. "It's—"

"No place for a kid?" Lonnie asked. "Screw you too, Sheriff. I need to make sure you off that son of a bitch."

"We aren't here to kill him; we're here to take him into custody."

"He's killed how many people, and you want to bring him back alive?"

"Yes. That's how civilized societies function."

"There's nothing civilized about our society."

"Maybe not here. That isn't true everywhere."

Lonnie smirked. He sat down against the platform wall. "Suit yourself. Good luck grabbing him. I'm willing to take bets one of you ninjas caps him while his back is turned."

Hayden shared a look with Bennett.

"We might have to incapacitate him if he resists," Bennett said. "But our first choice is to catch him alive."

"Thanks for guiding us, Lonnie," Hayden said. "I promise I'll be back for you and your family."

"Yeah, whatever," Lonnie said. "If I never see any of you again, it'll be too damn soon."

Hayden approached the side of the platform and pulled himself up. The Spacers joined him there a moment later, and they headed for the stairs at the far end of the platform. Hayden looked back a couple of times. He wasn't convinced the boy wouldn't follow them, but what could he do?

"We are going to take him alive if we can, right?" Hayden said.

"We'll do our best, Sheriff," Bennett replied. "But you're crazy if you think he's going to come willingly. He did a lot of damage escaping in the first place."

"Pozz," Hayden replied. None of them could control how Stacker reacted once they caught up with him.

They reached street level. The hospital was easy to identify; the area around it was in reasonably good shape. He could make out dim lighting spilling out of the front of the building.

"This is why we're here, Centurions," Bennett said. "Let's move."

"Uh, Sarge?" Happy said before they could take a step.

"What is it?" Bennett replied.

Happy pointed.

"What the hell is that?"

Chapter 46

Both Nathan and Rhonna remained still, listening for more noises within the building. The crash had been loud, a deep rumble as though something had come plummeting through the roof.

The way things had been going, he wouldn't have been all that surprised if something had.

They remained static for a good minute, looking at one another. When no other sounds followed the first, they started moving again.

"We need to get out of here," Nathan said.

"What about the chip?" she asked, picking up the small device.

"Leave it," he said. "I don't need it anymore."

He hopped out of the chair. His wrist hurt from the minor surgery, but it was better than having the Spacers corner him. He was more concerned about the noise. Random noises never meant anything good. He would have preferred if more had followed.

"Come on," he said, heading to the doorway and then out into the hall.

He turned left, freezing when his eyes landed on the doors to the lift. Something was wedged between it, trying to pry it open.

"Shit," Nathan said.

He grabbed Rhonna's shoulder, pulling her in the opposite direction and around the corner.

"The Centurions?" Rhonna asked as they ran along the adjacent hallway.

"It has to be," Nathan said. "I'm not surprised they survived the trife, but I have no idea how they caught up me this fast. Is there another way out?"

"There should be another stairwell up ahead."

Nathan heard a loud bang back the way they had come. He glanced over his shoulder. A wash of smoke cleared the corner.

"The corridors all connect along the outer perimeter," Rhonna said. "If they spread out…"

They would be coming from two directions, converging on the same spot where they were running. Would they make it to the stairwell before they arrived?

"Is there another way out?" Nathan asked.

"I don't think so."

He came to a quick stop, grabbing Rhonna's arm to stop her too. They had reached an internal corridor and intersecting hallway that didn't cut straight through to the other side.

"We'll have to hide for now. Without the chip, they won't be able to find us so easily. Hopefully, they'll think I'm long gone."

He realized there was a good chance the Spacers were packing detection tools, like sensors that could detect someone breathing on the other side of a wall. He could slow his breath to almost nothing. It was part of his training as a Centurion, intended more for environments where air might be scarce. He was sure Rhonna couldn't do the same.

It was a risk, like everything else. The chip wasn't far from them. Maybe the Spacers would guess he hadn't stuck around, and they wouldn't bother to search wherever they decided to hide.

Nathan guided Rhonna down one corridor to another. He picked a door almost at random, trying it out. The label beside it was grimy and faded but still legible. MRI. It swung open, revealing a small control room with a larger room behind it, a large piece of machinery inside. He didn't know what an MRI was, but he could see there was a space at the back of the machine where they could tuck in and stay out of sight. The distance might also be sufficient to keep the sensors from getting a solid reading.

They started for the next room, but Nathan paused when he heard the footsteps in the hallway outside, along with the murmured tones of someone speaking softly into a comm. The two of them had barely avoided being seen before they ducked into the room.

He heard the door beside theirs open, and then the one across from that. The Spacers were going room-to-room, searching for him. Had they already discovered the chip? Standard procedure would mean the soldiers were working in pairs. One to open the door, one to defend. Four soldiers outside, and two more near the chip. Six at least. He had a feeling there were more than that. The Spacers had come in and spread out and were probably covering the exits. He had seen two earlier. Had they come with an entire platoon? Could he really be worth that much to the Trust?

He pushed Rhonna against the wall, putting a finger to his lips to keep her quiet. He motioned to the door and pantomimed its opening, and her stabbing forward with the spear. He looked at her questioningly, to ask if she was willing to hurt someone to help him.

She nodded. She would.

He stood on one side of the door, his plasma pistol in hand. She stood on the other. He heard the movement in front of it, the soldiers getting into position to check the room. He had to take them out quickly and get into the hallway to hit the other pair before they could overcome their surprise.

The door was pushed open. The muzzle of a rifle entered first, sweeping toward him.

Rhonna shoved the spear hard into the soldier's side. He cried out in pain as Nathan threw a heavy punch into his unprotected head, rounding the door and firing his plasma pistol at the other soldier. It caught him in the chest, and he stumbled back and away.

Nathan roared out of the room, turning to shoot at the second pair of soldiers. They were already pivoting to defend, and one of them managed to get a shot off on him as he downed them with a quick burst from his pistol. The bullet grazed Nathan's side, close enough to tear his shirt and draw blood.

He looked over the downed soldiers, confused.

They were wearing uniforms. Black and gray fatigues to go with black boots. An eagle and star patch sewn to the shoulders. It was similar to the Centurion Space Force logo, but not the same. Their weapons were conventional projectile rifles, a model he had never seen before, probably because they hadn't come from Proxima.

These men weren't Spacers.

They were from Earth.

Rhonna came out of the room. She was shaking slightly, unnerved by her decision to stab the man in the side. She had dropped the spear, leaving it in the soldier. She looked at Nathan, and then at the men.

"I don't know who they are," Nathan said. "Or

how they found me. We have to move. The gunshot will draw them in."

He grabbed her wrist, pulling her with him. She was hesitant at first, and then she followed with him, running down the hallway.

"Stop!" someone shouted behind them in a deep, gruff voice.

Nathan glanced back. Another soldier, taking aim behind them.

They reached the end of the corridor, nearly slamming headlong into another pair of soldiers. Nathan reacted instinctively, stiff-arming the closer soldier in the neck with enough force to throw him back and to the ground, and then lunging at the second soldier. He grabbed the rifle, pushing the stock back into the man's chest, overpowering him and flipping the muzzle up and into the soldier's face. The soldier's nose cracked, blood flowing freely as he toppled to the ground.

That was seven already. How many were in here?

They made it back to the outer corridor, breaking for the stairs.

Chapter 47

"Who the fuck is that now?" Animal asked.

They were all looking to where Happy had pointed. An aircraft was hanging in the night sky, hovering a few meters above the rooftop of the hospital.

It was long, with a wide body up front that tapered as it moved back. Multiple rotors sat on top of it, spinning so quickly they were only visible as a solid circle above it. More were situated along short wings on the tail at the back, and on a second pair of slightly larger wings closer to the front. An open hatch was spilling light on the port side, and Hayden could make out narrow lines running from it to the rooftop.

Despite its presence, and despite the amount of air it was moving, the entire contraption was nearly silent. From the ground, all Hayden could hear was a soft *whoosh-whoosh-whoosh* that he would never have noticed without seeing the machine first.

"I'm taking bets it's the assholes that were shooting at us on the way in," Happy said. "What do you say, Sarge?"

"I say we need to get in there," Bennett said.

The Spacers broke for the entrance, stepping over the broken glass and debris and into the dilapidated lobby. There was a lift bank straight ahead, and a stairwell beside it.

"Goggles up," Bennett said, grabbing his and lifting them to the top of his head. The others followed suit. He lifted his wrist, checking the tracker. "The chip is stationary."

A soft pop echoed from somewhere inside. A gunshot.

"You think they're after Stacker?" Seventy asked, looking at Hayden.

He nodded. Why else would they be here? Not that any of it was making sense right now.

Animal reached the lifts and tapped on the controls. He shook his head. "Offline."

"Stairs," Happy said, pointing.

"There has to be another route," Bennett said. "That's been building code on Proxima forever, and we got it from somewhere. We'll need to cover both."

"We shouldn't split up," Hayden said.

"We don't have a choice. Sheriff, take Seventy and

Animal and find the other stairs." He pointed toward a corridor on the left. "Probably that way. We'll head up from here."

"Good hunting, Sergeant," Hayden said, breaking away from the group with Animal.

"Good hunting, Sheriff," Bennett replied.

He froze a moment later, a new sound echoing in the distance, coming from outside. Hayden heard it too, and he looked back out toward the street. It was tough to see without the night-vision goggles, but he could barely make out an increase in the illumination to the south.

"What is it?" Seventy asked.

"Cars," Hayden said. "A bunch of them."

"They're going to bring every fucking trife on this island back down on us," Bennett said.

"Maybe that's their intention," Happy suggested.

"I have a question," Animal said. "If this is an island, where the hell are all these people coming from?"

"Let's figure that shit out later," Bennett said. "We need to find Stacker."

Hayden led Seventy and Animal down the corridor. It intersected with another at the outer perimeter of the building, a second long hallway with illuminated exit signs pointing in both directions, along with signs indicating stairwells at either end. An old skeleton was resting under one of the signs, its spine shattered near the neck, its head resting a few meters away, a less recent victim of the trife.

"That guy had a bad day," Animal said.

They kept running along the corridor toward the stairs. Hayden could hear the sound of engines growing louder, echoing in the stillness of the early morning. There was no way the trife didn't hear it too. The only question was if they would bother coming to check it out with daybreak only a few hours away.

"Sheriff," Bennett said through the comm. "Stay alert. Stacker's chip is on the move. I don't know if Stacker is with it."

"Roger," Hayden said. "Seventy?"

The other Spacer lifted her wrist, tracking the chip. "It's moving away from us, sir."

They reached the stairwell, coming to a stop. Hayden drew his revolver, while Seventy and Animal unhooked their plasma rifles from their backs, bringing them forward.

Hayden nodded to them, and then leaned against the door, slowly pushing it open. He aimed his gun up the stairs.

"Clear," he said, sliding inside. Animal and Seventy followed.

"The chip is static," Bennett announced. "We're at the third floor, going to check it out."

Hayden, Seventy, and Animal continued to ascend. Hayden snapped around each corner of the stairwell, gun up and ready to fire. His heart was thumping, and he was trying hard not to think at all. He could wade into a hundred trife with just enough fear to keep him smart. Dealing with other people wasn't like that.

People always had the potential to surprise you with something that made no damn sense but could get you killed all the same.

He froze when something slammed into one of the stairwell doors above, hitting it hard enough that it clanged off the wall and reverberated along the risers.

"Spacers! It's a trap. A fucking trap."

Hayden could almost hear Bennett's shout without the communicator, coming from the floor above them. Gunfire followed an instant later, hard and heavy. The entire building shivered under the sudden assault.

"Cover!" Bennett yelled.

The plasma rifles were too quiet to hear from the stairs, but Hayden had no doubt they were being put to use.

"Sheriff, we need backup."

Hayden had already broken into a run, jumping up two steps at a time, Animal and Seventy right behind him.

They reached the next corner of the landing. Hayden didn't bother sweeping it, he barreled around, intent only on making it to the third floor and giving Bennett the help he had requested.

He slammed right into Nathan Stacker.

The impact sent him tumbling to the side, smashing hard against the wall as the bigger man used his arm to shove him out of the way. All the air was stolen from his lungs, and he looked back in time to see the fugitive doing the same to Seventy and Animal, casting them aside like toys as he charged down the steps to escape.

"Stacker!" he tried to shout, but he had no breath to do it with.

There was a woman following Stacker down the stairs. She looked back at him as she passed. Her face was pale. Her body language suggested she was terrified of what was happening. That had to be Lonnie's sister, Rhonna.

"Rhonna," he said. "Wait."

She hesitated slightly at the sound of her name.

Animal lunged up from where Nathan had shoved him, grabbing the woman by the legs and yanking her to the ground. They both fell into the corner together. Stacker stopped and turned back.

"Happy's down," Bennett said through the comm. "Sheriff, where are you? We're pinned up here."

Hayden aimed his revolver, taking a shot at Nathan. He missed on purpose, the round striking the wall next to the fugitive's head. Nathan glanced at

Hayden, their eyes meeting for the second time, Hayden sending a message:

The next shot wouldn't be a warning.

Nathan spun back around again, continuing down the stairs and leaving Rhonna behind.

"Seventy, Animal," Hayden said. "Bennett needs backup. Go!"

Seventy was on her feet, rushing up the stairs. Animal let Rhonna go, shoving her into the corner and joining the other soldier.

"Bennett," Hayden said. "Animal and Seventy are en route. I've got positive visual on Stacker. I can join them, or I can chase him."

There was only the slightest hesitation from the other side of the comm.

"Get Stacker," Bennett said.

Chapter 48

Nathan looked back, watching as the Spacer who had tackled Rhonna shove her against the wall and get to his feet. He only hesitated for a moment before turning away and heading down the stairs, leaving her behind.

For a fleeting moment, he was tempted to go back to help her. It would have been a bad move. They weren't going to do anything to her. She wasn't the one they wanted.

He hoped she would forgive him, especially after he had let her believe he had gone back for her. The Spacers were here after all. They weren't with the other group, whoever the hell they were. He had heard the gunfire. The two factions were busy fighting one another, giving him a chance to get away.

He rounded the corner, descended the stairs,

heading for ground level when a sharp crack sounded behind him and a bullet hit the wall right beside his chest. He glanced back in time to see the one they called Sheriff was on his tail and about to correct his aim.

He dove sideways, hitting the door to the second floor with enough force to break off its old hinges. It fell inward with him as he hit the ground and rolled to his feet, turning to the corridor on his left.

He flattened himself against the wall beside the doorway. He kept trying to get away without hurting them. He didn't want to kill any more Centurions. They weren't giving him a choice. He couldn't let them take him back to Proxima. Niobe had entrusted him with the intel she had gathered, and he had to see this through.

The revolver came through the doorway. Nathan grabbed it and tugged, surprise when he didn't meet any resistance. The move put him off balance, and Sheriff lunged through the door, slamming Nathan in the gut with a hard, metal fist.

Nathan grunted, his ribs flexing beneath the powerful blow as he was driven back. Sheriff didn't waste any time, charging him like a bull and getting his arms around Nathan's waist.

Nathan found his balance before Sheriff could knock him over, and he turned with the momentum and threw the Spacer to the side. Sheriff rolled on the floor and got back up, reaching for the rifle hooked to his back.

Nathan turned the revolver in his hand, pointing it at Sheriff.

"Don't," Nathan said, causing Sheriff to pause. "Don't make me shoot you. I don't want to."

"They tell me you killed your wife," Sheriff said. His eyes were narrowed, his face set like stone. He had a strange accent. He sounded more like an Earther than a Spacer. How could that be?

"I didn't," Nathan replied. "They set me up."

Sheriff kept staring. Nathan could almost feel the man's mind working.

"I need to bring you in," Sheriff said. "If you're innocent, you'll be cleared."

"Are you kidding me?" Nathan said. "The Trust didn't send you all the way here if there were any chance in hell I would be found innocent. But you don't work for the Trust, do you? If you did, you would have killed me already."

"I don't work for the Trust," Sheriff said. "Some people don't believe the Trust is a real thing."

"It is. I worked for them. I should know."

"Okay. What I know is that Proxima Command wants you real bad. If you come with me, I can bring you back alive."

The sound of gunfire was still echoing on the floor above them. Nathan shook his head. "I don't know if either one of us is getting out of here alive,

Sheriff. Whoever these other assholes are, I know they shot at both of us. But I also know they want me." He shifted the gun, putting his finger on the trigger. "And you're slowing me down."

"Where are you going? They're outside, too. We have a dropship."

"I'm sure you do. No. I can't go back. Not now. Niobe was counting on me."

"I can't let you leave."

"You don't have a choice. I've got the gun."

Sheriff smiled. "It isn't loaded."

Nathan's eyes widened, and he squeezed the trigger. It clicked. Once. Twice. Three times.

Then Sheriff was on him again, throwing another heavy punch that was too powerful for his size. The blow rocked Nathan to the side, bouncing him off the wall. He dropped the revolver, turning to catch Sheriff's next blow, driving the soldier's arm down and bringing his knee up into his gut. Sheriff managed to get his hand around the knee as it hit him, and he yanked it aside, sending Nathan to the floor.

Nathan landed on his back, turning and kicking up, catching Sheriff in the thigh with enough force to send him sprawling. He rolled over onto his hands and knees and then got up, sprinting down the hallway and away from the other man.

Nathan glanced back. Sheriff stumbled up

behind him; the wind knocked out of his lungs. He picked up the revolver and gave chase.

He was persistent. Nathan respected that. He kept running, toward an intact window at the end of the hallway. He knew he was on the second floor. A regular human couldn't take that kind of fall, but a replica could. It was his chance to get away.

"Stacker, stop!" Sheriff said behind him.

There was no way he was going to stop. He reached the filthy window and jumped, tucking himself in as he smashed through both the frame and glass. Then he was six meters above the ground and falling, arcing out and down toward the sidewalk.

He hit hard, his legs buckling at the impact, the pain more than he was expecting. He stumbled, his momentum throwing him into the side of an old car. His shoulder bashed into the rusted metal, denting it, and he rolled off the side and fell to his knees behind it.

He could hear the engines now, and he saw a pair of lights pointed directly at him. Sheriff hadn't been lying. The car began to growl more loudly, coming right at him.

He grabbed for his plasma pistol from the back of his pants and discovered he had lost it in the melee. He crouched and set himself, ready to dive away from the charging mass of metal. He still couldn't see it behind the lights, but he was sure it was heavy.

Then bolts of plasma were launching down from above him. Not at him, but at the car trying to take him out. They peppered the vehicle, and they must have hit something important because it swerved away from Nathan, turning left and smashing into the cars beside him. He looked over at the vehicle. It was long and low, with armor plating covering a good portion of it, the eagle and star logo painted haphazardly on the side. The driver was slumped over the wheel, dead.

"Stacker!" Sheriff called out again.

Nathan ran.

Chapter 49

Hayden watched Stacker start running again. He cursed under his breath. He understood that Stacker didn't want to go back to Proxima with Bennett, but he was as good as dead out there unarmed.

Hayden had already decided that no matter what else happened, he was going to do his best to not kill Nathan Stacker. Maybe he was innocent, maybe he wasn't, but their short conversation had given him enough reason to question the verdict. It wasn't so much about what Stacker had said. It was about how he had said it. Hayden couldn't take the man's life without it destroying his conscience.

Which meant the only other choice he had was to follow him wherever he ran.

Which meant he was going to have to jump.

He scanned the street. There were three more

cars nearby, and they all started moving, following Nathan as he ran. Three more were parked to his right, directly in front of the hospital. The people who had been in them must have come inside.

Stacker was getting further and further away while he stood there and watched. Damn it.

"Bennett, what's your status?" Hayden asked, taking a few steps back from the window. He wasn't a replica. He couldn't fall six meters and land on his feet without breaking something.

"We're clear, Sheriff," Bennett said. "Bastards were carrying Stacker's chip; they funneled us in and started shooting. Happy's dead, but Animal and Seventy turned the tide. What about Stacker?"

"I'm still in pursuit," Hayden said. "We're on the street and headed for the underground. You've got more bad guys coming up from street level."

Hayden took a few deep breaths. Then he ran toward the broken window, telling himself he was an idiot for doing it the entire time.

He stopped breathing when he reached the edge and jumped, a lump sliding into his throat as he started dropping.

Anyone else would have died easily by diving headfirst toward solid ground. For Hayden, using his arms was his best chance of surviving at all. He reached out, hitting the ground with his replacements, feeling the strain as they absorbed the force, tucking them in and somersaulting half-gracefully, rolling forward and coming up, his momentum duplicating Stacker's maneuver and sending him into the side of a car. He managed to lead with his forearm, slamming it with the metal and putting a deep dent in the rusted hide.

He flexed his fingers to make sure the augmentations were still functional. Then he grabbed his reloaded revolver from his holster and started running.

He was behind the cars pursuing Stacker, at the rear of the line of people chasing him down. He watched one of the passengers lean out of a passenger window, armed with an assault rifle. He started shooting at Stacker, the bullets sparking off the pavement behind him.

Hayden aimed and fired, his round striking the armored plating right under the soldier and skipping away. He fired three more rounds as the man tried to turn around to see who was shooting at him.

The last bullet hit him in the shoulder, causing him to drop the rifle. He grabbed at the wound and vanished back in the car.

Then the rear car slammed on the brakes, sliding sideways in the street and skidding to a stop. Hayden kept running toward it, charging toward the downed rifle on the ground ahead. He emptied the revolver to keep them from shooting back, grabbing his last speed reloader and dumping the rounds into the cylinder.

Someone decided it was worth the risk, and leaned out of a window to shoot back. Hayden aimed at the muzzle flash, firing two rounds that stopped the shooter before the shooter could stop him.

He holstered his revolver and reached for the assault rifle, diving to the ground and grabbing it. He came up and shooting, exchanging fire with the soldiers in the last car, sending a line of bullets from front to back. The armor plating was organized to protect the vehicle and its passengers from the trife, not slugs. His bullets found open spaces and soft flesh, leaving the interior of the vehicle silent.

He made it to the car. The doors were welded shut and plated over. The front had a piece of sharpened metal mounted to it, perfect for ramming trife. The driver was slouched sideways, bullet wounds in the side of his head.

Hayden tossed his rifle in, grabbing the top of the window and pulling himself up, leading with his feet. He used them to shove the driver aside, and then he threw the car back into drive. He spun the wheel, peeling away and back into pursuit behind the other cars.

Stacker was a good runner, and he managed to stay ahead of the cars, hugging the buildings on the side of the road and keeping the old wrecks between them and him. The soldiers were shooting at him, but he was a difficult target to hit, moving and obscured while they were moving too.

The lead car roared as it accelerated, deciding to try to get ahead of Stacker. Hayden accelerated too, coming up behind the middle vehicle.

"Shit," Bennett said over the comm. "Spacers, fan out. Watch your—"

Hayden heard the explosion from the car, and he flipped his head back to the hospital in time to see the flames and debris tunnel out from one of the windows.

"Bennett!" he shouted, about to slam on the brakes and go back.

"Sheriff," Bennett said. "We're okay. I think." He groaned. "Somebody hit a gas line or something. Animal, Seventy, report."

Hayden shoved his foot back down on the accelerator, the engine shaking the whole thing as it gained speed.

"Animal. Here, sir."

Hayden sped toward the middle car. It wasn't moving that fast, keeping pace with Stacker. The front of it was armored, but the back was relatively vulnerable.

"Seventy?" Bennett said. "Seventy, report."

Hayden's car slammed into the car ahead of it, the metal plow in the front digging into the crushed rear and holding tight. He kept pushing down on the gas, the engine roaring as he shoved the second car ahead, toward the vehicle in front. It had made a hard left, pushing an old wreck out of the way and blocking Stacker's escape.

The fugitive was almost beside him, and he glanced over at Hayden, surprised by his help. Hayden thought maybe Stacker would stop.

"Seventy?" Bennett said again.

She wasn't answering.

Stacker didn't stop. He ran right toward the enemy car even as the rifles turned in his direction, so close there was no way they could miss.

Hayden drove the middle car forward and slammed it into the ass end of the lead vehicle, the impact whipping it to the side and pulling it away from Stacker. The fugitive jumped, landing on the hood of Hayden's car, taking two steps and jumping off the other side, hitting the ground still running.

"Son of a bitch," Hayden cursed, grabbing his rifle and pulling himself from the car.

The lead soldiers had been dazed by the collision, but they were recovering and trying to get out of their car. Hayden ignored them, climbing over the wrecks and resuming the chase. His heart was racing, his lungs were on fire, and his shoulders hurt like hell. He wasn't going to let Stacker get away again.

Something came at him from the side, a dark blur in his peripheral vision. He barely got his arm up in time to take the impact of the trife as it crashed into him, knocking him back onto the ground.

The creature hovered over him, head diving

down for his neck. Hayden managed to get his arm in front of his face, letting the creature bite the metal. He used his other hand to slam it in the chest, and then throw it away from him. He rolled to the side to where the assault rifle had fallen, picking it up and shooting the demon before it could recover.

He heard screams behind him and looked back to see the enemy soldiers were under attack, dozens of trife appearing from the darkness and launching their attack. The soldiers had gotten caught out of their cars, and they were slow to get their weapons up to defend against the creatures.

Hayden got back to his feet, quickly scanning for more trife before resuming his run. He saw one dart out ahead of him and try to tackle Stacker, but the big man punched it in the head, and then grabbed its neck, crushing it like it was nothing more than a minor inconvenience.

"Sheriff, where the hell are you?" Bennett said.

"Still...in...pursuit," Hayden said, his breathing labored. "The...tunnels..."

"Roger," Bennett said.

"Seventy?" Hayden asked.

"No."

That was all he said.

Stacker was getting close to the station entrance. Hayden saw him look back again, taking note that he was still being chased and that the other soldiers were all off his tail. He made it to the stairs as a group of trife poured out of the closest alley, watching him descend before turning back toward Hayden.

He fired the assault rifle from his hip, shooting at the trife as he advanced on the stairwell. He didn't try to aim, and the bullets zipped past the creatures, only managing to hit one.

He heard the crack of gunfire behind him. He ducked slightly at first, thinking the enemy soldiers had cleared the trife and were taking aim at him. Then he saw the demons begin to fall, peppered with rounds from behind.

"Got them," Bennett said. "We're right behind you, Sheriff."

Hayden felt relief in his chest as he made it to the stairs and started down. He wondered where Stacker thought he was going, heading back into the tunnels. He had to know the people there would kill him on sight. Then again, there were a lot of tunnels. If he could make it to an intersection he could lose everybody in a hurry.

Hayden hit the platform. Stacker was already gone, off the edge and into the subway tunnels. Hayden let out a growl, finding just a little more speed in his tired and aching legs. He hadn't come this far to lose the fugitive now.

He got to the edge of the platform and jumped down without slowing, almost tripping on the tracks. He stumbled, planting his hand to keep from going all the way down, grabbing at the goggles on top of his head and bringing them over his eyes. The darkness shifted to an eerie reddish hue, and Stacker became visible in the tunnel ahead. This part of the subway was arrow straight, no turns or bends in sight.

"Stacker!" Hayden yelled again. He dropped the assault rifle, grabbing his revolver and aiming.

Stacker didn't slow. He didn't even look back.

Hayden put his finger on the trigger. "Stacker, I will shoot you!"

Stacker still didn't slow.

Hayden pulled the trigger. A second later, Stacker stumbled and fell to the ground.

Chapter 50

Nathan cursed, rolling over and looking down. The bullet had hit him in the leg, piercing his skin but thankfully not hitting any nerve or bone. It still hurt like hell, and he could feel the swelling already pressing on his muscles. He grabbed at his shirt, pulling it off and quickly wrapping it around the wound, tying it into a tight tourniquet.

He had lost his night-vision goggles somewhere in the hospital. Damn, he regretted ever stopping there now. He should have kept going, heading straight to the river and jumping in. He could have swam across to the other side by now.

Would that have helped him against the unknown force that had appeared out of nowhere, with their cars and guns and uniforms with the logo that was so similar, and yet so different from the one he had once worn? They seemed to have a tracker, just like the Spacers had a tracker. They had managed to find him too efficiently.

He would say they were with the Trust, but there was no way the Trust could have told them he was coming. Tech like that didn't exist.

But then, who the hell were they?

It didn't matter now. What mattered was that he was in the dark. On the ground. Unarmed.

And the one they called Sheriff was coming.

He pushed himself to a knee, testing his leg. It was painful to put weight on it, but at least he *could* put weight on it. He started to get up.

"Don't," Sheriff said, from somewhere in front of him. "Please."

Nathan lowered his head. He should have gotten up faster. "You don't give up, do you?"

"Neither do you."

"Did you hit me where you were aiming?"

"Almost. I missed by a couple of inches. I don't think you're going to die."

"No. Disappointed?"

"Not me. I believe in justice."

"There isn't going to be any justice, Sheriff. The Trust will see to that."

"I've got backup on the way. Just stay there, okay? The trife took care of the soldiers outside. We'll call in the cavalry, and then we'll be out of here."

Sheriff materialized less than a meter in front of him, revolver aimed at his chest.

"I can't go," Nathan said. "Niobe was counting on me. I'd rather die than let her down. I'd rather die than fail her memory."

He felt the tears coming again. Damn it, would he ever be able to talk about her without getting emotional?

Sheriff's eyes shifted to the ring dangling from his neck. Nathan could see his expression change, even in the darkness.

"Are you married, Sheriff?" Nathan asked.

"Yeah," Sheriff replied.

"Do you love your wife?"

"More than anything."

"What would you go through for her?"

"I've already gone through hell for her. It cost me both my hands."

Nathan smiled. "I think you made out okay on that." He paused. He could hear footsteps behind Sheriff. His backup was arriving. "I didn't kill my wife, Sheriff."

"I believe you."

"Then let me go."

Sheriff shook his head. "I can't."

"Why?"

"It isn't that simple. There's more at stake than you know."

"There might be more at stake than you know,

Sheriff." Nathan grabbed the ring. "She left me this." He paused. He didn't know why he was going to tell this man about the ring. Maybe because Sheriff said he believed him? "There's a data chip. They killed her for it. They—"

"Move aside, Sheriff," a woman's voice said behind the soldier. Nathan recognized it immediately. Judicus Shia?

Sheriff seemed surprised to hear her. He turned his head back, only for an instant.

Nathan didn't waste it. He lunged forward, grabbing at Sheriff's revolver for the second time, certain it was loaded now. He managed to get a hand on it when Sheriff recovered, yanking it to the side and hitting Nathan in the ribs. The blow nearly lifted him off the ground, but he managed to hold on, the force yanking the weapon from Sheriff's hands and sending it sliding away.

"Sheriff, move!" the judicus said again, as Nathan dove for the weapon.

He got his hand on it, but then Sheriff was on top of him, slamming a hand down on his wrist. The force made him open his hand and lose the gun. He rocked back, strong enough to flip over and knock Sheriff aside.

A plasma bolt cut through the darkness, hitting the ground only centimeters from his face.

"Judge, hold your fire!" someone shouted from further back.

Nathan kept moving, reaching for the gun again. A cold hand grabbed his neck, lifting and turning him, rolling him back over and into the wall.

A second bolt hit the side of the tunnel, not as close as the first.

Sheriff leaned over him, keeping a hand on his neck, gently enough that he could still breathe.

"Stay down," Sheriff said. He grabbed Nathan's ring with his free hand.

"No," Nathan said. "Please don't take it."

Sheriff yanked it easily from his neck.

"Why?" Nathan asked.

"Judge," he heard the other soldier say again. "What the hell are you doing? I said hold your…"

A flash of plasma lit up the tunnel for an instant. Nathan saw it leave the judicus' pistol and bury itself in the other soldier's chest at point-blank range. The soldier collapsed.

Sheriff leaned over him, face going pale, looking as though he had just been shot himself.

"I'm sorry Sheriff," Judicus Shia said, her voice getting closer. "This is just how it has to be."

Sheriff looked down at Nathan, his eyes shifting to the side, to where the revolver was resting.

"Wait," a fresh voice said in the darkness. "You got him, didn't you? You got that son of a bitch?"

Nathan recognized the boy's voice. Lonnie? What was he doing here? He looked up at Sheriff, whose eyes stayed fixed on the gun. Sheriff shifted slightly above him, turning his hip a little more to the side. The plasma pistol tucked into the rear of his fatigues came into view.

"I want to kill him," Lonnie said. "I want to blow his fucking—"

There was another flash of light from another plasma bolt as the judicus shot the boy. It was a momentary distraction, a break in her concentration.

Sheriff collapsed on top of Nathan, stretching for his revolver. Nathan reached up, grabbing the handle of the plasma pistol.

Sheriff rolled away from him, turning over at the same time Nathan sat up. A plasma bolt split the ground between them, a second hitting Sheriff in the arm.

Nathan used the light of the judicus' plasma to aim, finding the source and squeezing the trigger. Multiple bolts launched from the weapon, one of them hitting the traitor.

A pair of bullets followed an instant later, tracking his shots. Judicus Shia grunted, and then her attack stopped.

Chapter 51

Hayden swung his revolver back toward the fugitive, who was turning at the same time, aiming his pistol at him.

They froze, weapons pointed at one another from only centimeters away.

Hayden stared down at Stacker. His heart was in his throat, his body tense. At the moment that Judge had shot Bennett, he realized everything the fugitive had said was probably true.

"Sheriff," Animal said through the comm. "I followed the kid into the tunnel. I'm a hundred meters back. I've got a bead on Stacker. Give the word and I'll take him out."

Hayden and Stacker remained locked in position. Then Hayden stood up, taking a few steps back and allowing the other man to stand.

"The ring," Stacker said, motioning to Hayden's other hand. "Give it to me."

"Stacker, run," Hayden replied.

"The ring!" Stacker shouted.

"Sheriff, I can take the shot," Animal said.

"Negative," Hayden replied. "Damn it, Stacker, if you don't want to die, you'd better fucking run."

The other man looked confused. Hayden didn't blame him. He just hoped he was smart enough to go.

"I'll kill you to get it back," Stacker said.

"If you do right now, you'll die too," Hayden replied. "You want it? Live to fight another day, Captain."

"Sheriff?" Animal said again.

"Negative," Hayden replied. "If you discharge your weapon against my order, you can expect a court-martial to follow. We've got a man down here."

Stacker was still there, staring at the hand holding the ring. Then he glanced up, making eye contact. He was angry. Very angry. For a moment, Hayden wasn't sure if Stacker was going to run, or if he was going to get them both killed.

"I'll find you, Sheriff," Stacker said. "Wherever you go. Earth. Proxima. Anywhere in the fucking universe. I'll find you."

Then he turned and started to limp away as quickly as his legs would carry him.

"Sheriff!" Animal said desperately in the comm. "He's getting away."

"I told you," Hayden said. "Bennett is down. Help me."

He didn't waste time watching Stacker go. He rushed back to where his friend had fallen, right beside the dead Judicus. He knelt down beside the stricken Spacer, putting his hand on his neck. He felt a light pulse.

Animal joined him a moment later, falling on the other side of Bennett. "Sarge," he said. "Fuck!"

"We need to get him to the dropship," Hayden said.

"We can't move him," Animal said.

"We can't keep him here." He holstered his revolver and lifted Bennett, cradling him in his arms. "Danethi, we need emergency extraction. Bennett is wounded. We need emergency extraction."

"Consider the environment hostile," Animal added. "We need an immediate emergency pickup. Come in weapons hot."

"Roger," Danethi said. "I can only touch down in the clearing on the north side of the island. You'll have to meet me there."

Animal looked at Hayden. "How are we going to cover that much ground? The whole area is crawling with trife."

"We can make it," Hayden said. "We have to. Danethi, do it. Weapons hot."

"Roger, Sheriff. I'm on my way. ETA, ten minutes."

"Confirmed," Hayden said. He looked at Animal. "Let's go."

"What about Stacker?" Animal asked, pointing.

Hayden turned his head back. Stacker was vanishing into the darkness.

"I don't know," Hayden said. "There's something ugly about all of this. One thing I can tell you for sure is he didn't kill his wife. He's an innocent man."

"What? Sheriff, that's not your decision to make."

"This is my planet. My jurisdiction. With Bennett down, it is my decision to make. Now, do you want to save this man's life or do you want to argue some more?"

Animal hesitated for a moment. Then he nodded. "We'll settle this later."

"Gladly," Hayden said.

Animal led him back down the tunnel, right after spitting on Judicus Shia's corpse and taking her sidearm. There were no complications getting back to the station entrance. They couldn't say the same for getting onto the street and north to the clearing. Ten minutes, now eight, wasn't a lot of time, and there were plenty of trife waiting at the top of the steps.

"I think I said this before, but I wish we had brought some grenades," Animal said, looking up at the creatures. A few of them were bolder than the others, and they went down a couple of steps before retreating.

"How many charges do you have left?"

"Thirty."

"Get close and give them a stream. That'll clear the steps."

"Roger."

Animal started up the steps. Hayden stayed close, shifting Bennett into a fireman's carry. He hated to have to carry him at all, but he needed a free hand. "Pass me the pistol."

Animal handed it back to him. Then he turned the dial on his rifle to stream mode.

"As soon as the charge runs out, we run back toward the hospital. Get to the frontmost car and cover me. We put him in the back, and then we go. Got it?"

"Roger that, Sheriff," Animal said.

The trife were watching them intently. One of them made a break down the steps, and Hayden swung the pistol and shot it in the chest. It hissed and collapsed.

Animal moved up two more steps, glancing back at Hayden. Hayden nodded, and the plasma rifle began spewing super-heated gas at the trife, cutting through the entire front line in the few seconds the remaining charge lasted.

Then they ran, up the last few steps and into the throng. Animal grabbed his pistol and started shooting. Hayden did the same. It was impossible to miss at this range, every round finding alien flesh. The creatures tried to swipe and bite at them. Hayden could feel the claws against the bodysuit and hear them scraping on the metal of his arms. He saw Animal get cut on the back of his shoulder, an inky black fingernail drawing blood right before Animal shot his attacker point-blank in the face.

They kept pushing, resorting to kicks and punches when bullets weren't enough, somehow keeping the demons back long enough to break through. They got past the main lines of trife and into the open. The three cars were still locked together, the enemy soldiers dead on the ground around them. Headlights were visible further in the distance, another group of opponents coming their way.

Hayden gritted his teeth, growling in burning agony as he carried Bennett toward the cars, his legs and lungs complaining with every step. He could hear and smell the trife behind him, their noxious breath thick in the air. A sudden weight nearly pulled him backward as a trife jumped on Bennett, attempting to tear him away. Hayden made a quick choice, dropping the pistol and reaching back to grab the trife. It bit down ineffectually on his hand, and he yanked forward, bringing the creature with him. It flopped on the ground, and he brought a heavy boot down on it, crushing its head.

Animal reached the car, jumping on the hood and turning back. He fired a stream of bolts into the slick, giving Hayden a chance to open the distance between him and the trife. He hit three more creatures that got too close before finally making it to the vehicle.

"Come on," Hayden said, grabbing at the back door of the car. It didn't open, welded shut like the front. That was good and bad.

The trife kept coming, at least fifty of them charging their position. Hayden shifted Bennett in his grasp again, thankful for the strength of his replacement hands but nervous that the motion had already killed his friend. He guided Bennett through the vehicle's missing window and onto the back seat, dropping him there just as a trife vaulted onto the car and reached out for his face.

He snapped his hand up, slapping the creature's claws away and taking a glancing blow off the cheek. He already had one scar there, given to him by the trife, so the strike would hardly make it worse. He reached up with his other hand, getting it around the trife's neck. He pulled the creature off the car. It flailed and hissed in his grasp, and he turned and threw it into another demon closing on them.

"Get in the car," he told Animal, at the same time he leaped and slid across the hood to the driver's side.

Like before, he threw his feet into the window

and pulled himself inside, taking position behind the wheel. Another trife reached them, claws coming in through the window, reaching for Hayden's face. Animal fired past his head, the bolt close enough to burn his fresh wound.

"Ahhh, damn," Hayden said, wincing in pain. He started the car and threw it into reverse, slamming down on the right pedal. The wheels spun for a moment and then they started moving backward, metal tearing and screaming as the armored grill pulled the rear bumper from the second car.

Hayden shifted the car and turned the wheel, hitting the gas. The engine roared, the car slamming into the second vehicle again, catching it in the corner and flinging it into a group of oncoming trife.

Gunshots rang out, bullets pinging off the armored metal of the car as the enemy soldiers caught up to them. The trife died too, hit by the assault and cut down quickly by the multiple rifles.

"Danethi, what's your position?" Hayden asked.

"I'm at seven klicks and descending. Five minutes, Sheriff. Don't be late."

"We'll be there."

Hayden pressed down on the accelerator, the car jolting forward. A few rounds hit the back of the car's front seat, one of them punching through between the two of them.

"Fucking bastards," Animal said, turning back and firing a couple of bolts.

"Don't waste charges," Hayden said. "We may need them when we get there."

Animal sat back, looking at Bennett. "I'm not sure he's still alive, Sheriff."

"He'd better be."

Chapter 52

The car slammed into a group of trife that didn't move fast enough, two of them impaled on the front grill with the bumper, the others pushed aside or crushed. They rocketed north along the street, with Hayden using his memory of the city's layout to guide them toward the central clearing.

The enemy soldiers were staying behind them, their cars easily capable of keeping the pace, their guns seemingly possessing unending magazines full of rounds. They were lucky this car had armor on the back as well as the front, though it wasn't long before both rear tires were blown out despite the metal plates that hung down to protect them.

Hayden managed to maintain control, but he wouldn't be able to forever. He needed to get clear of the soldiers, to gain at least a few blocks on them.

Otherwise, they would never be able to climb out of the car without being shot to death.

He scanned the area ahead of them. There were so many abandoned cars here, and he realized now that it was unlikely they had all wound up on the side of the road, so neatly aligned. Someone had moved all of the cars. Someone had maintained the roads well enough to drive on them.

A long time ago, or only recently?

He flew along another street, catching a glimpse of an upcoming cross-street. There were cars blocking this one, stretched across the road to prevent anyone from going past. Hayden had no idea why, but it only made the path more appealing.

"Hang on," he said, glancing back at Bennett and hoping he didn't get thrown too hard as he slammed on the brakes and turned the wheel.

The car skidded, Bennett pushed back in the seat while Animal held the frame to keep himself stable. Bullets pinged off the doors, one of them catching Animal in the shoulder, grazing off the bodysuit and drawing blood from his arm. He shouted angrily, getting a good look at the enemy soldiers as they approached, intent on ramming the car.

Hayden pushed down on the gas, getting them out of the way and carrying them toward the barrier. He slammed into an old van, pushing it aside before the grille caught on it, turning it slightly and shoving it ahead of them. Hayden didn't let up, shoving the van another fifty meters before it hit the curb and was pushed up and off the spikes. It toppled slowly, rolling sideways and then falling across the street.

"If you did that on purpose, you are the most amazing fucking soldier I've ever seen," Animal said, watching the enemy soldiers come to a stop behind the new barrier.

"I wish it were on purpose," Hayden replied. "Just lucky."

"We needed a little damn luck."

They went across four blocks before turning north again.

"Sheriff, this is Danethi," the pilot said. "I'm on final approach. Weapons are hot, but I don't see any targets."

"Roger, Captain," Hayden replied. "You probably will any second now."

The unknown force hadn't fired more missiles at the dropship on the way down? That didn't make sense unless they didn't think they had anything that could get through the armored starship's hide.

Hayden crossed another street, his eyes landing on an old rusted sign on the side of the road. It was dented and faded, with weeds growing all around it, but he could still make out the word that composed it:

LOVE.

He put a hand on the pocket of his fatigues,

pressing down on Stacker's wedding band. That's what this was about, wasn't it?

The Kiev became visible a moment later, a spot in the sky falling fast, headed for a field of dark green ahead. Retro-thrusters pushed against gravity, slowing the ship, bringing it carefully toward the tall, heavy bushes growing in the central fields.

Hayden turned the headlights on and off. "Danethi, I'm flashing my lights. Do you have a visual?"

"Roger, Sheriff," Danethi replied. "I have visual on you. I'm going to turn around for easier extraction."

"Pozz."

The dropship started to turn and then paused. It rotated back, twin plasma cannons opening fire, sending thick bolts into the ground ahead. Hayden couldn't see what Danethi was shooting at, but he yanked the goggles off his head as a bright explosion filled the street ahead of them, nearly blinding him.

"Target destroyed," Danethi said. "You're clear, Sheriff."

The car flew between an opening in a crumbling brick wall, entering the clearing half a klick from the dropship. It was starting to rotate again, thrusters bright and hot as Danethi positioned the ship for them to rush up the ramp and into the hold. Hayden glanced back at Bennett again, unsure if his friend was alive or not.

He looked back in front of them, slamming on the brakes just in time to avoid hitting a statue that had been hidden by the growth. Bennett rolled forward, but Animal reached back and caught him, keeping him from further harm.

"Got you, sir," the Spacer said.

"We're close enough to run," Hayden decided. "Help me get him out."

He jumped out of the car and went to the back. Animal stayed inside, pulling Bennett toward him. Hayden could hear the cars still approaching, finding another way around. The Kiev was only a few hundred meters off the ground, the back ramp starting to open.

Animal fed Bennett into Hayden's arms. He cradled the Sergeant again, gathering him securely and then taking a step forward, the first in a short sprint to the finish line.

A bright flash caught his attention from the left. He looked over in time to see the helicopter that had been hovering silently over the hospital in the light of a long blast of thrust.

"Danethi, incoming!" Hayden shouted into the comm. There was no way the pilot could do anything about the weapon. It was just too close.

The missile dove toward the Kiev, breaking apart and splitting into a dozen smaller propelled discs as it did. Each of the discs spread out and hit the side of the ship, clinging there.

The helicopter started to rise and fade away from the dropship. The Kiev touched down, waiting for Hayden and Animal to bring Bennett on board.

"Sheriff, what are you waiting for?" Animal said.

Hadn't he seen the missile?

"Sheriff, the signature is gone," Danethi said. "It must have been a..."

The discs exploded, one by one, each one creating a ball of fire Hayden could hardly believe. In an instant the Kiev was invisible, buried under the flames. Then pieces of the ship began to emerge, debris flaring out from the explosions.

Hayden shifted and ducked behind the car, letting it capture the fallout. The ground shook, the roar so loud it hurt his ears. What the hell had they hit the dropship with?

He waited for the fireballs to subside before standing upright again, to look directly at the Kiev. The entire thing looked like it had been melted from the outside in, collapsed to nothing but a smoldering mess of a burned out, dead husk.

"Danethi?" Hayden asked hopefully. He didn't expect a reply.

He didn't get one.

"Well, that's just fucking great!" Animal shouted.

He looked up at the helicopter, which was moving away. He pointed his pistol at it, but realized soon enough how stupid shooting at it would be.

"What the fuck do we do now, Sheriff?"

Hayden ignored him. He lowered Bennett to the ground, tears falling from his eyes.

"Sergeant?" Animal said, realizing Hayden was on his knees beside the other Spacer. He came beside him, looking down. "Shit. Son of a bitch." He sighed loudly, carrying his anger and pain with it, his worries about their situation momentarily forgotten.

Hayden owed Sergeant Austin Bennett a debt of gratitude he would never be able to repay. The man had helped him when no one else would. He had been directly responsible for both Hayden's survival and the survival of his wife and daughter, as well as thousands of others. A soldier-turned-diplomat who had truly cared about the fate of humankind on Earth, even though he technically wasn't human himself. He was a hero in every sense of the word.

But most of all, and more importantly, he had been Hayden's friend.

And now he was gone.

Hayden reached down into his pocket, pulling Stacker's ring from its resting place and holding it over Bennett.

"What's that?" Animal asked.

Hayden glanced up at him. "Do you want to know what all of this is about?"

"Yes, sir."

"Sergeant Bennett died for this," he said, turning the ring in his hand and catching the inscription in the light of the dying flames.

Real love never dies.

"The answers are here." He pointed out in the direction the helicopter had gone. "And out there. But first, we have to get out of this place."

Animal nodded, standing up and looking back the way they had come. Hayden looked back too. A line of trife was emerging from the city, attracted to the heat and noise.

"I'm ready," Animal said.

"Get in the car."

Animal looked like he wanted to question the order, but he climbed back into the car instead.

Hayden pushed Bennett's eyes closed. Then he picked him up, carrying him the last hundred meters to the burning wreckage of the Kiev. The heat was intense, but he wasn't about to leave his friend's body out in the open for the wildlife. He reached into the flames and gently lowered Bennett to the ground.

Then he turned back toward the car. The trife were approaching cautiously behind it, not quite sure what to make of the whole thing. He walked back to the vehicle, watching them. They didn't charge. They didn't attack. He would have liked to think they had come to pay their respects.

Not likely.

He slid back behind the driver's seat. The vehicle wouldn't take them far running on its rims, but it would get them away from the trife and hopefully to the river. They would figure out the rest from there.

Three days.

Natalia was going to think he had died. He hated knowing she would be upset. If he could get a message to her sooner, he would. If not? It would make their reunion all the more joyful.

Assuming he survived.

He put the car in drive and turned the wheel, making a wide U-turn through the overgrown brush and facing the trife once more. He glanced at Animal, who nodded in reply.

Then they were on their way.

Chapter 53

Nathan limped along the dark tunnel. He had no idea where he was headed. He didn't even know what direction he was going. He knew he was angry.

Very angry.

He seethed inside, the loss of Niobe's ring driving his rage. Why the fuck had Sheriff taken it from him? Why had he stolen it, only to allow him to go? Was he working with the Trust? Just because he had helped Nathan kill the judicus, that didn't mean he wasn't. Maybe they had a difference of opinion on how to handle him?

Live to fight another day, Captain.

That's what Sheriff had said to him. Sheriff had to know he would come for him. Was he that smug? Was it all a game to him and the Trust?

He clenched his free hand, balling it tightly into a

fist. He decided he was going to kill Sheriff. No matter where, no matter when. He was going to get his ring back. He was going to find out what Niobe was trying to show him.

The Trust wasn't going to get away with any of this.

He stopped for a moment, leaning against the wall to rest his leg. He had stopped the bleeding, and there didn't seem to be any damage to the muscles. The swelling was pushing on the nerves, making it painful.

He could deal with pain.

He didn't stay there long, taking a handful of breaths to regain himself and then pushing off and continuing along the tunnel. If he had to guess, he would say he was going north. But it was just a damned guess.

He aimed his pistol forward and fired a bolt, using it to light his path through the darkness. He spotted a sharp turn up ahead, just before the charge vanished against the wall. He measured the distance and kept going, heading for the curve, trudging along in the pitch black.

He took a dozen steps and fired again, lighting the way. He reached the turn, going around it by following the wall with his hand, saving his charges until he had gotten to the straightaway.

He fired another round, which zipped along the tracks and revealed a station up ahead.

Live to fight another day, Captain.

Who the fuck did Sheriff think he was? He had left him with a limp and moving through the tunnels in the dark. Did he think it was funny? If Sheriff really wanted him to survive, he would have given him his night-vision goggles. Asshole.

He picked up speed, dragging his leg as he powered toward the station. He was done with these fucking tunnels. He was done with the fucking darkness. He didn't care if the trife came for him. He would kill every damned one of them, with his bare hands if he had to. He regretted coming to Earth, and at the same time, he was glad he had come. It was better than being a prisoner. It was better than being a research subject back on Proxima. At least he had a chance.

Live to fight another day, Captain.

He intended to follow that advice. No matter what, he was going to survive. Niobe was counting on him, and that was the greatest motivation of all. Without the ring, the only thing he had left of her was his memories. It was enough.

He raised the pistol, firing into the darkness again.

He caught a glimpse of a dark shadow in front of him, out of place with the rest of the tunnel.

"Is my luck really this bad?" he said, turning the weapon and firing at the lump.

The Stalker uncurled and leaped to the side, avoiding the plasma bolt. It hit the wall and bounced off, diving toward him while he adjusted his aim. He got one bolt into its chest before it reached him, rough hands grabbing his arms, its weight pushing him down. He could smell its breath right over his face, and he bucked up hard, throwing the creature over him. Its sticky fingers held onto his flesh, pulling hard against the momentum before it let go. Nathan could hear it smack against the wall, and he rolled over, trying to get up but stumbling on his bad leg.

He fired the plasma pistol again. The bolt hit the Stalker in the leg. The wound on its chest was already nearly healed. It bounced sideways, forcing him to turn. It jumped up and flipped over, grabbing the top of the tunnel and vanishing into the darkness.

Nathan stayed down, turning in a desperate search for the creature. He fired his weapon straight up, creating microsecond bursts of light to find the Stalker.

It seemed to have disappeared.

He knew it wouldn't have left. Not while he was still alive and it hadn't fed. He kept turning until he was facing away from the station and shooting back into the tunnel.

Still nothing.

He started backing up, listening carefully for any

sound that might give the creature away. Where had it gone?

He didn't know which direction it attacked him from. One moment, it wasn't there. The next, it was. It landed on his back, claws digging into his arms again, puncturing deep into the flesh. He shouted, the sound echoing in the tunnel, trying to dislodge the Stalker as its teeth found his neck.

It bit into him, and he threw himself backward into the wall, smashing the Stalker against it. The move loosened the teeth but didn't get it off. Its nails went deeper into his skin. It had learned from its earlier mistake.

He turned the plasma pistol toward himself, squeezing the trigger and sending bolts burning past his face. The Stalker released his neck to avoid them, staying on his back and riding him like a scooter.

Live to fight another day, Captain.

Nathan fell to his knees, blood soaking his chest and pouring down his arms. He wanted to live. He needed to. For Niobe.

There was no way in hell he was going to.

He let out a soft cry, tears forming in his eyes. He had survived all of the monsters, the soldiers, the judicus and the Spacers, only to fail now? He reached back for the Stalker, planting his hand on its blind head and pushing. He wasn't strong enough. Not now.

He leaned forward on his hands, the life draining

out of him. He was getting lightheaded. Dizzy. This was the end. He was going to die.

"Need a hand?" a voice said in the darkness behind him. It was deep and confident. It sounded familiar.

Then the Stalker was gone from his back. He could hear it whining behind him, and he turned his head to see it held up by a huge metal hand. At first, he thought it was Sheriff, but the hand was too big, its shape primitive compared to the soldier's smooth replacement.

His savior threw the Stalker hard into the wall. It bounced off and charged the man, and he laughed. He fucking laughed. He caught the thing in his other hand, again metal like the first. He lifted it by the neck, holding it out past its ability to reach him, though it tried to slash him with its claws.

"Doc, get the hell over here and patch him up," the man said, still holding the Stalker up.

A light appeared behind the man, bathing him and making him visible. He was wearing armor of some kind; a type Nathan had never seen before. It was big and chunky, with a full helmet that hid the man's face, leading down into bulky arms and torso and legs, which he realized now made a soft whining noise as the man moved.

He noticed the eagle and star logo etched into the arm, and his head began to slump. Had he just been saved from the Stalker, only to wind up in the hands of a different enemy?

A squad of soldiers approached. One of them broke off and came to kneel beside him. She was a hard woman, with a shaved head and a weathered face. She dropped a satchel beside him and opened it, pulling out medical patches.

"Don't die on me," she said.

Nathan didn't reply. He watched the man in the armored suit play with the Stalker for another few seconds, pulling it in to let it get close before holding it out again, continuing to laugh.

"It's been a long time, Betty," he said to the thing. "I see you still hate me as much as ever."

Nathan wasn't sure he wasn't hallucinating. Had he already died and didn't realize yet?

"I'll give you one chance to get out of here," the man said to the Stalker. "You come at me again; I'm going to have to kill you."

He tossed the Stalker back again. It was motionless for a moment. Then it jumped on one of the other soldiers. The man screamed as it slashed him in the throat, right before the man grabbed it again.

"You shouldn't have done that," he said. He reached up with his other hand, wrapping it around the Stalker's head.

Then he twisted.

Its bones cracked. Its body convulsed. He held the torso in one hand and pulled with the other, separating its head from the rest of it. Then he dropped both to the ground.

Nathan continued watching, even while the woman was applying ointment and patches to his neck and shoulders. He barely noticed how the pain was subsiding.

"Someone shot him," the woman said, getting the armored man's attention.

The man turned toward them. He reached up, tapping the side of the helmet. The faceplate came up, and Nathan froze. He was dead, wasn't he? Was this Hell?

He was looking back at himself.

"You're a hard man to kill, Stacker," the other Stacker said. "But then, I guess I should have known." He laughed again. "It's probably for the best. I assume Judicus Shia is dead?"

Nathan stared at him without speaking.

"Okay. You don't have to talk to me now. We'll have plenty of time later. I know you think we're your enemy because we were trying to kill you. I know you won't believe this, but we're not. There's stuff going on; you have no idea. But you will." His eyes shifted to the woman. "Is he stable?"

"Yes, sir," she replied.

"Good." The man put out his hand. "My name is James Stacker, but most folks down here call me General. These here are the Liberators. Part of my army. If nobody else has said it, then let me be the first. Welcome to Earth."

Nathan didn't take his hand. He continued staring, still trying to make sense of it. He was failing miserably.

"Have it your way," General said, pulling back his hand. "Give him a sedative and let's get him loaded up. We've wasted too much time and lost too many people already. It's been a lousy night."

"Yes, sir," Doc said.

She reached into the satchel and withdrew a needle. Nathan's eyes widened when he saw it, and he tried to shove it away.

General grabbed his arms, holding them easily with the powered armor. Doc jabbed the needle into him, emptying its contents in his thigh.

He stared at General as his vision started to blur, his strength and will to stay awake fading along with it.

Live to fight another day, Captain.

They hadn't saved him to kill him. He would wake up again. This wasn't the end of his fight.

It was only the beginning.

Thank you for reading Earth Unknown!

If you enjoyed this book and want to support this series, please, please, please consider leaving a review and letting me and others know how much you enjoyed it. It may seem like a waste of time, but I promise, it REALLY, REALLY HELPS! A star rating and a sentence is all it takes.

You can do that at:

mrforbes.com/reviewearthunknown

Do you want to know when I have a new release? Make sure you join my mailing list at mrforbes.com/notify

Thank you for your support.

Cheers,

Michael.

Other Books By M.R Forbes

M.R. Forbes on Amazon
mrforbes.com/books

Forgotten (The Forgotten)
mrforbes.com/theforgotten

Some things are better off FORGOTTEN.

Sheriff Hayden Duke was born on the Pilgrim, and he expects to die on the Pilgrim, like his father, and his father before him.

That's the way things are on a generation starship centuries from home. He's never questioned it. Never thought about it. And why bother? Access points to the ship's controls are sealed, the systems that guide her automated and out of reach. It isn't perfect, but he has all he needs to be content.

Until a malfunction forces his Engineer wife to

the edge of the habitable zone to inspect the damage.

Until she contacts him, breathless and terrified, to tell him she found a body, and it doesn't belong to anyone on board.

Until he arrives at the scene and discovers both his wife and the body are gone.

The only clue? A bloody handprint beneath a hatch that hasn't opened in hundreds of years.

Until now.

Starship Eternal (War Eternal)
mrforbes.com/starshipeternal

A lost starship...
A dire warning from futures past...
A desperate search for salvation...
Captain Mitchell "Ares" Williams is a Space Marine and the hero of the Battle for Liberty, whose Shot Heard 'Round the Universe saved the planet from a nearly unstoppable war machine. He's handsome, charismatic, and the perfect poster boy to help the military drive enlistment. Pulled from the war and thrown into the spotlight, he's as efficient at charming the media and bedding beautiful celebrities as he was at shooting down enemy starfighters.

After an assassination attempt leaves Mitchell critically wounded, he begins to suffer from strange hallucinations that carry a chilling and oddly familiar warning:

They are coming. Find the Goliath or humankind will be destroyed.

Convinced that the visions are a side-effect of his injuries, he tries to ignore them, only to learn that he may not be as crazy as he thinks. The enemy is real and closer than he imagined, and they'll do whatever it takes to prevent him from rediscovering the centuries lost starship.

Narrowly escaping capture, out of time and out of air, Mitchell lands at the mercy of the Riggers — a ragtag crew of former commandos who patrol the lawless outer reaches of the galaxy. Guided by a captain with a reputation for cold-blooded murder, they're dangerous, immoral, and possibly insane.

They may also be humanity's last hope for survival in a war that has raged beyond eternity.

(War Eternal is also available in a box set of the first three books here: mrforbes.com/wareternalbox)

Hell's Rejects (Chaos of the Covenant)
mrforbes.com/hellsrejects

The most powerful starships ever constructed are gone. Thousands are dead. A fleet is in ruins. The attackers are unknown. The orders are clear: *Recover the ships. Bury the bastards who stole them.*

Lieutenant Abigail Cage never expected to find

herself in Hell. As a Highly Specialized Operational Combatant, she was one of the most respected soldiers in the military. Now she's doing hard labor on the most miserable planet in the universe.

Not for long.

The Earth Republic is looking for the most dangerous individuals it can control. The best of the worst, and Abbey happens to be one of them. The deal is simple: *Bring back the starships, earn your freedom. Try to run, you die.* It's a suicide mission, but she has nothing to lose.

The only problem? There's a new threat in the galaxy. One with a power unlike anything anyone has ever seen. One that's been waiting for this moment for a very, very, long time. And they want Abbey, too.

Be careful what you wish for.

They say Hell hath no fury like a woman scorned. They have no idea.

Man of War (Rebellion)
mrforbes.com/manofwar

In the year 2280, an alien fleet attacked the Earth.

Their weapons were unstoppable, their defenses unbreakable.

Our technology was inferior, our militaries overwhelmed.

Only one starship escaped before civilization fell.

Earth was lost.

It was never forgotten.
Fifty-two years have passed.
A message from home has been received.
The time to fight for what is ours has come.
Welcome to the rebellion.

Or maybe something completely different?

Dead of Night (Ghosts & Magic)
mrforbes.com/deadofnight

For Conor Night, the world's only surviving necromancer, staying alive is an expensive proposition. So when the promise of a big payout for a small bit of thievery presents itself, Conor is all in. But nothing comes easy in the world of ghosts and magic, and it isn't long before Conor is caught up in the machinations of the most powerful wizards on Earth and left with only two ways out:

Finish the job, or be finished himself.

Balance (The Divine)
mrforbes.com/balance

My name is Landon Hamilton. Once upon a time I was a twenty-three year old security guard, trying to regain my life after spending a year in prison for stealing people's credit card numbers.

Now, I'm dead.

Okay, I was supposed to be dead. I got killed after all; but a funny thing happened after I had turned the mortal coil...

I met Dante Alighieri — yeah, that Dante. He told me I was special, a diuscrucis. That's what they call a perfect balance of human, demon, and angel. Apparently, I'm the only one of my kind.

I also learned that there was a war raging on Earth between Heaven and Hell, and that I was the only one who could save the human race from annihilation. He asked me to help, and I was naive enough to agree.

Sounds crazy, I know, but he wished me luck and sent me back to the mortal world. Oh yeah, he also gave me instructions on how to use my Divine "magic" to bend the universe to my will. The problem is, a sexy vampire crushed them while I was crushing on her.

Now I have to somehow find my own way to stay alive in a world of angels, vampires, werewolves, and an assortment of other enemies that all want to kill me before I can mess up their plans for humanity's future. If that isn't enough, I also have to find the queen of all demons and recover the Holy Grail.

It's not like it's the end of the world if I fail.

Wait. It is.

Tears of Blood (Books 1-3)
mrforbes.com/tearsofblood

One thousand years ago, the world was broken and reborn beneath the boot of a nameless, ageless tyrant. He erased all history of the time before, enslaving the people and hunting those with the power to unseat him.

The power of magic.

Eryn is such a girl. Born with the Curse, she fights to control and conceal it to protect those she loves. But when the truth is revealed, and his soldiers come, she is forced away from her home and into the company of Silas, a deadly fugitive tormented by a fractured past.

Silas knows only that he is a murderer who once hunted the Cursed, and that he and his brothers butchered armies and innocents alike to keep the deep, dark secrets of the time before from ever coming to light.

Secrets which could save the world.

Or destroy it completely.

About the Author

M.R. Forbes is the creator of a growing catalog of science fiction and fantasy titles. He lives in the pacific northwest with his family, including a cat who thinks she's a dog, and a dog who thinks she's a cat. He has a raging sugar and coffee addiction, and he's always happy to hear from readers.

To learn more about M.R. Forbes or just say hello:

Visit my website:
mrforbes.com

Send me an e-mail:
michael@mrforbes.com

Check out my Facebook page:
facebook.com/mrforbes.author

Chat with me on Facebook Messenger:
https://m.me/mrforbes.author

Printed in Great Britain
by Amazon